THE DANCE OF LOVE

Book of Love, Book Fourteen

Meara Platt

ARE YOU SIGNED UP FOR DRAGONBLADE'S BLOG?

You'll get the latest news and information on exclusive giveaways, exclusive excerpts, coming releases, sales, free books, cover reveals and more.

Check out our complete list of authors, too!

No spam, no junk. That's a promise!

Sign Up Here

www.dragonbladepublishing.com

Dearest Reader;

Thank you for your support of a small press. At Dragonblade Publishing, we strive to bring you the highest quality Historical Romance from some of the best authors in the business. Without your support, there is no 'us', so we sincerely hope you adore these stories and find some new favorite authors along the way.

Happy Reading!

CEO, Dragonblade Publishing

Additional Dragonblade books by Author Meara Platt

The Book of Love Series
The Look of Love
The Touch of Love
The Taste of Love
The Song of Love
The Scent of Love
The Kiss of Love
The Chance of Love
The Gift of Love
The Heart of Love
The Hope of Love (novella)
The Promise of Love
The Wonder of Love
The Journey of Love
The Dream of Love (novella)
The Treasure of Love
The Dance of Love
The Miracle of Love

Dark Gardens Series
Garden of Shadows
Garden of Light
Garden of Dragons
Garden of Destiny
Garden of Angels

The Farthingale Series
If You Wished For Me (A Novella)

The Lyon's Den Connected World
Kiss of the Lyon

The Lyon's Surprise
Lyon in the Rough

Pirates of Britannia Series
Pearls of Fire

De Wolfe Pack: The Series
Nobody's Angel
Kiss an Angel
Bhrodi's Angel

Also from Meara Platt
Aislin

CHAPTER ONE

Exeter, England
October 1821

"WHO ARE YOU?" Rafe Quinton barked, staring at the young woman seated behind his desk holding his young son on her lap. "And who let you into my office? Cavendish! Where is that idiot?"

She frowned at him, not in the least daunted by his presence. "Magistrate Quinton, I presume? What have you been doing? Rolling in soot?"

Her nose twitched, and she waved her hand lightly in front of her face as he ignored her remarks and approached. "If by rolling in soot you mean putting out a fire, then yes."

Her eyes widened, and her lips curved in a soft 'O' as she met his gaze. "Oh, I see. Was anyone hurt?"

"I am not discussing an active investigation with you. Get out of my chair." He was a big man, and most people jumped when he gave a command.

But not this elegant, young miss with eyes the magnificent blue of an ocean.

That counted for nothing. She had no right to be in here with *his* son wrapped in her arms. "Sam, come to me now."

"But, Papa! Auggie was reading to me, and she gave me some of her mince pie to share. And she told me not to worry, that you would never forget about me. And she would not leave me until you returned. But you were so late…and I was scared. You smell funny, Papa. And you're bleeding."

"It is nothing, Sam." He reached out to take the boy in his arms but realized his hands were stained with blood. Not his. The man he'd just captured and tossed in a cell. The very one who'd probably started the fire at Lady Priscilla Nesbitt's residence in an attempt to kill the poor woman.

He and his men had gotten her out from the wall of dark, billowing smoke before it swallowed all of them up. Indeed, they'd gotten the dowager out just before the ensuing flames had engulfed the entire structure and burned it to cinders.

The poor woman lost everything.

Why anyone would ever want to harm a beloved, eighty-year-old was anyone's guess. It was up to him as Exeter's magistrate to find out.

But first, he had to wash the blood and smoke off his body.

Never mind about his clothes.

They were probably ruined.

He set his hands at his sides and did not ask Sam—who had not budged off the woman's lap anyway—to come to him again.

"Who are you?" he asked the young woman in a more polite tone since he *had* been late, and his little boy must now be hungry and tired.

The grandfather clock in the corner chimed six o'clock.

Hellfire.

He was almost two hours late.

No wonder Sam was so frightened, especially as twilight approached.

He supposed he ought to thank the young woman for feeding and comforting him.

"I am Lady Augusta Nesbitt," she replied, her voice soft and bordering on sultry.

He shook out of the thought. "Nesbitt?"

"Yes. Perhaps you know my father's aunt, Lady Priscilla Nesbitt. I was—"

"Hellfire," he said, studying her more closely by the gleam of lamplight. Was it mere coincidence she was here, in his office?

Her eyes once again widened in response to his darkening expression.

Were they really that beautiful a shade of blue? Flecked with gold, too. Or was it merely a trick of the light? It also brought out the dark, honey gold of her hair, not that it mattered in the least. She had to be a suspect in the fire that had destroyed Lady Priscilla's house.

She paled as she stared at him. "Why are you looking at me that way?"

"How do you think I am looking at you?"

"As though I am a criminal. Will you kindly tell me what is going on?"

"Your elderly aunt is fine, but her house is not. This smoke I reek of…someone set her home ablaze a few hours ago. I have the man in custody now. Perhaps I ought to bring you down to him and have him identify you as—"

Lady Augusta gasped and gently set Sam on his feet as she rose. "Are you jesting? Because I do not find your humor at all to my liking. Where is my aunt now? I must go to her at once. How dare you suggest I would ever harm a hair on her head. My father shall hear of this! I'm sure you are familiar with the Marquess of Chelsford. I'll have you—"

She paused in her indignation as Sam took her hand. "Oh, I am so sorry. I did not mean to upset you, Sam. I think your father and I got off to a bad start, but we shall straighten it all out shortly. I apologize, Mr. Quinton. I know you are only doing your duty. Let me assure you, I will do everything in my power to assist you. But please, I need to see my aunt. Well, she is my father's aunt, but I refer to her as that, too."

"I'll take you to her as soon as I wash up. Give me a moment. If anyone is to give an apology, it ought to be me for leaping at you with accusations. But answer me this, if you had no idea her house just burned, then what are you doing here?"

Her splendid eyes widened again, although she was not quite as angry as before. "I suppose this is what comes of doing a favor for a friend. What is the adage? No good deed ever goes unpunished? Your Brayden cousins, Shayne, Lorcan, and Donal asked me to deliver a package to you."

"You know my cousins?"

"Not very well. I am good friends with Donal's wife, Lucy. And I have had the pleasure of meeting Shayne's wife, Willow, and Lorcan's wife, Cammy. They are quite lovely."

He groaned.

Now his cousins were going to kick his arse from here to London because he'd insulted their friend. But it also eased his mind, for his cousins were sharp as nails and would never have asked a favor of Lady Augusta if they did not trust her. "What's in the package?"

"Do you really have no idea?"

Sam's eyes brightened at the thought it might be a gift. "Will you let me open it, Papa?"

"No, Sam. It may be official business." He glanced at his hands again. "Give me a moment. I keep a change of clothes here because sometimes this can be quite a dirty business. Sam, stay in here with me. Lady Augusta, would you mind stepping outside? I prefer not to be gawked at while I undress."

She came around his desk, her handkerchief now withdrawn. "Rest assured, I haven't the slightest interest in looking at you. But you will ruin your change of clothes because you are still bleeding. Just let me stanch that wound first. Then I'll clean the dried blood off your forehead. Don't touch it," she said sharply when he raised his hand to the lump forming on his right temple. "You'll only make it worse. Sit down a moment, Mr. Quinton."

"Listen to her, Papa."

He grinned at his son. "All right."

His head was beginning to hurt like blazes.

He pulled out one of the wooden chairs beside his worktable and settled his large frame in it, while the fashionable Lady

Augusta removed her fancy lace gloves, set aside her reticule, and poured some brandy onto her handkerchief from the bottle he kept behind his desk. "This will sting a little," she warned, placing the soaked handkerchief against his forehead.

He rocked back, almost knocking over his chair as stars blurred his eyes and a searing pain tore through him. "Ow! Get the damn thing off me now!"

"Papa!"

She grabbed his chin and pressed the handkerchief more insistently against the lump. "Now see what you've done? You've upset your son. I'm sure he would have been a lot braver than you. You are awfully delicate for a big oaf of a man."

"And you are awfully bossy for a slip of a girl."

She was more gentle as she began to wipe around the area of the wound. "I am hardly a girl. I am twenty-one and soon to be considered on the shelf."

"Whose shelf?" And why was her glorious bosom practically smothering his face? "You are annoying but hardly unattractive. I cannot imagine any young buck passing you up."

She studied him, uncertain whether he had just complimented her. "I've had offers of marriage," she said, lightly dabbing at another cut on his cheek, her body still too close to his for comfort. "But I would rather remain a spinster than marry someone I did not love."

"You could marry my papa," Sam said, squeezing in between them. "He is in desperate need of a wife."

Lady Augusta burst out laughing. "Sam, is this what he's told you?"

"No, that's what my grandmother and her friends say. Because we lost my mama when I was a baby, and they all think I need a new mama. But I don't like the ladies they bring around. They're not nice like you are, Auggie."

She sighed and knelt beside Sam. "Perhaps if you gave them more of a chance to warm up to you. Sometimes, it is very difficult for people to get to know each other when they are in a crowd. Everyone fights for their attention."

Sam lowered his gaze to stare at his shoes. "Maybe. But I don't think so. I heard one of them tell my grandmother I should be sent away to school."

Rafe saw a spark of indignation in Lady Augusta's eyes as she said, "Oh, I hardly think you are old enough for that yet."

"Would you send me away, Auggie?"

She caressed his cheek. "No, Sam. I would hug you close to me and smother you with kisses."

"That's what my papa does. But sometimes his cheek is scruffy, and it scratches my face." He patted Rafe's face. "See, like now."

Lady Augusta surprised him by brazenly placing the palm of her hand against his cheek. "Yes, he does need a shave. And he needs to wash up now that we've stopped the bleeding on his forehead and treated the cut on his cheek. Fortunately, Mr. Quinton, I do not believe you'll need stitches. I'll leave you to your undressing."

She walked to the door and was almost knocked over as two of his investigators, Cooper and Marbury, ran in.

Rafe rolled his eyes. "What now? Speak up, Cooper. You almost trampled the young lady in your rush to get to me."

"That man we just brought in…"

"What about him? I'll see my son home and then I'll come back to question him."

"You can't, sir. You see…he's escaped."

Rafe shot to his feet with a roar that sent Sam scrambling into Lady Augusta's arms. She hugged the boy and scowled at him as he released a string of curses. "Who in bloody blazes let him out? Cavendish! Get in here! Bring your roster! I'll have that stupid arse strung up by his—" He was going to say *strung up by his nuts* but there was a woman present, and he'd already shocked her with his crudeness. "What are you doing standing here gaping at me? Go after him. The bastard was wounded. He cannot have gotten far. Follow his trail of blood."

His men ran off leaving him alone once again with his son and a blisteringly angry debutante. Where was his clerk, Cavendish? Probably cowering under his desk. Lord, how did that villain get out of a locked cell?

The lady was still tossing daggers at him.

He was not going to apologize to her. She should not have come here in the first place. "Do not berate me on my language," he growled, frowning back at her. "That man burned your aunt's house to the ground. We had him, and some incompetent let him get away."

"I understand your frustration, Mr. Quinton. But scaring your son does not help matters. My carriage is outside. Why don't you wash up and get changed, then you can take me to my aunt. Perhaps she knows something of this sad business. Is there a reputable inn close by? I'll settle her there with me."

She glanced down at Sam, who was still clinging to her gown, and ran her hand playfully through his dark mop of hair. "While your father makes himself presentable, I shall take you across the street for ices. We've already had a supper of mince pies, so we are ready for dessert. What's your favorite flavor, Sam?"

"Strawberry."

"A fine choice. I think that's my favorite, too." She started to leave, then halted and marched back into his office to grab her reticule and the package she was meant to hand to him.

"What are you doing? Isn't that mine?"

She nodded. "But you are too riled yet. I'll hand it to you when your mind is calmer and you won't lose it."

First, she burns him with that brandy-soaked handkerchief, then she insults his intelligence. "I am not a little boy, Lady Augusta."

She gazed up at him, the package neatly tucked under her arm. "Indeed, you are not. I would venture to say you are quite grown up and wickedly handsome once you get past all the soot and grime."

She took Sam's hand in hers and walked across the street to

the confectionery shop with its bright yellow window display. He watched from his window as Sam skipped beside her. Waiting on the street was her coachman perched atop an elegant carriage.

He recognized the crest on the polished, black metal door gleaming under the last bright rays of the sun.

The Marquess of Chelsford.

Despite his wretched day, Rafe shook his head and grinned. Auggie, as his son called her, had a hot, little wiggle to her walk.

He'd never be so crude as to tell her…although he'd already been in a temper and hurling expletives from the moment he'd walked into his office.

She was obviously a lady.

Not one of those silly, giggling geese, either. Nor did she walk with her nose in the air. No, she was one of the rare young ladies graced with intelligence and compassion. Well, certainly compassion. He wasn't certain how clever she was. But she seemed more capable than the idiots who worked under his authority.

How had they let their prisoner escape?

He turned away in disgust and threw off all but his trousers, then poured water from the ewer on his desk into a basin. He grabbed soap and a cloth and began to wash the grime off himself. The cloth immediately turned black. Lord, he needed to drop himself into a vat of water to properly clean himself.

He did the best he could, then went to his cupboard to dig out a fresh shirt and cravat. He could not find a cravat. "Bloody hell, where did the bloody thing go?"

"Papa! You are swearing again."

He turned in surprise to find Sam and Lady Augusta staring at him. "What are you two doing back here?"

"I forgot my gloves," Auggie, with the splendid eyes and even more splendid lips any man would enjoy kissing thoroughly, said. Her face was now aflame as she stared at his bare chest. "There they are." She grabbed them, dropped them, picked them up, unknowingly dropped one, and darted back downstairs with Sam in tow.

Served her right for walking in on him unannounced.

He found the cravat at the back of a drawer and finished dressing.

"Cavendish!" he called to his missing clerk, who should have been at his station in the anteroom, monitoring all who came in or out. No doubt the little milksop was still hiding under his desk. "Cavendish! I know you are there. Get rid of the dirty water and see that my clothes are cleaned."

The young man popped his head up from behind his desk, straightened his spectacles, and hurried in. "At once, sir."

"Next time a woman marches up here while I am undressing, keep her out. Especially if she is the daughter of a marquess." He tucked Auggie's lost glove in his pocket and headed across the street. She and his son were just finishing up their ices. The boy was smiling again. Well, he had to give her credit. She knew how to manage children.

"Are you ready, Lady Augusta?" he asked, handing over her glove. "You dropped it as you were fleeing my office."

"Oh, thank you. I did not realize I had…" She stopped speaking, and her cheeks turned pink again, no doubt because she was recalling the sight of him without his shirt.

He liked that she'd taken notice.

He also liked her surprising innocence. She was not in the habit of walking in on men as they dressed. "If you don't mind, I'd like to drop Sam off at home first. It isn't far, and my home is not too much out of the way. My mother ought to be back from her ladies' club meeting by now and will see to putting him to bed. We can stop next at the Swan Inn and reserve rooms for you and your aunt. Then I'll take you to Lady Priscilla. She's settled at a neighbor's for the moment."

"Thank you, that sounds acceptable."

Sam was excited to climb into the exquisite carriage. He bounced on the padded leather seat beside Augusta. "Sam, sit quietly," he said.

"All right, Papa."

Rafe tossed him a wink. "That's my boy."

"I love you, Papa." A tear dropped onto his pudgy cheek, and in the next moment, he leaped into Rafe's arms.

"I'm not hurt, son. Don't be afraid. It will take more than a bump on my head to stop me." He gave his boy a hug when he sensed Sam was about to cry, and then looked around for something to distract him. "Shall I open my package now? What do you think? Shall we see what my cousins sent me?"

The boy looked up and nodded.

Lady Augusta cast him a soft smile as she handed over the package.

Their hands grazed as he took it from her, but he ignored the sudden jolt that seared through him at their slight touch. "Go ahead and unwrap it for me, Sam."

The boy tore into it with enthusiasm. "Papa, it's a book. A pretty red book."

"I see that."

"I can read the title. Auggie, did you know I can read? It says…*The Book of Love*. Oh, Papa. How did they know?"

Rafe lolled his head back and groaned.

So much for that brilliant idea.

What were his cousins thinking? And now he'd opened this lewd book in front of his son and this elegant marquess's daughter. "I didn't…this has to be a jest. I wouldn't…hellfire…"

Augusta gave an unladylike snort as she tried to muffle her laughter.

Sam was beaming. "Papa, you swore again."

"Sorry, son. It has been a trying day."

"It's all right. I know you are sad and desperate because you have no love in your life."

Augusta burst out laughing. "Did your grandmother tell you that?"

Sam nodded.

Rafe couldn't help but laugh along with her.

"My father is badly in need of a woman," the lad continued in earnest.

"Oh, blessed saints," he grumbled, wanting to shut the boy up.

"I need a woman, too," the lad continued sweetly. "Auggie, would you be mine?"

The laughter died in her throat. "Come onto my lap, Sam."

He went to her without hesitation and nestled in her arms. "I shall always be your friend, I hope you know that. You may come to me for hugs and kisses whenever you like. But I do not live in Exeter and will only be here for a month or two. After that, I will return to London. Will you write to me when I'm gone? I shall write to you. This is what friends do."

He rested his head against her shoulder. "I don't want you as a friend. I want you as my mama."

She kissed the top of his head. "I think you need to know me better before you take that leap."

Rafe said nothing as he studied her.

Sam, with his clear-headed childhood wisdom, was not so far off the mark.

He glanced at the book set beside him on the leather seat. *The Book of Love.* Well, he wasn't desperate or sad. Neither was he a fool.

Lady Augusta could very well be someone special.

She looked back at him as he now gazed at her, her expression soft and gracious as she held his boy.

"Papa, ask her to marry you."

"I'm thinking about it, son. I'm thinking about it."

CHAPTER TWO

AUGUSTA FELT AN unexpected flutter in her heart when Rafe Quinton helped her down from the carriage and led her to his house. It was a surprisingly elegant townhome built of red brick and situated in one of the finer parts of Exeter. The house was not ostentatious but solid and well maintained. "This is where you live?"

He grinned. "Yes. Where did you expect me to reside? In a barn?"

Heat rose in her cheeks. "Of course not. But there's a graceful beauty to the house…"

"And I'm a coarse, oath-spewing tyrant? You caught me on a bad day." He took her arm and led her inside as soon as his housekeeper opened the door.

Sam tore inside and shouted for his grandmother. "You'll never guess! Papa has found himself a lady! And a book to teach him all about love!"

Auggie put a hand to her mouth once again to stem her laughter.

Mr. Quinton looked to be in utter pain. "Bollocks, I am going to put a gag on that boy. I beg your pardon, Lady Augusta. Let me settle him in, and we'll be off to secure rooms for you and your aunt at the Swan Inn. It's the best in town."

"Thank you, Mr. Quinton. Take your time seeing to your boy. I am quite enjoying him."

He quirked an eyebrow and cast her a surprisingly appealing smile. "What you are enjoying is my complete humiliation, I suspect." He spoke with mirth, and she could see he loved his son fiercely.

She smiled back at him. "Yes, there is a little of that. But he is truly wonderful and he adores you. What a sweet, little heart he has."

Mr. Quinton nodded. "He also absorbs everything he hears, right, Mrs. Lacey?" He turned to his housekeeper who was eyeing Auggie curiously, but her gaze appeared kind.

"Yes, indeed. Let me see to the scamp right now, and then I shall come back to properly attend to your guest." She scurried off calling after Sam.

"He's like a sponge, so you had better watch what you say around him, or it will be repeated, often at the most embarrassing times. He's probably telling my mother all about you right now." He held up the book his cousins had sent to him. "Do you know what this is?"

She nodded. "Donal's wife, Lucy, explained it to me. I did not want to say anything when you asked me about it earlier in your office because your son was present. But whoever is given this book is bound to find their true love match. This is what Lucy told me. Good luck to you, Mr. Quinton. I hope you meet a lovely woman who will be a good wife to you and a kind mother to Sam."

"Thank you, but I doubt it will happen anytime soon." He glanced at the book again. "I'll have to hide it now to be sure Sam doesn't get his sticky fingers on it. He'll look for it as soon as I am off to work again. He and my mother have made it their mission in life to have me marry again."

She noted the flicker of pain in his eyes and realized he must have loved his wife deeply. "I'm so sorry for your loss. She must have been someone truly special."

"Mary died about two years after Sam was born," he said tersely. "My mother moved in to help me with the boy, but she has her own full plate of social activities, and I never meant for her to be looking after him day in and day out. We had a governess for him, but she left recently, and I haven't found the time to interview a suitable replacement yet."

He led her into the parlor and introduced her to his house-keeper when the kindly woman scurried back in to ask if she ought to prepare refreshments. "Not on my account," Auggie said. "Sam and I quite filled ourselves with strawberry ices."

"Thank you, Mrs. Lacey." His dismissal was surprisingly courteous. "Perhaps we shall tempt Lady Augusta next time."

No sooner had his housekeeper bustled off than Sam rushed in with his grandmother in tow. "Auggie, this is my grandmother. Grandmama, this is my friend Auggie, who gave Papa that love book that Papa thinks is lewd. What does that mean?"

Mr. Quinton was grinning again, a softer smile that lightened his handsome face and reached into his incredible eyes. Not that they were soft or gentle in any way. No, they were a stormy gray tinged with hints of dark emerald. Keen and assessing, they seemed able to pierce one's soul at a mere glance.

They were stunning eyes.

She could stare at them for hours and never get bored.

Auggie's cheeks heated. "Sam, I merely delivered it as a favor to his cousins. And they assured me it is not...oh, dear. Mrs. Quinton, I do hope..."

"Oh, my dear. It is a delight to meet you," said with a gentle laugh and came forward to take her hands. "You are as lovely as Sam assured me you were."

"Thank you," she said with open relief.

"My mother was born a Brayden and is not one to be easily rattled or offended," Mr. Quinton said. "You are already a favorite of hers because Sam likes you, and he rarely likes any of the young ladies brought around. Not that there are many."

His mother was a charming lady with bright green eyes and a full head of silvery hair. "It is truly a pleasure to meet you, Lady Augusta. I gather from Sam that you are new to town."

"Yes, I arrived a few hours ago and only meant to drop off the book before riding on to my aunt's house, but…" She turned to Mr. Quinton, not certain how much to reveal about the fire.

He nodded and proceeded to relate the bits of information he wished to make public. "Lady Augusta is Priscilla Nesbitt's grandniece. Unfortunately, Lady Priscilla's home was completely destroyed. We're on our way to see her now and get her settled safely for the evening. I may be home late. Will you attend to Sam? He needs to wash up and be put to bed."

"Yes, dear. Of course."

He took a moment to playfully muss Sam's hair. "And you behave, young man. I'll come in to kiss you goodnight when I return."

The boy nodded. "All right, Papa. Auggie, will I see you again?"

"Yes, Sam. I cannot promise to come by tomorrow because I must take care of my elderly aunt first. But I will make it a point to come around shortly afterward. That is my promise to you."

Sam wrapped his arms around her waist and gave her a heartfelt hug.

She returned it and gave him a light kiss on the top of his head. "It was a pleasure to meet you, Sam."

"We had better go," Mr. Quinton said quietly and took gentle hold of her arm.

His mother nodded. "Please do stop by again, Lady Augusta. I'll send a formal invitation once you and your aunt are settled. Do let us know what we can do for her. Poor thing, she must be devastated. How can she not be when a lifetime of memories has gone up in flames? Our Ladies Auxiliary will be happy to help with all her needs."

"Thank you, Mrs. Quinton. It is very kind of you."

She walked out with the magistrate, her mind already turned to thoughts of the fire and the fiend who had caused it.

Who would ever want to harm her aunt?

This was the very question Mr. Quinton asked once they

were back in her carriage and on their way to the Swan Inn to secure rooms for her and her aunt. She pursed her lips in thought to fashion a reply. "She recently loaned some money to a cousin of mine, Morgan Nesbitt. He had gone to my father first, but he refused to lend him anything more. You see, he'd come to my father last year with hat in hand pleading for assistance to help with debts."

"Let me guess, instead of paying off his creditors, he spent it all at the London gaming hells."

She nodded. "You are a cynical man, Mr. Quinton. But yes, that is exactly what he did. My father was enraged when he found out. I cannot believe Morgan dared approach him again. My father tossed him out this time. So, he came to Exeter and wheedled funds from Aunt Priscilla."

"How much did she give him?"

"I don't know." She shook her head. "Whatever the amount, it will never be enough when he insists on tossing it all away at the gaming tables. But why would he try to harm the only relative in the family who was willing to help him out? Also, he may be lazy and a profligate, but he never struck me as mean. Certainly not the sort to kill a harmless old lady."

Mr. Quinton was seated across from her, his shoulders broad and his body quite magnificent in its breadth. He seemed to dominate the entire space. Well, he did strike her as a leader, naturally strong and commanding. "Any man might be pushed to murder if he were desperate enough. Your aunt might have demanded repayment."

"I don't think she would have done."

"Then perhaps he wanted more and stole it when she wouldn't give it over."

Auggie studied him, unable to draw her gaze away. "You think he meant to cover up the theft by setting the blaze, only it got out of hand?"

"It is a possibility."

Their gazes locked.

Warmth curled in her belly. "I cannot believe Morgan would do such a thing."

Their conversation ended when her carriage drew up in front of the Swan Inn. "Oh, we are here. It looks to be a lovely place. Thank you for suggesting it."

The inn, situated in the same elegant part of town as his home, was built of the warm, gold-tinged stone traditionally found in the Cotswolds. For this reason, it stood out among the other buildings along what appeared to be Exeter's popular market street. It had a welcoming porticoed entrance, bright blue shutters, and flowers all around. "My aunt will be quite comfortable here, I'm sure," she said, melting a little as he wrapped her hand in his to help her down.

Fortunately, he did not appear to notice her excitement at his touch.

"The food is quite good here, and the proprietor maintains a staff in the overnight hours as well," he said. "There will always be someone on duty to attend your aunt should the need arise."

"That is excellent." She hoped not to sound too breathless, but his nearness sent fiery tingles through her body. This had never happened to her before, not with any other man, and she was not certain what to make of it.

Rafe Quinton was gruff and rugged, but that did not mean she thought him coarse, even though his language was that at times. No, he was intelligent, exceptionally handsome, and despite being big and muscled, he moved with elegance. In her mind, she could see him as a medieval warrior, a valiant knight, his body twisting and straining as he thrust and parried his weapons of steel in a deadly but graceful dance of survival.

He would be quite graceful on a dance floor as well because that finely honed body of his moved with natural ease. All in all, he was quite devastating to any young woman's senses. She was no exception.

She imagined herself caught up in his arms as they twirled in a waltz, but quickly shook out of the thought and hurried inside.

"Good evening, Mr. Quinton," the innkeeper said, scurrying toward them as they stood at his desk beside the open registry book.

"Good evening, Mr. Perkins. I'll need two of your best rooms, preferably adjoining, if any are available."

The man's smile faltered, and he eyed Auggie speculatively. "Adjoining rooms?" Then he arched an eyebrow and had the audacity to cast the magistrate an approving nod.

She gasped. "The rooms are for my aunt, Lady Priscilla Nesbitt, and me."

Mr. Quinton turned the registry book toward him. "This is her niece, Lady Augusta Nesbitt. I'm sure you've heard the news by now of the fire in Aimsley Square. It was Lady Priscilla's house that burned."

The man appeared sincerely apologetic. "Oh, the dear lady! I did hear about the fire but had no idea it was her home. Of course, we shall make certain she has every comfort. Rest assured, Lady Augusta. She will lack for nothing."

Auggie cast him a grateful nod. "Thank you, Mr. Perkins."

"I'll have a private suite of rooms just off our splendid garden made ready for you immediately. Your dear aunt won't need to climb stairs. I know how she struggles with her walking. She comes in here from time to time for tea with her friends. Why, she was just in here last week with another relation of yours."

"Morgan Nesbitt?" Mr. Quinton asked, suddenly on alert.

The man nodded. "Yes. They came in here both smiling and cheerful enough, however, she did not seem too pleased with him by the time they walked out."

Auggie was not certain she ought to be asking questions but jumped in anyway. Mr. Quinton would stop her if he did not want her interference. "Did you hear any of their conversation?"

"No, but their table was assigned to my daughter, Esther. She might have overheard something. Unfortunately, she is not here right now. This is her night off. But she will be here in the morning."

"I'll stop by to question her then," Mr. Quinton said. "Lady Augusta, we had better fetch your aunt before it grows too late."

Mr. Perkins cleared his throat. "Before you go, would you please tell me how long you plan to stay? Shall I set the suite aside for a week? Two weeks?"

Auggie was not certain yet but knew this matter was not going to resolve itself in a day. Also, she would have to make more permanent arrangements while her aunt's home was being rebuilt. If the inn proved to have all the comforts, then it would be a good place to settle her aunt while the work was done. "I think two weeks to start. We'll know better once we have had a chance to inspect the damage."

Mr. Quinton took her by the arm. "We'll return in about an hour. See that the ladies are given the very best."

Truly, he had a gentle way of holding her. She found it most surprising considering his gruff manner when they'd first met. He'd calmed down now and was being quite pleasant. In truth, she liked his company. There was something about him that made her heart flutter whenever he stepped close.

Tingles. Flutters. She was no giddy young miss. What was happening to her?

Perhaps, it was his protective manner she liked.

Protective, yet not overbearing.

She also loved the gentle way he'd treated his son.

The kindness with which he handled the boy spoke well of him.

He escorted her back to the carriage.

However, they waited for her trunks to be unloaded before climbing in. Oh, she had so many. One would think she was moving to Exeter permanently and not merely for a month or two.

Mr. Quinton was staring at the quantity and absently running his hand through the waves of his dark hair. "Did you empty out the London shops?"

"I shall ignore that remark," she said with a light laugh, taking no offense. As the daughter of a marquess, she had a certain standard to uphold. Everyone would immediately notice if she wore the same attire day after day. Did she not need at least three gowns for each day?

Still, Mr. Quinton must now think her quite spoiled.

Mr. Perkins was beside them, ordering his lads to bring her trunks to her suite of rooms.

"I just realized," Mr. Quinton said, his eyes still on the parade of valises, "where is your lady's maid? Did you not bring one along?"

"No, she did not come with me. I had planned to ask Aunt Priscilla's maid for assistance when I needed it. I can assure you, I am quite capable of managing for myself."

"You do appear to be competent. But how do you manage with…" His gaze raked over her body, those compelling eyes of his seeming to bore straight through the layers of fabric.

"You mean when lacing my corset?"

He chuckled and cast her an appealing smile. "Lady Augusta, I was not asking for specifics. It was merely a general curiosity."

She found herself blushing again. "Oh, I…well, the fact is…I can manage most of it on my own. That includes fashioning my hair. I only require additional help when preparing for a grand occasion. The intricate plaits and twists are too much for me to handle by myself."

"Did you style your hair today?"

She nodded.

"You did a nice job," he said in a husky murmur and helped her into the carriage. His touch once again shot tingles through her body.

"Was that a compliment, Mr. Quinton?"

His smile was warm as he settled across from her and then signaled for her coachman to drive on. "I am capable of being polite on occasion, Lady Augusta. Yes, it was."

She liked this man, she decided. "Please, call me Auggie. All my friends do."

"Mine call me Rafe. Since I expect we shall be seeing a lot of each other over the coming weeks, I am glad we can drop the formality when not in the company of others. Auggie," he repeated in a husky rumble. "The name suits you. It is warm and approachable. Sam noticed this about you immediately."

They were seated across from each other, but he now leaned closer. "Despite the mountain of gowns you brought along to Exeter, I—"

She gasped. "I am not a spoiled debutante."

"I never said you were, but you still have a mountain of clothes," he said, his stunning eyes alight with mirth. "In truth, I expect you are not at all frivolous. You seem clever and kind. I cannot thank you enough for looking after Sam the way you did. My heart aches knowing I left him alone in my office all that time."

She reached out and briefly touched his hand. "You were saving my aunt, and I'm sure he would have been attended to by your clerk, Mr. Cavendish, were I not conveniently there."

"Your aunt will need your steady hand to guide her through this ordeal. She is fortunate to have you. I mean it sincerely."

"Well…Rafe, was that another compliment you just gave me?" She grinned at him. "You have my senses reeling. I think I shall swoon if you toss me another."

He leaned back against the squabs, his body so big and fine as he relaxed against the soft leather. "Then I shall save the rest for tomorrow."

The scent of smoke filled her nostrils as they rode up a hill and turned onto the charming Aimsley Square. She peered out the window. The houses were all quite grand and neatly maintained except for the heap of ashes in one of the far corners.

It hadn't taken them long to reach her aunt's house.

In truth, all their rides had been short ones. She realized it would take her no more than ten minutes to walk from the Swan Inn to Rafe's office or home, or to Aimsley Square. The inn itself was situated in the quaint market center of town, a welcome refuge for the well-heeled after a day of shopping, but still conveniently close to their elegant homes.

Walking around Exeter would be something pleasant to do on a nice day.

"Auggie, you mentioned your cousin, Morgan Nesbitt. Anyone else come to mind who would have reason to harm your aunt?"

She shook her head. "No. And I refuse to believe my cousin would do this heinous thing. He is a reprobate, but—"

"I've already told you, desperate men will take desperate measures. Never think any man is harmless."

"Not even you?" She dismissed the notion. "Will you please keep an open mind until we have gathered all the facts?"

"I always do."

"It does not feel as though you are doing so now. I'm almost sorry I mentioned my cousin."

His eyes turned stormy, and he frowned at her. "Never hold anything back from me. I need to gather all the facts possible. If I seem to be fixed on your cousin, it is only because I have nothing else to go on yet. But more will come to light as we question your aunt's staff, her neighbors, even a passerby who might have witnessed something out of the ordinary. Will you promise to tell me everything? Please, Auggie. I need to trust you."

She nodded. "I promise."

Her carriage came to a halt near the site of the fire. Several men were tossing water on the now subdued flames. There appeared to be little left to burn, but as she and Rafe descended from the carriage, she could hear the spit and crackle of wood and knew there had to be live embers still buried amid the dust and ashes.

It would take no more than a small gust of wind for those embers to float to a neighbor's roof and cause another fire. She expected these men, no doubt a part of Exeter's fire brigade, would work all night to ensure the disaster did not spread.

Rafe took her arm to lead her away from the burned-out

shell. "We'll see what your aunt and her neighbors can tell us."

"What about the man you took into your custody? How did you know he was the culprit? Did someone point him out to you?"

"Criminals sometimes remain close to the scene of their crime, especially this sort of crime. He was watching the house burn and began to fidget the moment I noticed him. When I approached, he ran."

"He could have decided to flee for innocent reasons."

He nodded. "Perhaps, but I know he must be our man. Someone paid him to do the job. He wasn't the sort to be allowed into any home on this elegant square. He was just some scoundrel in need of money, the lowest form of life, not bothered with a conscience. I hope my men have him back in custody by now. He was wounded and could not have escaped far."

"Unless he had a carriage waiting for him. Whoever helped him out of your prison would have thought to carry him off fast. You might never find him."

"Oh, we will. I'm just afraid we'll find him dead. Now that we've seen him, he has become a liability to his employer."

"One who is ruthless enough to set fire to an old lady's home."

Rafe nodded again. "Yes, his employer is the one I really want. He will think nothing of killing his accomplices to keep from being identified."

"I see."

He led her to the neighboring home, a large townhouse made of the same reddish stone common to the area. Ivy gracefully trailed down its facade. "Lord and Lady Whiting reside here. They are pillars in our local society and great friends of your aunt."

"Yes, I've met them before." Auggie's heart beat faster as they were shown into the Whiting's well-appointed parlor and asked to wait. She was too much on edge to sit, but it wasn't long before Lord Whiting rushed in. "My dear Lady Augusta, what a relief you are here."

"How is my aunt?"

"Quite on edge, as is to be expected. I cannot imagine why anyone would do such a thing to her. My doctor came by and gave her a sedative to calm her nerves. She is asleep at the moment."

"Oh, dear. I've come to take her to the Swan Inn. Mr. Quinton was kind enough to arrange rooms for us there."

Lord Whiting shook his head. "I think it is best she not be disturbed this evening. Let her spend the night with us, and you can bring her over in the morning."

She turned to Rafe, seeking his guidance.

He did not seem to mind and gave a curt nod. "I'll escort you back here in the morning."

"Thank you, but did you not wish to question her?"

"Lady Augusta, I doubt she will give us very much useful information in her present condition. We'll start the questioning tomorrow."

She hated to think this trip was wasted, but the gentlemen did not appear to be put out. Nor did she wish to shake her aunt awake and force her out of bed when she'd obviously been through an ordeal. "What about you, Lord Whiting? Is there anything you can tell us? Did you or your wife notice something unusual at the time of the fire?"

He shook his head. "No, not a thing. Not that we were paying close attention, for I was preparing to leave for London tomorrow on business. We were distracted by all that had yet to be done. I'll postpone my trip, of course."

Auggie tried not to show her disappointment at the lack of information Priscilla's kindly neighbor could provide. "So, you noticed nothing at all?"

"I'm sorry, but no. I wish I could be more helpful. One moment, all was peaceful. In the next, her house was ablaze. We thought perhaps she had dropped a candle and it caught on her drapes. But her hysterical maid assured us this was not so. She claimed someone had tossed a lit torch through the parlor's open window."

"And you believe her?" Auggie asked, thinking of the man Mr. Quinton had subdued, brought to his prison, and had now escaped.

"Clara has been with your aunt for more than twenty years and is utterly devoted to her. I don't think she would lie about such a thing, especially something as wild as a stranger hurling a fiery torch through an open window." He arched an eyebrow as he now turned to Rafe. "To be honest, I doubt Clara has the intelligence to concoct such a story."

Auggie had to agree with Lord Whiting's assessment. She'd visited her aunt before and had met the trusted lady's maid. In truth, Clara was more of a companion than a maid to her aunt now. She was devoted, but rather a dim, plodding sort. Auggie doubted her head had ever been filled with fanciful notions. "Where is Clara now?"

"We've put her up in our servants' quarters. The poor thing had nowhere else to go."

Rafe nodded. "Will you bring her down here? I'd like to question her."

"Yes, I'll have it done at once." He crossed the room and tugged on the bell pull. His butler immediately came in and took the instruction.

They had only a few minutes to wait before Clara rushed into Auggie's arms and began to cry hysterically. "Praise the Lord! You are here! We are homeless, Lady Augusta. Everything's gone. It is all gone!"

Auggie put her arms around the woman and did her best to soothe her. "You are not to worry. Mr. Quinton will find who did this, and he has already arranged housing for us at the lovely Swan Inn. I've taken a suite there. You and Aunt Priscilla shall be quite comfortable until we can get you back on your feet."

"Bless you, m'lady. Bless you. I thought it was the poorhouse for us for certain."

She tried not to roll her eyes. "Clara, neither I nor my father would ever allow you to live in penury."

"In what?" the woman asked with a sniffle.

"You need never worry about enduring hardship. We will always take care of you, but you must calm down and allow Mr. Quinton to ask his questions. All right?"

Clara wiped her eyes with the sleeve of her gown and nodded.

"Here, sit down." Auggie motioned to one of the elegant silk chairs.

"Oh, no m'lady. I couldn't. It is too fine for me."

Rafe brought over a stool that had been beside Lord Whiting's hearth. "Here, sit down."

Clara was obviously too afraid of him to disobey.

Lord Whiting excused himself and shut the doors behind him to allow them privacy. Auggie settled in the silk chair the woman had considered too fine for herself. Rafe dropped on his haunches so that his gaze was at eye level to Clara's. "Tell me exactly what happened today."

Since Clara appeared ready to faint, Auggie reached over and took her hand in an attempt to soothe her. "You can trust Mr. Quinton. He is here to help us."

They both listened attentively while she rambled through the tedious trivialities of her morning. "Then I served Lady Priscilla her lunch."

"Did anyone come to your door this morning?"

"Only the milkman, Mr. Rodgers. This is his usual day for deliveries."

She exchanged a glance with Rafe, both of them obviously thinking they had to find Mr. Rodgers and question him next. Hopefully, he was not as dim as Clara and would be able to tell them if something had struck him as suspicious.

But for now, they were dealing with this well-meaning but not very helpful woman. "Were you able to salvage any of Aunt Priscilla's belongings?"

"No, not a one. We fled for our lives, m'lady."

"Of course, that is most important. Her artwork and furnishings are merely possessions and cannot compare to the loss of life."

Clara nodded. "I suppose if it had to happen, it was a good thing it happened today and not last week."

Auggie leaned forward. "What do you mean?"

"Well, that nice young man from Wendall and Crowell took all of her paintings and several pieces of her best furniture away for restoration."

"Took them away?" She turned to Rafe in amazement, for this was too much of a coincidence and had to be investigated. "What is the name of this young man?"

She rubbed her temple and groaned. "I cannot recall. But Lord Whiting will know. He was the one who recommended the company to your aunt."

They got little else out of her, so they dismissed her with a final admonition. "Clara, do keep your mind on this matter and make a note of anything else you remember. Mr. Quinton and I will come by tomorrow to bring you and my aunt to the inn."

"I will, m'lady." She bobbed a curtsy and hurried out.

Rafe asked the butler to summon Lord Whiting.

"At once, Mr. Quinton."

Left alone with him for the moment, Auggie took advantage to review what they'd learned. "Do you suspect that young man from Wendall and Crowell? The connection cannot be overlooked, but it makes no sense for him to then burn down her house."

"Unless they were trying to force your aunt to sell them her paintings. When asking politely did not work, they resorted to threats and intimidation."

Auggie's eyes rounded in surprise. "It does not seem the sort of thing art gallery owners would do. It is too overt and brutal. Perhaps it is something more along the lines of insurance fraud. It is possible she was not expected to be home but plans obviously went awry. I'll have to ask my father if Aunt Priscilla's belongings were insured. Several of her paintings were valuable."

"You've visited her before. Do you recall what she had in her home?"

She nodded. "Yes, down to the last detail. But what is gained by setting a blaze when too many people know her valuables were removed before the fire? They could not pretend those valuables had burned. Do you think the agents for Wendall and Crowell thought to keep the goods for themselves and return forgeries to her? It would make sense to burn her house and create a delay if they needed time for their artist to paint fakes."

"The thought had crossed my mind, but it does no good to speculate. Let's see what Lord Whiting has to say about these art dealers."

It was not long before Lord Whiting joined them.

Rafe quickly related what Clara had mentioned. "Do you happen to know the name of the young man?"

"No, I usually deal directly with Mr. Wendall or Mr. Crowell, and I haven't done so in quite some time. About five years, I'd say. However, I can describe him to you. My wife and I happened to see him from our window as he and the firm's carters carried everything out. He is a tall fellow and thin. Bright red hair and wears owlish spectacles. Perhaps Lady Priscilla will recall his name when she wakes in the morning. The sleeping draught my doctor gave her was quite strong."

"Then we won't trouble you any longer this evening," Rafe said, offering Auggie his arm. "You must be tired as well, Lady Augusta. I'll escort you back to the inn. I know your head must be awhirl but try to get a good night's rest. Pacing and fretting will accomplish nothing."

"I'll try my best." It wasn't every day she was thrown into a mystery. While she did enjoy puzzles, this one felt a bit too dangerous to attempt to solve on her own.

In truth, it left her quite on edge but feeling relieved she had Mr. Quinton by her side.

"We will unravel it in time," he strove to assure her, taking a moment to cast her a surprisingly appealing smile before he turned his attention to Lord Whiting. "When may we come around to collect Lady Priscilla and her maid? Is eleven o'clock too early?"

"That sounds fine. We shall see you then."

Auggie wished Lord Whiting a good evening and reluctantly returned to her waiting carriage. She deflated once the carriage started for the inn.

Rafe, once again seated across from her, reached for her hand. "Are you all right?"

She nodded, liking the warmth of his touch. "I will be, I expect. Does it not feel strange to you that her furniture and artwork were removed just before her house was set afire?"

"Of course, it does. The coincidence is too glaring." He moved his hand off hers and eased back. "I'll return to my office once I drop you off. I'm hoping my men will have found the culprit by now."

"You look doubtful."

He shrugged. "This investigative work can often be frustrating. We had him in hand."

She glanced at the subsiding lump on his brow, relieved he did not seem to be suffering from it too badly. The cut to his cheek would likely fade by tomorrow. "And by the look of you, he was not easily subdued."

"Desperate men fight dirty and take desperate measures. He coshed me with a rock before I managed to subdue him. What bothers me more is that he got away. I personally tossed him in the holding pen. He was locked in and yet managed to escape. I hold out little hope we'll find him alive. Now I have to figure out which of my men were bribed to let him out."

"And, in turn, who bribed your man."

He nodded. "Crime is a dirty business. Bringing the culprits to justice is my job, but there are times I would love to chuck it all in and go off fishing with my son."

"I will help you in this investigation as much as I can."

"I'm not sure I want you to, Auggie. It could prove dangerous."

"I know, and I promise to be careful. I have no intention of prowling through the streets of Exeter at midnight. I'll leave that to you. But I can help with questioning witnesses. We now have the innkeeper's daughter, the milkman, the Wendall and Crowell agent, and Lady Whiting and her staff to be interviewed. This seems a very good start, do you not think so?"

He cast her a soft smile. "Yes, we've done a good day's work."

"May I ask you a question?"

He arched an eyebrow.

"Why are you being so nice to me now? I thought I had made a terrible impression on you and was convinced you wanted nothing to do with me. Yet, here we are, and you do not appear to be angry with me at all."

"I was never angry with you."

"Yes, you were."

He grinned. "No, Auggie. I was out of sorts because that scoundrel hit me over the head and fought me the entire way back to the prison. I was covered in soot and blood. Not to mention, some idiot guard allowed him to escape. Now I have to worry about who is bribing my men and which men of mine are being bribed. You were a ray of sunshine in an otherwise miserable day."

"Do you always frown and curse so vigorously when encountering a ray of sunshine?" She laughed heartily. "How does your head feel now?"

"It hurts, but nothing I can't handle."

She wanted to reach out and stroke his forehead, but it was too intimate a gesture, and she was already feeling more of an attraction to him than was proper. "Put a cold compress on it when you return home."

He smiled. "You cannot help yourself, can you?"

"What do you mean?"

"You have a compassionate manner about you. You care

about people, and they naturally warm to you. My son certainly did. So did Clara. She ran into your arms. I tend to intimidate people. You put them at ease, and they let down their guard."

"Is this why you are amenable to my helping your investigation? You think we'll make a good team."

He shook his head in denial. "We are not a team. I will shut you out the moment things get too heated. I will not put your life at risk. Understood?"

"Yes. I am not keen on getting mixed up in anything more perilous than asking questions. My aunt needs me to take care of her. My father would be bereft if I were hurt. It has been just him and me for almost all my life. He loved my mother and… well, it does not matter. My point is, loss is heartbreaking. I suppose you feel the same way about Sam's mother…your wife."

He said nothing, but she felt a sudden tension between them and knew she had stepped on a sore topic. "I'm sorry. I had no right to mention her. Ah, we are at the inn."

He peered out the window. "So we are."

"Mr. Quinton, please—"

"Rafe, or do you hate me once again?"

"I don't hate you at all…Rafe. Please feel free to make use of my carriage. I doubt I'll be using it once I am settled here with my aunt. In fact, use it now."

"Not necessary. I'm sure your driver must be tired, not to mention the horses will be quite spent by now. My office isn't far from the inn."

"How will you get home afterward?"

He shrugged. "As I always do, by walking. If it gets too late, I'll simply sleep in my office. It isn't the most comfortable, but it'll do."

"You told Sam you would kiss him goodnight."

"I will if I return home. The boy will be asleep and not know the difference." He shifted in apparent discomfort. "Why do you care?"

"He's a lovely child and obviously dotes on you. What you say to him is important. And are you not the one who told me he absorbs everything like a sponge? I would not like to see him hurt."

"He won't be. He knows I love him." He flipped open the door and descended quickly, then held out his hand for her. "I'll walk you inside, see you safely settled before I leave. Will you be all right on your own?"

She laughed lightly. "Yes, I am quite capable of tending to myself. Not that I'll have much to do other than tug on a bell pull and await a maid to address my every need."

He helped her down and led her inside.

The inn was surprisingly active.

"It is a favorite dining spot for the local gentry," he explained, his gaze taking in all who walked in and out of the bustling inn. "Dances are held here every Saturday night in the summers and twice monthly during the other seasons of the year. I suppose these are our version of an assembly ball. Of course, ours are not nearly as fine as those held in London. I'm sure you'll find us quite provincial."

She regarded him with some surprise. "Do you attend them? You do not seem the sort to dance the night away. But I suppose as an eligible bachelor—"

He laughed and shook his head. "Not on your life! I cannot stand those affairs. Let me obtain the key to your suite for you. Shall I walk you to your door? It is just down the hall."

"No, not necessary. Besides, people will talk if they see you there. It is amazing how quickly the facts become distorted. You innocently standing beside my door will soon turn into your being seen coming out of my room in the middle of the night. I'll be ruined after only a few hours in Exeter. Then you'll have no choice but to do the honorable thing and marry me."

She'd spoken in jest, but he wasn't laughing. "Oh, dear. I've scared you."

"No, Auggie. Marriage to you would not scare me in the least." His voice was low and deliciously raspy.

She swallowed hard. "It wouldn't?"

They weren't touching, but she could feel sparks of lightning leap between them.

Well, she was certainly sparking.

She wasn't certain what he was feeling.

"No, it wouldn't. You look surprised." He cast her a deliciously wicked smile that shot more sparks through her.

This was ridiculous.

Why was she turning into a fluttering peahen?

"Goodnight, Auggie," he said after obtaining the key and handing it to her. "I'll watch you from here until you make it safely to your guest chamber. We'll be an entire hallway apart. That ought to be distance enough to save your reputation."

"Now you are making fun of me."

"Not at all. I'm actually struggling hard to maintain that gentlemanly distance."

She hurried down the hall, opened the door to her suite, and cast him a final glance...perhaps longer than a glance, for she could not draw her gaze off him.

What was it about this man that had her reeling every time he looked at her?

She'd spent the last three seasons feeling absolutely nothing for any man, certainly not a one among the onslaught of suitors begging for her hand in marriage.

But Rafe Quinton?

He wasn't like the others.

He was not the sort ever to beg for her affection.

He was a widower with a child. A man who knew his way around a woman's body. Exeter's magistrate. Big. Handsome. Smart.

Probably smarter than any of her other suitors. It was no small accomplishment to hold the position of magistrate in this thriving market town.

He was trusted and respected.

Would he truly consider taking her as his wife or was he merely jesting?

Did she want to be considered for the role?

She shook off the ridiculous notion and hurried inside.

CHAPTER THREE

THE SUN HAD now disappeared below the rooftops as Rafe strode back to his office in the impending darkness. The building, a large structure in the center of town, housed Exeter's prison as well as administrative offices for himself, his investigators, and the prison guards. The courts, including the region's Court of Assizes, were in an ancient edifice around the corner from the prison.

The main shopping streets were directly to the west of his office, and amid the shops was the Swan Inn. Just beyond were the elegant squares and hilly streets where he, Auggie's aunt, and most of the well-heeled in Exeter resided.

He stopped by the prison first, hoping the escaped man had been found and brought back. "No, Mr. Quinton," the guard on duty replied. "He hasn't been found. Not sure how that little worm escaped in the first place."

"Who was on duty when it happened?"

"Thomas Pritchart, but he would never be so careless as to unlock the cell and then forget to lock him in again. Someone else did this...and if ye want my opinion..."

"I do, Mr. Lawrence."

"Then I would say to look closer at the new guard, James Kerrigan. A slacker if I ever saw one."

Rafe nodded. "Thank you, Mr. Lawrence. I will take a closer look at him. Don't say a word to the others, especially not to Mr.

Kerrigan."

"I won't, sir."

Rafe walked out into the night. The air had begun to turn damp, a sign of impending rain. He only hoped it would hold off long enough for him to get home. He entered the administrative entrance to the building and waved to the familiar night guard on duty before climbing the marble steps up to his office.

His clerk, Cavendish, would be gone by now.

Since the escaped prisoner had not yet been returned, he expected his two investigators, Cooper and Marbury, were still on his trail, and he would not hear from them until tomorrow. They were good men, quite dogged when on the search, as they would be for this scoundrel. However, Rafe knew the longer it took, the slimmer the chances of finding the man alive.

Too bad.

He would have been their best lead.

And now he'd have to put another investigator quietly on this new guard, James Kerrigan.

He unlocked the door to his office, lit his lamp, and withdrew Kerrigan's employment application. He would have required references before hiring him in such a sensitive position as prison guard.

"Hellfire," he muttered, staring at the names of his listed references. "Wendall. Crowell."

This connection was too glaring to be dismissed. The blaze must have had something to do with Lady Priscilla's paintings after all. But there was more going on than a plot to swindle an old lady out of her paintings.

Planting a crooked prison guard within his prison spoke of a broader operation, and Wendall and Crowell were likely involved up to their eyeballs.

But how?

And what exactly were they doing?

He put the application back in its folder, doused his lamp, and locked up his office.

The moon was covered in a thin veil of clouds and barely visible as he walked past the now closed shops while making his way home.

He quickened his pace as it began to drizzle.

Hellfire.

He did not want to get caught in a downpour to end this miserable day. The only good thing to come out of it was Auggie, indeed a ray of sunshine amid the gloom.

However, despite his attraction to her, nothing was going to come of it.

She was the daughter of a marquess.

What chance would he ever have with her?

Even if she felt something for him, her father would never allow her to marry a commoner.

Why was he even contemplating marriage to a woman he'd known less than a day?

He marched into his house and locked it securely for the night.

Once done, he went up to Sam's room and quietly walked in. "Papa?"

He knelt by his son's bed. "Why are you still awake, Sam?"

The boy was cozily tucked in and only his face peeked out from under the blanket. "I couldn't sleep."

"Did my shouting earlier today upset you? I'm sorry, son. I wasn't shouting at you."

"I know, Papa. I'm not upset. I'm happy because we met Auggie, and I like her."

He gave the boy a kiss on the forehead. "I like her, too. I'm sure we'll all become good friends in time. Just remember, she hardly knows us. You cannot ask her to be your mama without giving her the chance to form her own opinions about us. If you rush her, you might scare her away."

"Oh, I don't want to do that."

"I know. Be patient and just enjoy her friendship. Don't forget, she has to take care of her aunt. That is her first priority, and we cannot take her away from it." He gave his son another kiss on the forehead. "Close your eyes and try to sleep."

He left the boy and went into his own bedchamber.

After stripping off his clothes, he washed up, then wrapped the towel around his waist while he crossed to his bureau and opened the bottle of brandy sitting atop it. He poured some in a glass, then settled into his chair by the hearth.

The night was unusually warm for this time of year, so he'd merely lit a candle to cast some light in his chamber.

He distractedly swirled the amber liquid as he pondered the clues he'd gathered so far. Several potential suspects had now emerged. Auggie's cousin, Morgan Nesbitt, and the duo of Wendall and Crowell.

All three were likely involved and conspiring to steal Lady Priscilla's artwork, perhaps by paying someone to forge the most valuable pieces and then split their winnings once they sold the real works to private collectors. Of course, these private collectors would know the paintings were stolen, but it was a risk they were willing to take for the sake of possessing the art.

Every man would take his cut. The greedy art gallery owners charged exorbitant commissions for serving as the middlemen. A desperate nephew in need of funds. If the art was insured, even Auggie's aunt would be made whole.

But no, that insurance angle would not work now that too many people knew the art had been removed before the fire.

It might have been their initial plan and could not be entirely dismissed.

He briefly considered whether Lady Priscilla and her maid were involved but dismissed that notion as well.

Auggie's dotty maiden aunt and her dim maid were the victims here, the perfect targets for this ring of thieves since they were easily fooled.

Except now the dotty aunt's very sharp niece had come to visit.

His fingers tightened around the fine crystal of his glass.

Auggie could be in danger.

His gut began to churn.

Damn it.

She had just come into his life and now he had to get her out of it. Sam would be heartbroken, but it could not be helped. Perhaps it was for the best since nothing could come of this surprisingly strong attraction he held for her.

He had to convince Auggie to take her aunt back to her father's estate. It was a sensible suggestion. There was no reason for them to stay in Exeter while the crime was being solved.

Would Auggie agree to the plan?

He did not think so. Still, he had to suggest it. No one had been killed yet, but these criminals would not care if lives were lost.

Would they be so brazen as to kill the daughter of a marquess?

Perhaps he ought to write to her father.

He groaned and set aside his glass. "Damn it."

He rose, tossed aside his towel, and climbed into bed.

His head throbbed at the spot where he had been struck by that fire-starting scoundrel.

He'd think more on the matter of Auggie tomorrow.

Rafe fell asleep to the patter of hard rain and opened his eyes shortly after sunrise to sunlight slashing across his face. He shifted, only to find a soft lump beside him on the bed. His son had climbed in and was now fast asleep and clinging to his arm. He felt a pang to his heart, for he'd frightened the boy by returning two hours late to his office. If not for Auggie, the lad would have been in hysterical tears.

She deserved to be properly thanked for tending him.

Scorching kisses might do the trick.

He rubbed a hand across his face and groaned. Here he was, a grown man with his son as a bed companion and his own mother sleeping just down the hall. This arrangement did not do much for his bachelor life.

Nor was anything likely to change any time soon, not with active cases taking up most of his day and a son to care for at night.

As for Auggie…he was aching to kiss her.

But he was not about to mix business with pleasure. If she refused to leave Exeter, they would be in close quarters for weeks. They needed to trust each other, and he did not want her feeling awkward around him.

Their interactions needed to remain professional, no matter that his heart seemed to cry out for her.

He quietly rolled out of bed, washed and dressed, then carried Sam back to his room. "Papa," he said sleepily, his little arms circling around Rafe's neck.

"Yes, son."

"Are you going to work now?"

"I must, but I don't expect to be late tonight. Be a good boy for your grandmother."

"Will you see Auggie?"

He set the boy down under his covers. "Yes, and I will tell her you send your good wishes."

"Do that, Papa. And I want to take dance lessons."

Rafe bit the inside of his cheek to keep from laughing. "Why would you want to do that, son?"

"For Auggie. She likes to dance, she told me so. Maybe she will fall in love with us if we do something nice for her."

Oh, Lord.

"We'll talk about it later." He gave his son a kiss on the head before leaving his bedchamber.

The hour was still early when Rafe walked to his office. It was his habit to work in the quiet hours. But nothing new had been reported, so he strolled to the Swan Inn and thought to question Esther, the proprietor's daughter.

He entered the dining room and was surprised to see Auggie seated at a table by the window, a cup of tea and a plate of eggs beside her. She sat alone, looking achingly vulnerable and lost in thought. He asked one of the serving maids to bring him the same as she was having, then strode over and took the chair opposite hers. "Good morning, Lady Augusta."

She turned to him, obviously caught off guard. But her smile was genuine and quite breathtaking. "Good morning, Mr. Quinton. I did not expect to see you here so soon."

The formality in their manner of address felt odd, but they were in public, and others were listening in. That they were now sharing breakfast would be all the gossip around town. It was not every day that he, perhaps Exeter's most eligible bachelor, was seen in the company of a woman. Nor was it every day that a young woman as pretty as Auggie came to town. Not to mention, she was the daughter of a marquess. "I have a theory about the fire at your aunt's house."

Her eyes rounded. "You do?"

He glanced about the room. "But I would rather not speak of it here. It is a little early yet to pick up your aunt, so let's finish our morning meal, question Esther, and then I'll take you for a stroll along the shopping streets."

She nodded.

"How do you like your accommodations?" he asked, merely making polite conversation while they waited for Esther to finish attending the other tables.

"The bed was comfortable, and I was provided with every amenity."

He grinned. "Even a maid to properly lace your corset?"

She blushed. "Yes, if you must know. She also assisted with my hair." She gave her upswept curls a light pat.

"Very pretty." He liked that Auggie, who was obviously clever and sophisticated in many ways, still had a shyness about her. "And yes, that is a sincere compliment. You look lovely."

She raised her cup and took a sip of tea. "Thank you."

They said nothing more as Esther approached their table.

Rafe drew out a chair for her and immediately got to the questions since the dining room was filling up and he did not think they would have her attention for much longer. "What can you tell us about Lady Priscilla and her nephew, Morgan Nesbitt? I understand they had words, and Lady Priscilla was not pleased."

The girl nodded. "He was asking her for a loan. I did not hear how much he wanted, but I did catch a snippet of some plan he wanted to put in place."

"What sort of plan?" Auggie asked, her brow furrowed in concentration.

"I'm not sure, but he said something about art. And he mentioned her jewels. Then I was called away and heard nothing more. Lady Priscilla was scowling at him and insisting he take her home by the time I returned. I am sorry, Lady Augusta. That is all I know."

Auggie patted her hand. "You've been very helpful. Thank you, Esther."

The girl nodded. "Sir, may I be excused?"

"Yes. We appreciate your time. I'll let your father know if we need to question you again."

He and Auggie watched as she darted back to work. "Well, we now know there was a 'plan' in the works," she muttered. "I only hope my aunt will tell us more about it."

"Afraid she'll try to protect your cousin?"

"Yes. She has always adored him. He can be quite charming when he wants to be. But why isn't he here now? How can he be so callous as to run away knowing Priscilla was about to be left homeless?"

"Perhaps he did not know that part."

"Do you think so? I hope he is innocent of that, at least. But why then would he leave town?"

"Perhaps to avoid the debt collectors. The men sent around by these gambling establishments to collect what is owed are not the sort to be put off. They won't wait around politely while he secures his funds."

"Oh, dear. I see." She took his arm as he escorted her out of the dining room. "I suppose we'll have to ask my aunt about her jewels as well. Rafe, what's next?"

"It's a little early to pick her up yet."

"Will you head back to your office?"

"No, I've already been there. Nothing new to report." He did not want to bring up the matter of the guard and his connection to the art gallery owners just yet.

"Oh, too bad. Then as you suggested, let's walk by the shops. I was thinking to stop at my aunt's modiste and order new gowns for her and Clara. It won't take me long. But I can meet you back here in an hour if you would rather not escort me."

"I'll go with you. I don't mind at all."

"You don't?"

"Unless you are eager to be rid of me."

She laughed. "No, I rather like your company. But you do not strike me as the sort who enjoys shopping."

"I don't usually. It's about as much fun as a boil on one's neck, but you make it tolerable."

"A tolerable boil. Be still my heart," she teased, placing a hand over her heart. "You certainly know how to flatter a lady."

He grinned.

The air had dried out nicely, and the sun was presently darting in and out behind a patch of clouds. But there was a sturdy breeze to carry those clouds off and leave a sparkling autumn day.

However, Rafe was glad it had rained last night, for there was no better way to douse any stray embers at the site of the fire. Unfortunately, any clues would also be washed away, but they had plenty to go on at the moment.

"I'm told the modiste is located just down the street. Madame Josephine's. I would like to ask her to come to the inn later to take my aunt's measurements. Clara's, too, of course. I don't think Aunt Priscilla will be in any condition to leave our suite of rooms once she settles in."

"My mother shops there as well." He pointed to a prettily adorned shop just down the street on the opposite side. The bricks on its facade were painted a bright yellow and trimmed in white, similar to the bakeshop across from his office.

While most of the buildings within the old market square retained the more common hues of gray, red, or golden Cotswolds stone, it was not uncommon for merchants to paint the facades in brighter colors to draw the eye of shoppers. Yellow seemed to be popular, but one also found blues, greens, and an occasional lavender adorning the facades.

Auggie held him up as they were about to cross the street. "May we talk a moment before we go in?"

He nodded. "What do you wish to know?"

"You mentioned having a theory about the fire. We know my cousin was after Aunt Priscilla to lend him funds, and we cannot overlook the coincidence of my aunt's art being taken out just a few days before the fire. These have to be connected. But to what end? If the art gallery owners had a talented artist on staff, what is to stop them from copying the finer paintings, and selling those originals to an interested buyer? The gallery owners take their commission, Priscilla receives the replacement paintings, and Morgan pockets the proceeds of the sale. It is all quite simple if one has the proper people in place to pull it off. Do you think my cousin is the mastermind behind this scheme?"

"He is in it deeply, but not the one who thought this up. The art gallery owners, Wendall and Crowell, are likely the ones who suggested it." He took a moment to tell her about the prison guard's references.

Auggie's eyes rounded in surprise. "Oh, my."

"Your cousin is a minor player, likely involved only in the forgery of your aunt's paintings. But these gallery owners must have a lucrative side business going on. That is why they planted an informant in my prison. As their shady business dealings expand, they need an inside man who can make evidence and witnesses disappear before they can be examined."

"So that odious guard was the man on duty when your prisoner escaped? What are you going to do about him?"

"Put him on suspension for a week and quietly have him

watched. I don't want these men who are bribing him to realize I am already on to their connection. I need to appear to be struggling to make sense of his escape and the fire."

"Won't they be put on alert when we show up to question them?"

"Not necessarily. It is just routine. A part of the investigation." He turned to face her. "About the 'we' part. I'm not sure you ought to come with me. In fact, I think you should take your aunt and her companion to your father's estate as soon as she is fit to travel."

She gasped and shook her head furiously. "I was afraid you were going to suggest this very thing. Put it out of your head at once. I am not going anywhere."

"Auggie—"

"No. I am doing this with you. I need to know if Morgan is involved and how deeply. Do not assume my aunt is his only victim. My father will decide what to do once we collect the incriminating evidence against him."

She looked up into his frowning countenance. "Let me do this with you. Those men who took my aunt's paintings might not be suspicious of me. I can take the lead and play the haughty, unpleasant niece who has come around to ask for an inventory. Or I can pretend to be flighty and an utter peahen."

He continued to frown at her.

She sighed. "Or I can simply be myself. My point is, they'll be more suspicious if you prevent me from seeing them. Besides, I can keep them occupied while you look around. And there is another thing you will need me for."

He arched an eyebrow. "What is that?"

"I am an art scholar and will be able to tell you which paintings hanging in their gallery are forgeries and which are not."

"So help me, Auggie…if this is a jest, I—"

"It isn't. What do you think the pampered daughter of a marquess does with her spare time?"

"Blast it." He groaned and gave a reluctant nod. "All right. It would help me to know just how deep into this criminal activity they've delved."

She cast him a bright smile. "Thank you, I look forward to working with you. It would also be interesting to know how much of their…um, enterprise…goes on with the cooperation of their victims. Estates are often entailed, which means the entailed assets cannot be sold. A member of the nobility might live in splendor but be forced to scratch and scrape for every available shilling since he or she is prohibited from ever selling their magnificent assets."

She paused to search his expression.

When his stoic look revealed nothing, she shrugged and continued. "Is it so farfetched to believe their clients are in on the deception, purposely bringing their finer works to this firm in the hope of a clandestine sale? They pocket the proceeds, giving the firm and the forger a percentage in return for an excellent forgery and a substantial payout. There is little risk of discovery since these paintings, if they are part of the entailed estate, would never be brought to market anyway."

"Gad, you're a clever thing." They crossed the street and started toward the modiste shop. "That is exactly what I believe we are looking at. I've had years of practice at outwitting criminals, but you put it all together by yourself on your first attempt. Consider me impressed. I have no doubt that is the scheme Morgan suggested to your aunt that day at the Swan Inn, and she was not happy about it."

Auggie cast him a devastatingly sweet smile. "I'm pleased to know I have the mind of a criminal. However, it was not too difficult to puzzle out. It is not unusual for a wife in need of funds to do the same with her jewelry. You know, sell the real thing and have a good quality replica made. Then she has a secret nest egg and does not need to worry about how much of an allowance her husband chooses to give her."

"Would you ever do such a thing?"

She appeared surprised by the question. "It would not be

necessary in my situation. My father saw fit to provide me with enough to leave me independently wealthy. And it is not in my nature to squander my assets. I'm probably considered tightfisted. But few women are indulged as I have been. And what of you? Would you be so miserly with your wife as to require her to resort to desperate measures?"

"I would hope not, but that depends on her spending habits, does it not?"

"I suppose. Still, it is quite unfair that a husband has all the say and the wife is at his mercy."

"Not unfair. Often it is done for a woman's own protection. Don't cast me that scowl. I am not a condescending ogre." He placed his hand on the door to open it. "Women have been tossing themselves at me since before I was married and after I became a widower. I can say with confidence that you are the only woman I would ever trust with unrestrained access to my funds. I don't trust most men either, for that matter."

"You would trust me?"

"Yes. I judge people on their character, not on whether they are male or female."

She laughed. "Here I thought we were about to have an argument about the inequities between men and women, and I think you've just complimented me again."

"Try not to look so shocked," he said with a grin. "Come on, let's get your aunt scheduled for a fitting, and then we'll go pick her up."

Madame Josephine was a vivacious woman in her forties who carried herself with impeccable style. She brightened the moment she caught sight of Rafe. "Good morning, Mr. Quinton. What brings you about so early in the day?" She eyed Auggie. "In need of something for your…er, friend?"

"This is Lady Augusta Nesbitt, Lady Priscilla's niece. We've come on Lady Priscilla's behalf. I'm sure you heard about the fire at her home yesterday."

The woman nodded. "Yes, quite a terrible thing."

"She's lost everything," Auggie said. "I was hoping to open an account on her behalf and schedule a fitting for new gowns. Her companion will also require a few garments. Everything is to be charged to me. I am staying at the Swan Inn for the next few weeks. My aunt will be staying there with me. We're about to pick her up from her neighbor's home."

"Yes, of course. Um, I don't suppose you have bank references."

Auggie looked surprised. "I can assure you, I pay all my bills."

Rafe realized that no matter how clever she was, her father must have been the one to arrange these credit matters for her. Auggie probably had no idea how to establish credit for herself at a correspondent bank in Exeter. She would have to write to her father and her London bankers for references. It could take weeks. Priscilla needed her gowns and other items of ladies' wear made immediately. "I'll guarantee all payments, Madame.

"Thank you, Mr. Quinton."

Auggie regarded him with her mouth agape.

He tucked a finger under her chin and nudged her mouth closed. "Lady Augusta ought to have her aunt settled at the inn by midday. Would you send a seamstress over around two o'clock this afternoon? Have her bring a selection of fabrics."

"As you wish."

He turned to Auggie. "Make a list of everything else they will require."

Auggie's lips were pinched, and she did not look pleased when they walked out of the shop a few minutes later. "Why are you angry with me?" he asked.

"I am the daughter of a marquess."

He nodded. "And that will gain you invitations to the finest parties in Exeter. However, our merchants do not have the luxury of waiting months to be paid. I will guarantee your charges until you are established here."

Her cheeks were a bright pink, no doubt from her mounting irritation. Whether it was with him or with herself, he could not tell. But she did not appear happy at the moment. "You are going above and beyond your duties, Magistrate Quinton. Am I to have limits on my spending?"

"No. I've told you, I trust you."

She tried to maintain her scowl but could not manage it. A soft smile crept upon her lips. "I was ready to be angry with you."

"I know. But you are not any longer?"

She sighed. "How can I be when you go ahead and say something very nice about me? Do you really trust me?"

"Yes, without doubt."

"Well, that does it. I cannot be angry with you now. But I am irritated with myself, truth be told. It never occurred to me to make arrangements with my bankers. I suppose this is what comes of being indulged by one's father."

"He may have already opened up lines of credit for you here. Perhaps Lady Priscilla has longstanding credit arrangements as well."

"Everything she has is what my father has given her. Morgan's probably taken most of it by now."

"Our largest bank is the Bank of Exeter, and this would be where your father has established his connections. Shall we stop in now? We have time before we pick up your aunt."

She nodded. "Yes, let's take care of this financial matter right away. It is not right that you should be guaranteeing my family's expenses when you have a son and mother to support."

"I am not a pauper, Auggie."

"I don't mean to suggest you are, but…are magistrates even paid wages?"

"That is a very personal question, but to answer it…yes, we are paid in Exeter. It was instituted recently by the Lord Mayor. However, I've waived my wages and asked that the funds be applied to my staff. I need more men to assist me. We're a prosperous town, and the local merchants depend heavily on maintaining our good reputation. Thieves naturally follow the flow of wealth, and it is our responsibility to stop them before they can strike. I've been given a force of about ten investigators under my direct supervision and another fifty to guard the prisoners brought to Exeter's prison. It is a fortress, and we often receive the more hardened criminals from the entire southwest of England."

She regarded him askance. "You've chosen not to be paid for your work?"

"I don't need the income."

"Right, because you are not a pauper."

She had her arm in his as they strolled toward the bank. He was quite enjoying her company, even though their topic was hardly an appropriate one to be having between them. "But I do need capable men to handle the more serious offenses in Exeter."

"Is this your roundabout way of telling me you are very rich?"

He laughed. "I doubt my holdings are anywhere near as extensive as your father's. But Finn Brayden is my cousin, and he manages my funds. He takes care of the entire family and has done quite nicely for us all. I have assets beyond those I've turned over to Finn. Several properties in and around Exeter."

"I've only been briefly introduced to Finn. However, I do know Belle, that's his wife. And Belle's sister, Honey. Of course, Honey and I are often invited to the same affairs, since she is married to the Earl of Wycke."

"Of course."

She pinched her lips. "Now you think I am being haughty."

"Not at all, but you do travel in lofty circles."

"Belle and Honey are kind and hardworking. They share their time between London and Oxford because their family produces the Farthingale soaps. Belle is the talent behind each scent created. But you know them possibly as well as I do through your family connections. It is odd how we are connected through similar friends and family."

"Yes, it is."

"And yet, we'd never met until yesterday, even though I've visited Aunt Priscilla several times over the years. Usually, a month each summer. How extraordinary that you and I were strangers to each other until yesterday."

He shrugged. "We've met now, and I doubt I will soon forget you."

"Nor will I ever forget you," she said quietly as they entered the bank and asked to speak to the manager.

"Mr. Quinton, good to see you," the affable gentleman said, reaching out to shake hands with him. "What can I do for you?"

He introduced Mr. Vole to Auggie. "She's often spent summers in Exeter, so we were wondering whether her father had set up credit for her. If not, we'd like to establish it now. Shall we say five hundred pounds to start?"

Auggie kicked his foot.

He ignored her.

"I am familiar with the Marquess of Chelsford. Allow me a moment to check through my records."

She kicked his foot again as soon as the manager scurried out. "It is too much, don't you think?"

"Five hundred pounds? It is too little, frankly. You will have at least two weeks of room and meals owed to the inn. Gowns for your aunt and her companion. And what of the reconstruction of her house? That will not come cheap."

"I was thinking of selling the plot of land, merely clearing it out and not rebuilding. Aunt Priscilla will be more comfortably settled in one of my father's homes. Morgan will not be so easily able to steal from her once she is under my father's protection."

"I suppose that makes sense. Just keep in mind Lady Priscilla has lived in Exeter all of her adult life. She may not be as keen to leave as you are." He tried to keep the irritation out of his voice, not even understanding why he was so put out. Auggie's decision was sensible in every way but one…it would take her away from Exeter, too.

Of course, she had never intended to remain beyond a month or two.

And was he not eager to get her out of town for her own

protection?

It was amazing how quickly she'd gotten into his blood.

He only hoped he could forget her as quickly.

Auggie looked up at him, her lips pursed. "Do you think I am being heartless? You are right, of course. This must be her decision to make. I cannot pull her from this place she loves simply because it is convenient for my father and me."

He took her hands in his as she clasped them, for he could see she was berating herself unnecessarily. "You are only thinking of what is best for your aunt. I know that, Auggie."

He released her when the manager bustled back in. "All is in order, Mr. Quinton. Lady Augusta shall have whatever she needs at her disposal. Her father has ample credit here." He turned to Auggie. "Come to me if you require anything further, and I shall help you fill out the instructions. Or you can ask Mr. Quinton to assist you. He understands these matters of finance."

She cast the man a brittle smile. "Thank you, Mr. Vole. I'm sure I shall manage quite well."

Rafe led her out of the bank and into the morning sunshine. "You can stop seething now," he said with a chuckle.

"Why does every man assume a woman is inadequate to the task of managing her own finances?"

"Well, you did not know about these credit transactions. And before you lop my head off, let me assure you, I know you are quite capable. But you are also young and pretty, so men naturally assume you are helpless...or we want to assume you are because we hope you'll need us to be your hero and come to your rescue." He shook his head. "I wonder if that book my cousins gave me explains why men lose their wits over an attractive woman?"

"I am not that young, and I don't think most men find me appealing. I spent years on the odious marriage mart and attracted nothing but fortune hunters." She placed her arm in his as they strolled toward the inn to call for her carriage.

He liked her touch.

Yes, he definitely had to read that book.

"It is more likely those aggressive fortune hunters chased off the decent men who hoped to court you. You must have been considered a *ton* diamond when you had your come-out."

She groaned. "I was so miserable that first year."

"Why, Auggie?"

"I think it was all too much for me. I was indeed hailed as a diamond and barraged with suitors and invitations. My season was spent going from one party to another and, in between, rushing to my modiste for more new gowns. It felt so hollow. I really did not enjoy it. I wanted to be a wallflower and remain peacefully ignored. But the only child of a wealthy marquess can never be ignored."

"Indeed not."

"Perhaps I did chase away some decent men, but how was I to know the difference?"

"Did you not feel anything for a single one of them?"

She gazed up at him, obviously confused. "What should I have been feeling?"

"The quickening of your heart when a gentleman of particular interest approached you. The same when he held you in his arms while dancing the waltz. Was there no one at these elegant balls you were secretly eager to see?"

Now she regarded him oddly.

"No," she said quietly. "Is this how love is supposed to feel?"

"I cannot say for certain." He'd been through war and through marriage, had been a responsible father, husband, and son. He'd also enjoyed being irresponsible a time or two, ploughing his way through women and drink in his younger days.

Indeed, he and his brother Deklan had been quite wild as boys.

But one thing he had never been was in love.

Not that he considered himself in love with Auggie now. How could he be? Perhaps infatuation was a better word for it. Yes, infatuated with the look of her, the scent and touch of her.

He could tell she liked him, too. The little gestures gave her away, the way her eyes glittered. The way she patted her hair when he approached. The—

"Rafe, should we not have turned right to return to the inn?"

He shook out of these wayward thoughts. "Yes, but we still have half an hour before we need to be on our way. Do you mind if we stop by my office? It is only around the corner."

"I don't mind." A few moments later, she emitted a soft trill of laughter. "I have it. I shall know I am in love when my heart flutters with excitement just as it is fluttering now at the thought of learning more about these criminals."

"Auggie, I sincerely hope love's kiss is far sweeter than the prospect of digging through criminal records."

She was still laughing as she said, "I wouldn't know. I've never been kissed in a romantic way. I expect it is much different from the kiss of a friend or family relations bussing my cheek. I never thought about it that way. Love's kiss. That is a very nice way to describe it. I did not take you for a romantic, Rafe."

"I'm not."

She eyed him speculatively. "Oh, I'd be willing to wager you are and merely hide the poet in you behind a curmudgeonly facade."

"You would lose. I am terse, impatient, and cannot abide flowery prose." He held open the door for her, fighting to keep his senses from exploding. How was it possible she had survived three seasons without a single stolen kiss?

He needed to kiss this girl.

Hellfire.

He needed to be dunked in a vat of icy water.

Why was he suddenly feeling savagely possessive over her?

CHAPTER FOUR

AUGGIE TRIED TO stay out of the way as chaos appeared to be swirling all around them. Rafe's investigators, Marbury and Cooper, had arrived minutes before them with the body of the escaped man. She knew who they were because she had met them briefly in Rafe's office yesterday.

"Lady Augusta, wait in my office," Rafe said with an authoritative growl as he tried to block her view of the dead man.

"I will not." If no one else was fainting at the sight of a corpse, then why should she?

But as she skittered around Rafe's big body and saw the damp molder and pale purplish hue of the culprit's skin, she turned away and gagged. "I'm all right," she insisted when Rafe put a gentle arm around her waist, the light touch searing her to the core. "It took me by surprise, that's all. Where was he found?"

"We pulled his body out of the Thames," Marbury said.

"He must have been in there since yesterday evening," Cooper added, his gaze shifting from her to Rafe and then remaining on Rafe as he gave the rest of his report. "His name is Alfred Finster, a ne'er-do-well who sometimes lived with his sister's family. We'll head there next to question her and her husband about Alfred's last job."

"Ask them about all his recent jobs and if any included an art gallery, specifically—" She drew in a breath and looked to Rafe. "I'm sorry. I will keep my mouth shut now."

But he did not appear to be angry. "You heard the lady. Get as much information as you can on all his jobs in the past six months. Especially work he did for any carters and haulers or art galleries and jeweler's shops. There's also the milkman to be questioned. Track him down after you speak to Finster's family. I'll be assisting Lady Augusta with her aunt. You will find me with them at the inn in about an hour."

"Yes, Mr. Quinton. Any reason we should be asking about carters and haulers?"

He quickly told them about their suspicions. "Lady Augusta and I will poke our noses around that art gallery first. Hopefully, they will think she came around to ask about her aunt's paintings and nothing more."

"Won't your presence alarm them, sir?"

"We'll make it clear I am merely escorting her as a favor to her father."

"Or, I could go in myself," Auggie said, knowing he would shoot down that idea like a game bird out of the sky. "Is it not more sensible than you coming in with me? You are too well known about town and will scare the gallery owners even if you pretend you haven't a clue about their involvement."

"No." The word came down like a hammer atop her head. "Utter a word of protest, and I will ship you back to your father before the day is through."

She closed her mouth and gestured as though she were buttoning her lip.

His investigators chuckled.

She caught the twitch of a smile at the corners of Rafe's lips. Which led her to wonder how his lips would feel against hers.

Quite spectacular, she imagined.

She gave it no more thought as he finished with his men and dismissed them. "Wait for me in my office, Auggie."

"Why?"

He sighed. "You are headstrong, aren't you?"

"No, just very spoiled and used to giving instructions rather than taking them. Why do you not want me with you?"

"Because I am going to search through this man's clothing and examine his body. It is bad enough you saw his dead body. You are not going to see his *naked* dead body."

She put a hand to her mouth and gagged again. "Right, perfectly sensible. I'll be on my way. You'll find me in your waiting room chatting with Cavendish."

"Auggie…" He took her gently by the arm. "Try to avoid mention of this to Cavendish."

The remark surprised her. "Do you think he is another spy in your midst?"

"No, but he does not know when to keep his mouth shut. He is academically brilliant, and I trust him completely, but he is as innocent as an ingenue at her first ball and easily gulled. I am not asking you to lie to him. Just do not go out of your way to bring it up."

"But if the topic is raised?"

"Then respond truthfully. All I am saying is that the fewer people who know about this body, the better."

"Oh, I am certain he is sharper than you give him credit for. But you are quite intimidating, and you obviously leave him rattled whenever you come in growling like an angry bear. He must fear losing his job every time you shout at him."

She left him pondering the notion, although she doubted he was much concerned about his behavior toward his clerk. Cavendish also needed to show a little spine instead of diving under his desk whenever Rafe strode in.

After all, Rafe was responsible for keeping the peace in Exeter, as well as guarding some of the most dangerous criminals in England. The task was meant for a man of grit and not a mild-mannered scholar.

She walked to his waiting room.

Cavendish looked up from his work and smiled. "Good morning, Lady Augusta. Mr. Quinton is not here. May I assist you with anything?"

"No, please do not mind me. I was told to meet him here. I'm sure he'll be along shortly."

The young man set aside his piles of paperwork and came around his desk. "Would you care for a cup of tea while you wait? It is no trouble for me to send over for it from the shop across the street."

"Truly, I am fine. I do not mean to distract you from your work. You seem quite busy."

"The work can wait. It would be rude of me to ignore you."

"Not at all." But he seemed quite perplexed and not inclined to resume his tasks, so she engaged him in conversation. "What sort of work do you do here, Mr. Cavendish?"

"The scholarly end of things, since I am not really fit for fieldwork. But I enjoy the intellectual exercise. We receive writs daily from the court concerning these prisoners. Some of these men will be set for release as their sentences near an end. Others will be scheduled to hang. Dear me, I should not have mentioned that. I do not mean to unsettle you."

"You haven't. I find it all quite interesting. Do continue. What else comes across your desk?"

"Oh, everything. Letters from the prisoners' families requesting leniency or the right to visit. Some enclose funds for extra comforts for their loved ones. I make certain those funds do not find their way into a guard's pocket instead of being properly applied. I also attend to the investigative reports, put them in coherent order to be read by a judge when a man is on trial. Then there is the preparatory work for the weekly hearings over which the magistrate presides."

"Mr. Cavendish, it seems you do quite a bit of work here. And you handle all of it yourself?"

He smiled. "I do. Most days it is manageable. But crime is not orderly, and criminals do not work in turns. Nor are judges patient. There are times when having extra help would be appreciated. But it would require me to take the time with an apprentice at the very moment I have no time to spare. Also, while the prison expenses have always been funded, the town council only recently approved making the office of magistrate a paid position and setting aside revenues for his investigators."

"So I've heard. One would think such arrangements would have been put in place long ago for a town of this size and importance."

"Informal arrangements were in place, but nothing coordinated, and all required private backing. When he first took on the role of magistrate, Mr. Quinton was fighting for every spare farthing he could wheedle from the council members, as well as the local business leaders and trade guilds, since it was to their benefit to have the streets kept safe. But it has all been consolidated now. However, only the magistrate and his investigators are paid positions."

"And not the supporting staff?"

"No, not one of us. Although we are only three on his staff currently. Me and the two boys we use as runners to take our reports to the court or over to the prison warden. Mr. Quinton continues to pay me and the boys out of his own pocket, and he is a generous man."

"I see. This is all quite fascinating. Mr. Cavendish, have you begun a report on the fire at my aunt's house?"

"Yes, just starting it. The investigators have not given me much to write up yet. The culprit escaped, but I know Mr. Quinton will want to move fast once he is found again. A man like that needs to be put away for the duration of his life. I'll prepare a report for the court once he is recaptured."

Auggie cleared her throat.

Mr. Cavendish stared at her. "Why do I suddenly feel as though you know something I don't?"

She groaned.

"Please, Lady Augusta, tell me. Good grief. Is he dead?"

"Um, there was a bit of a commotion when I walked in. Yes, it is possible the man was found...dead."

Mr. Cavendish's eyes rounded in surprise. "Well, it would

have been nice for someone to let me know. But I seem to be the last to be told anything, and then it is a mad rush to properly write down all the details and send the report off to the judges and barristers. Although, in this instance, there is nothing to report other than he is dead."

"What of your other matters?"

"Serious matters are held over for the Assizes. The justice holds court four times a year, quarterly sessions that can last anywhere from a day to a month or several months depending on caseload. However, Magistrate Quinton is responsible for ruling on the minor crimes and civil matters himself. He sits every Thursday to hear those disputes."

"And you are there by his side as well?"

"Oh, yes. Usually, full reports aren't necessary. I merely jot down notes for him, just enough to record the important details. Too many complainants come before him to keep all in his head. But he is remarkably good at doing so."

She nodded. "He strikes me as a clever man."

"Indeed, he is. It is a pleasure to work for him. He cares for people, too. Do not let his brusque manner fool you. He's honest, too. Everyone respects him. I wish I could be more like him, but..." He held out his hands in a gesture of dismay. "I am nothing much to look at, and I become a tongue-tied idiot whenever he barks at me."

"And he is always barking at you," she said with sincere empathy. "I think he has fallen into the bad habit of dumping his frustration out on you."

"On occasion. In truth, you caught him on a very bad day. He is rarely like that. It is small sufferance for all the good he otherwise does."

"Nevertheless, I will mention it to him. He must not be aware he is doing this to you."

Mr. Cavendish stared at her, obviously appalled. "Please do not say anything to him. It is bad enough I am too weak-willed to fight my own battles. But to have a lady fight them for me? That is too much of an embarrassment, even for the likes of me."

"Oh, I am truly sorry, Mr. Cavendish. I only meant to be helpful."

He winced. "You have been. It is nice to have someone listen to me every once in a while. But I can stand up for myself. Truly, I am capable of it. But there is no need. I enjoy my work very much. Mostly he does not growl at me but at the stupidity and pettiness of some of these villains brought in. Life can be very cruel, at times. You are fortunate to have been spared a view of this."

She had indeed led a protected and pampered life. But was this not precisely the reason she should do something, even if only in a small way, to help those suffering? This was a topic to be discussed with her father once she returned to London. "Mr. Cavendish, I shall be settled at the inn with my aunt and her companion for the next few weeks. I hope you will consider me a friend and not hesitate to call on me if ever you feel the need to talk."

"I would not think of imposing on you, Lady Augusta." He blushed and appeared quite rattled by the offer.

"It is no imposition, I assure you. Most people expect me to be frivolous and caring for nothing more than the next party or the newest fashions. It is a pleasant relief to converse with someone who has more than pudding stuffed between his ears."

He laughed. "Thank you, my lady. I think you will quickly become the jewel of Exeter and too popular for me ever to get within shouting distance of you."

"Well, shout loudly so I can hear you," she said with a grin.

Rafe walked in as they were both still chuckling over their exchange. "I see you are distracting my clerk."

Mr. Cavendish blanched and rushed back to his desk.

Rafe held out his arm to her. "Shall we go?"

She nodded, but first spared a moment for his young clerk. "It was a pleasure chatting with you, Mr. Cavendish." She turned to Rafe. "I had no idea he shouldered so much responsibility.

Preparing your investigative reports. Sorting through the daily writs. Preparing your decisions for the matters you oversee. I assume he does them very well and makes you appear quite clever in the eyes of others. I have not heard you once complain about a shoddy report."

Rafe laughed and turned to his clerk. "I do believe I have just been spanked for my surly behavior yesterday. And it was very elegantly done, too. Wipe that grin off your face, Cavendish. You are taking too much pleasure in it," he said in good humor. "Send word to the Swan Inn if you need to get hold of me."

"I will, Mr. Quinton."

Auggie waited for Rafe to admonish her as they walked back to the inn, but he remained silent, so she began the conversation. "He really does a lot for you."

"I assume you are referring to Mr. Cavendish."

She nodded.

They strolled in silence a moment longer before Rafe bothered to respond. "I know he does. He's an excellent man. I would not keep him on if he weren't. Are you fighting his battles for him?"

She winced. "No. As a matter of fact, I know he would be quite angry if I dared say another word on his behalf."

Rafe arched an eyebrow. "Then why are you meddling? What did he wish to talk to me about?"

"Nothing. He will never speak up for himself. Nor am I suggesting he has any wish to do so."

"Auggie, you have me utterly confused. What are we talking about?" They had reached the inn, and Rafe took a moment to request her carriage be brought around. "You obviously have it in mind that I am an ogre and everyone needs to be protected from me."

"Not at all. I wouldn't give you the time of day if you were that. But I did notice you seem to be tougher than necessary on Mr. Cavendish. You were yelling at him the first time I saw you."

"I yell for him, not at him. There is a difference. Besides, men are far more coarse among themselves than when in the company of women."

"He seems very mild-mannered."

Rafe nodded. "He is intelligent and thoughtful. I like him, and he is tougher than he may appear to you. After all, we work in prison surroundings. My investigators and I haul in some very nasty culprits."

"Speaking of which, did you find out anything more about the drowned man Mr. Cooper and Mr. Marbury brought in?"

"No, nothing of use on him. I expect the men who killed him went through his pockets before they tossed him in the water. Let's get Lady Priscilla. I hope the sedative has worn off her by now. I'd like her alert when questioned."

"You will be gentle with her, won't you?"

He sighed. "Auggie, I'm good at what I do. I will not browbeat your aunt."

She took his hand without hesitation as he assisted her into the carriage. She'd poked her nose where it did not belong, and now he thought she was chastising him for his efforts. Nothing could be farther from the truth.

She thought he was marvelous.

Truly someone special.

She'd known it the moment his son had run into his arms yesterday.

Perhaps that was why she felt so fidgety around him. She wanted to be in his arms, too. For the first time in her life, she wanted to be held and kissed. She wanted the arms to be his and the mouth covering hers to be his.

She had always been curious how a first kiss would feel. But in three seasons, she had never met a man worth surrendering to until this moment.

With Rafe, she knew it would feel right.

She tried not to be obvious when studying his lips.

Oh, they would feel splendid.

Utter rapture.

She closed her eyes and allowed her thoughts to wander.

"Auggie, are you all right?"

Her eyes shot open. "Yes, why shouldn't I be?"

He leaned toward her. "You had an odd look on your face. I thought you might be feeling queasy. I should not have allowed you to view the body."

Good gracious, he thought she was thinking of dead bodies? "I'm glad you did. I am fine. I merely closed my eyes a moment to think."

"About what?"

You.

Heat rose in her cheeks. "Nothing important."

He cast her a soft smile that had her heart fluttering again. "All right, if you say so."

Honestly, it was as though he could read her mind and knew she wanted him to kiss her. She had to do a better job of hiding her thoughts...or not think when in his presence.

They soon arrived at the home of Lord and Lady Whiting. "Rafe, may we have a quick look at my aunt's property before we go in?"

"As you wish." He led her next door to the remains of her aunt's home and greeted the men who were still at the property sifting through the ashes to make certain there were no more live embers.

"Good day, Jonah," he said to the searcher obviously in charge. "This is Lady Priscilla's niece, Lady Augusta Nesbitt. Have you come across anything of interest for us?"

"Nice to see ye, Rafe," the man replied with a nod. "A pleasure to meet ye, m'lady. No, nothing to report. But last night's rain did the job of dousing those last embers. We were able to spend the morning sifting through the debris. In fact, we haven't found anything of interest, and that is interesting in itself."

"What do you mean?" Auggie asked.

"Not everything burns in a fire. One would expect to find remnants of yer aunt's jewelry, m'lady. Diamonds don't melt.

Most gemstones are typically hardy. We've found nary a one."

"I see. That is most interesting, is it not Mr. Quinton?"

He nodded. "It is another thing to ask your aunt. Are you done looking around?"

"Yes. Thank you, Jonah. Gentlemen. We are most appreciative of your efforts." She took another moment to thank each personally.

Rafe led her back. "Careful, Auggie, or you'll have every man in Exeter in love with you."

She laughed. "I hardly think there is a danger of that."

They were shown into the Whiting residence and once again settled in the parlor. Lord Whiting came forward to greet them. Auggie had barely the chance to sit down when she was on her feet again and asking questions. "How is my aunt? Did she pass a restful night? How is she today?"

Lord Whiting chuckled and shook his head. "She is fine. My wife and our maids are assisting her downstairs right now."

Auggie could hear them on the steps and wanted to run out, but her aunt could barely manage the climb last time they had been together, and she did not want to distract her and cause a tumble.

Her aunt's face lit up with joy the moment she entered the parlor and saw Auggie standing there. "My darling, what are you doing here? When did you get into town?"

She hugged her aunt. "I arrived yesterday, just after the fire. Do you not recall I had planned to visit?"

Her smile faltered. "Oh, yes. Yes. It slipped my mind in all the excitement."

"Mr. Quinton was kind enough to help me make other arrangements for us. We came by to see you yesterday, but Lord Whiting's physician had already given you a potion to settle your nerves. You were asleep, and we did not wish to disturb you."

She helped her aunt to a chair. "I have reserved a suite of rooms for us at the Swan Inn. I believe you are familiar with it."

"Oh, yes. I meet friends there regularly for tea," she said, settling in with a grunt.

Auggie nodded. "That is what the proprietor told me."

"It is a charming establishment."

"I thought so, too. I think our stay will be most pleasant. I've also made arrangements for your modiste to come by later and take measurements of you and Clara. You'll each need an entire new wardrobe. We'll make a list of everything you'll require once you are settled. Where is Clara?"

Lady Whiting gestured toward the door. "She is waiting in the hall. I saw no need to have her come in since you will all be off in a few minutes."

Auggie maintained a gracious smile, but she was angry. Hadn't Clara been through the same fire? Was she not her aunt's companion? Did she not deserve better than to be left standing alone in the hall?

Well, Clara had only become more of a companion recently but was really a maid. Most people, even if they viewed her as a companion, would not consider her proper company. She forced herself to swallow her irritation. At least the poor woman had not been sent to wait outside. There was a nip in the air, and she doubted Clara had so much as a shawl to keep her warm.

Auggie silently berated herself.

Why was she becoming so sensitive to everything around her? Not even Aunt Priscilla appeared to be put out, and Clara was the woman who had tended to her needs for over a decade.

She settled in a chair beside her aunt and then took hold of her hand. "We will be on our way as soon as you catch your breath, Aunt Priscilla. I see you've been having some difficulty walking. They've put us on the main floor at the inn so you will have no steps to climb. We'll be just down the hall from the dining room, and we also have lovely glass doors in our suite leading straight to the inn's garden."

Her aunt waved her perfumed handkerchief lightly. "Oh, that sounds divine."

Rafe remained standing by her side with his arms folded

across his chest. "Lady Whiting, I questioned your husband briefly yesterday but did not have the chance to talk to you. It is my experience that women tend to notice a lot more going on around them than men do. Did anything strike you as out of the ordinary yesterday or any time over this past week?"

"No, not at all." She glanced at Auggie's aunt in a manner that immediately put Auggie on alert. Had Rafe noticed the exchange of glances between the two women? Lady Whiting was in on a secret and not about to share it without her aunt's permission.

She would make a point to mention this to Rafe once they got her aunt and Clara settled at the inn.

Rafe asked Lady Whiting several more questions, to which he received unhelpful answers. Not that the lady appeared to be evasive in responding to them, but simply did not have anything useful to report.

"Well, we had better be on our way," Auggie said once Rafe had finished his interrogation. "Are you ready, Aunt Priscilla? Mr. Quinton is a busy man, and I've already taken up too much of his time."

"Yes, of course." Her aunt required Rafe's assistance to help her out of the chair. "Thank you, Mr. Quinton. So terribly kind of you."

"My pleasure, Lady Priscilla." He escorted her out of the house while Auggie expressed her appreciation to the Whitings.

The Whiting footmen assisted her aunt into the carriage and did the same with Clara. The ladies took seats beside each other, leaving only the opposite bench free for her and Rafe to share.

Auggie did her best to tamp down her delight.

To be this close to him felt wonderful, and she was afraid it showed on her face.

His body was big and warm.

She wanted to burrow closer.

Of course, it was out of the question.

However, she did enjoy the occasional rub of their shoulders as they rode back to the inn.

Butterflies erupted in her belly every time this happened.

Butterflies. Tingles. Heat. Truly, she was responding like an utter peahen.

Since they were seated side by side, he could not see her expression. Thank goodness for that. He had a discerning eye and would know at once what she was thinking.

"I must invite Lady Whiting to join us for tea once we are settled," Priscilla said, startling her out of her thoughts.

"Yes, of course. I would also like to ask Mr. Quinton's mother and her Ladies Auxiliary. They have kindly offered to help out with anything you lack."

"That is very kind of them. But I think we shall be fine, shall we not Clara?"

The woman appeared surprised to be addressed, no doubt since she'd been ignored at the Whitings. "We shall be fine, indeed."

The pair exchanged a glance.

Auggie's stomach began to roil.

Something was going on.

Her aunt and Lady Whiting had done the same back at the Whiting residence.

Auggie was determined to get at the truth. "It is a good thing your paintings and jewelry were taken away before the fire. Where did Morgan send the jewels? To the same gallery as your paintings?"

Priscilla pursed her lips, obviously determined to ignore the question.

Clara spoke up. "We don't know. He said he'd take care of everything."

Auggie frowned. "Auntie, you are always careful with your possessions. What needed to be done?"

Once again, it was Clara who spoke up. "Your cousin said everything looked a bit worn down. Then he brought those nice gentlemen to the house, and they said the same thing. They told

Lady Priscilla that her beautiful paintings would be ruined if she did not take immediate steps to have them restored."

"Hush, Clara," her aunt said in a hiss. "How you do go on."

"Aunt Priscilla! Why are you being so secretive? Who were these gentlemen Morgan brought with him?"

"Just friends of his. What does it matter?"

Auggie glanced at Rafe, wondering how he withstood this sort of response from those he was trying to help. He probably endured it day in and day out. But this was her aunt, and she was Priscilla's beloved grandniece. "Do you have their names?"

Clara started to tell her but was immediately silenced by her aunt.

"You should be as forthcoming, Aunt Priscilla." Auggie frowned. "I was with you just last year and none of your belongings appeared to be in bad shape. Indeed, they looked quite well cared for."

Priscilla shook her head impatiently. "You are no art expert."

"Neither is Morgan. Besides, I do know a good deal about their care since I help my father with the Chelsford art collection, which is quite extensive."

"My darling, Auggie. You know I adore you, but you can be excessively tedious at times. Let's talk about something else. How was your season?"

"My latest?" She cast Rafe a quick smile. "Just as miserable as the first two seasons, thank you for asking. Apparently, all the young men find me as tedious as you seem to find me."

"Nonsense, child. You are a delight. You simply do not know when to let go of a topic, that is all. My niece is really quite charming, Mr. Quinton."

"I've noticed," he said with a hint of amusement in his husky voice.

Her aunt's eyes lit up.

Clara tittered.

The carriage clattered over a rut in the street and threw Auggie against him. He caught her in his arms. Rock hard arms, she noted as she held on to them to steady herself. Well, she knew his body was spectacular having seen him half undressed when she'd returned to his office to retrieve her gloves.

Sweet, glorious heaven.

She allowed herself to the count of five to remain melted against him, then eased herself away.

Everyone was now staring at her.

Well, perhaps she'd counted to ten…or twenty…and rested her head a moment against his firm chest.

Perhaps she'd sighed.

No, she wouldn't have been so obvious.

She cleared her throat and sat straight as an arrow, her hands clasped on her lap. "Aunt Priscilla, where is Morgan now?"

CHAPTER FIVE

RAFE HELPED AUGGIE settle her aunt and companion in their suite of rooms and immediately realized they would not have time to stop at the Wendall and Crowell gallery today. The elderly women required too much attention and seemed unable to manage the simplest tasks for themselves. Nor were they helpful in answering Auggie's question as to Morgan's whereabouts.

He suspected they knew but were purposely not telling her or him.

Auggie cast him a frustrated look. "They are so obviously holding back. Do they not understand we wish to help them? And now they are doing all in their power to thwart me. I don't think I will be able to leave them this afternoon. I did not expect my stepping out for a few hours would matter but look at them. They are little more than helpless children."

"Walk me to the foyer," he said while her aunt and Clara were momentarily being attended by the maids who had brought in their midday meal.

She nodded and eagerly tucked her arm in his as they ambled down the hall toward the inn's front entrance. "You seem to be taking their obstructiveness better than I am."

He shrugged. "I'm used to people lying to me. It seems to come with the territory."

"She is my aunt, and I am here to help her. Perhaps she is a bit intimidated by you, but she should not be hiding the truth from me. Why would she do this?" She sighed and shook her head. "Oh, well. Perhaps she will have a change of heart tomorrow."

"I'm sure she will."

Auggie shook her head again. "I think you are saying this merely to placate me."

"Perhaps there is a little of that," he admitted. "I can see you are hurt by her lack of cooperation." Auggie obviously loved her aunt and being shut out of her confidence had overset her. But that was how people often behaved when they held back secrets. They closed themselves off, even to their loved ones.

He was used to it, had come to expect it as a part of his job.

"As for today," Auggie continued, pursing her lips as she mused, "I suppose it is better for me to be here when the modiste arrives because I have no idea what my aunt will order. I think not all of her behavior is purposefully evasive. She and Clara seem genuinely dithering, do you not think so?"

"I did notice."

"Rafe, would you mind delaying our gallery visit until tomorrow?"

"Not at all. It may be for the best. We cannot appear to be too concerned about your aunt's paintings or they'll know immediately we are on to them. I've had a man watching their activities since last night. He knows to report to me if anything is moved in or out after hours. I'll see what we can do to track down the jewelry in the meantime."

"Thank you, but there is something else you should know. Lady Whiting and my aunt exchanged glances when I asked them if they'd noticed anything out of the ordinary. Then Clara and my aunt did the same when I asked the same question of Clara on the carriage ride over here. I think the three ladies are hiding something else from us."

"It is likely nothing but see what information you can pry out of Clara. She seems to be the weak link and will run off at the mouth. Hopefully, she'll reveal something useful. In the meantime, I'll ask Cavendish to check the land records."

Her lovely eyes rounded in surprise. "Why those?"

"Just trying to be thorough. Do you think it is possible your cousin has convinced your aunt to transfer the house to his name? Perhaps Lady Whiting and Clara are aware this was done and meant to keep it a secret from you and your father."

"Why would Lady Whiting indulge in this deception?" She shook her head. "No. Besides, my father owns the property. Morgan cannot touch it. But do have a man look into it. I don't know what to think anymore. It would break my heart if he were so far gone as to forge my father's name. And how would he obtain his seal?"

"Then it is likely not that."

She nodded. "The secret they are hiding seems to be something only the women are in on. Lord Whiting did not appear to know anything about it. So maybe it has to do with my aunt's jewels. Or perhaps the ladies are involved in a ladies-only gaming club."

"I do not see your aunt as a card sharp," he said, suppressing a chuckle. "There are obvious signs when someone gets in over their head. The avid players are often short of funds when their luck turns cold. She would have been pestering your father if this were her problem. Has she been?"

"No."

They'd walked beyond the inn's entry and were now standing on the street. "Auggie, you are still frowning."

"Because I cannot make sense of my aunt's behavior. If it is not a question of gambling because she has never exceeded her monthly allowance, then what did those exchanged glances mean? Truly, I do not think I am making something out of nothing."

"We'll figure it out," he assured her.

She was facing the sun as she smiled up at him causing her to squint and put a hand over her eyes to shade them. "Thank you,

Rafe. I look forward to seeing you tomorrow. I also promised Sam I would see him. I'd like to keep my word."

He moved to stand in front of her, his size blocking most of the sun. The day had been cool a moment ago, but there was something about Auggie's nearness that turned the air suddenly hot. That heat could not be blamed on the golden orb in the sky. Auggie was wreaking havoc on his senses. He could not be around her without his body responding. It was ridiculous, a grown man with all his experience unable to control his organs.

There was simply something about her that his heart recognized and wanted. "We can take care of that tomorrow as well. I'll stop by around noon with my son. Would you mind if we dined together at the inn?"

"My aunt and Clara prefer to take their meals in our suite, so it would just be the three of us."

He grinned. "Thank goodness."

"Is it awful of me to feel the same way?" She laughed lightly.

"Sam will be delighted to have you to himself. I'll reserve a table for us. Afterward, we can drop my son back home and continue to the gallery."

"Sounds perfect."

"I'll see you tomorrow then."

"Rafe..." He'd started to walk off but paused and turned to her when she called him. "Yes, Auggie?"

"Nothing...I..." Her cheeks were red, so whatever she meant to tell him was causing her some embarrassment.

He frowned, his hand settling on her waist to draw her to him. But he could not take her into his arms out here on the street, so he dropped his hand to the side. "What's wrong? Are you worried we've overlooked something?"

"No...I...just wanted to thank you for today. Having you by my side...oh, I'm not expressing myself properly. Thank you. More than thank you for all you've done for me and my family." She glanced around, saw no one was looking, and hastily bussed a kiss on his cheek, then fled back inside the inn.

"I'll see you tomorrow," he said in a whisper, his body once again in a hot roil. So was hers, he suspected, for he was experienced enough to understand the signs of attraction.

He returned to his office and forced his mind to the other matters he'd neglected today. "Cavendish, how many cases are we scheduled to hear on Thursday?"

"Heavier load than usual, Mr. Quinton. I've reviewed the plaintiff's pleadings for each case to come before you and jotted down some notes."

Rafe grinned. "You are a good man, Cavendish."

"So are you, Mr. Quinton. And Lady Augusta is a gem. I suspect you have already noticed her fine qualities."

"I have, not that it is any of your business."

"It isn't, I know. But I think she likes you, and it seems a terrible shame for Exeter to lose her to those London dandies."

"I'll see what I can do. It is early days yet, Cavendish. Early days." Rafe returned his attention to the pile of documents waiting for him atop his desk. He and Cavendish sorted through each matter, but even though they worked quickly, it still took them hours.

He could tell by the position of the sun shining in through his window that it was past five o'clock. He was used to working much later, often until close to midnight, but he did not want this to be another late night. Sam had been upset yesterday, and he wanted to see his boy before the lad fell asleep. He'd work another hour or two and then leave.

His back was aching, so he rose and walked around his desk to peer out the window. From his vantage point, he could see much of Exeter stretched out before him in all its shining glory.

He was happily settled here.

But Auggie was only here for a few months to take care of her aunt.

Would she consider staying longer?

Staying a lifetime?

He returned to his desk and worked a few hours longer, then

finally gave up. "I'll review the last of your notes in the morning. Go home, Cavendish. You've done a fine day's work."

"Thank you, sir. I'll see you in the morning. Give my regards to Lady Augusta."

He glanced up from the papers on his desk and shook his head. "I'm not seeing her tonight."

Cavendish grinned. "That look in your eyes tells me you will."

He laughed. "Go home, you arse. I don't need more people meddling in my life."

A few minutes later, he strode out of his office into the last glimmers of twilight. As he passed the inn, he realized he had not yet reserved a table for tomorrow's engagement with Sam and Auggie.

There was no help for it; he had to stop by the Swan Inn.

In fact, he could grab a quick meal there instead of disturbing his housekeeper, who had likely cleaned up after supper and would be eager to retire for the evening. Auggie would have dined already, but he knew she would not mind joining him while he ate.

The shadows fell long across the street as he reached the inn and made arrangements for tomorrow. "Lady Augusta is taking a turn in the garden, Mr. Quinton. You'll find her there."

"I…" He hadn't asked to see her, but he supposed he was fooling no one. "Thank you."

He strode out the parlor doors that opened onto rows of flower beds, all of which were in bloom and dazzling in the colors of autumn. There were several couples walking about, but he did not notice Auggie until he crossed beyond the flowered paths and saw her sitting with a book in hand on a bench beside a trellis that was mostly bare now but in summer contained an abundance of wild, tumbling roses.

She reminded him of a summer rose herself, a golden rose amid the vivid reds and pinks that would cover the trellis in the hottest months of the year. There was a slight nip to the air now, so she'd wrapped a light shawl around her shoulders. "Good evening," he said, taking in her sweet scent that was lovelier than any flower. "Isn't it too dark to read?"

She looked up and set her book aside. "Good evening, Rafe. I wasn't expecting to see you tonight." She shifted over to give him space beside her on the bench. "I was caught up in my thoughts and lost track of time. What brings you here? Has something happened?"

"No, I finished a little later than expected and realized I hadn't made our reservation for tomorrow. I attended to it just now. I haven't had supper yet either and thought to have a quick bite here. Care to join me?"

"I would love to." She glanced at her book. "I borrowed this from the inn's library."

He glanced at the title. "A History of Exeter."

"I thought it would be useful to learn more about your town, but I'm afraid little of it has sunk in. Perhaps it is just me unable to concentrate. My aunt and Clara retired early this evening, thank goodness. I have a new respect for nannies who take care of unruly children. They have exhausted me."

He could not help but grin, for he remembered his own struggles dealing with Sam on his own, his son barely came up to his knee but was still able to run him ragged. "I'm sure they'll calm down in a day or two. It could not have been easy for them to escape that blaze and watch helplessly while all they'd saved over the course of their lives went up in flames. Also, that sedative Lord Whiting's physician gave your aunt will take a few days to work out of her system."

"I suppose you are right. I can only hope once Aunt Priscilla settles down, so will Clara. The woman does not seem to have a mind of her own and parrots whatever my aunt does. If Priscilla is overset, then Clara will be the same. Come, let's walk inside, and I shall bore you to tears with the rest of my day."

"Auggie, I shall never find you boring."

She tossed him a sweet smile. "Well, I hope I do not prove

you wrong."

If only she knew how much she affected him, but he was not about to say anything to her yet. They'd only just met. However, he'd never felt more at ease with another woman, not even his wife. His marriage to Mary had been what he would call a dutiful one, each of them faithful to their vows and taking on their assigned roles without complaint.

He'd never shared his thoughts or worries with Mary because she did not want to hear them. Nor had she wanted to know about his work or anything beyond her household responsibilities. She was most comfortable in her domestic surroundings. The outside world held no interest for her, not the arts, or reading, or political matters. Nor did she ever challenge his ideas or offer any of her own.

He ordered the stew of the day for himself and a cup of tea for Auggie, since that was all she wanted. They spoke as he dug into his meal, and he liked that she took the lead in their conversation. "I sent off a quick letter to my father," she said after taking a sip of her tea. "I wanted him to know what was going on, although I think he'll leave the matter up to me to handle."

Rafe was surprised. "It is a lot to put on your shoulders. Not only resettling your aunt but figuring out what Morgan is planning to do next. Did you tell your father of your suspicions about him?"

"I did," she said with a nod. "We keep nothing from each other. I also mentioned you. That's why I think he'll let me handle the matter. I told him you were wonder—" She shook her head. "I said you were an excellent magistrate and had all well in hand."

Had she written that he was wonderful? Is that what she was about to let slip?

He swallowed the bite of venison stew and then took a swig of his ale. "Let's hope I do. I'm fairly certain we are on the right trail about that art gallery and their side business of forgery. Who knows what else illicit is going on there?"

"You think there's more?"

"Yes, there has to be."

"Oh, because of that guard they placed as a spy within your prison."

He nodded. "I should have the name of the jeweler who is holding your aunt's belongings within the next few days. But it would also be helpful if you could get a name out of her. I always like to have confirmation from two sources."

"I'll do my best."

"We'll stop by the art gallery tomorrow. However, I must sit in session on Thursday and that duty usually takes me all day. I'll take you back to the gallery on Friday if we need to nose around some more."

"And a stop at the jeweler? Assuming we have a name by Friday."

He nodded. "I'm fairly certain we will. I've been at this long enough to have an idea of the honest ones in town and those who are not always known to keep their noses clean. Also, the news you've been visiting Morgan's shady contacts ought to bring him back to Exeter soon. I would not be surprised if your cousin went straight to his accomplices. I'll have a man on him as soon as he shows his face in Exeter. We'll know where he goes, who he speaks to, and what his next intentions are."

"Is it really necessary?"

"Yes, Auggie. It is also necessary that you be careful. When he returns, I don't want you going anywhere alone with him. All right?"

She pursed her pretty lips. "He'll suspect we are on to him if I refuse to be alone in his company."

"He won't. Just blame it on me. Tell him I am an overbearing oaf who ordered you to remain at the inn and not take a step outside without me or one of my men to escort you until the mystery of who set your aunt's house on fire is resolved."

"Very well, I'll do my best to convince him I have become a scared, little lamb who is afraid to disobey the big, oafish wolf.

You have the eyes of a wolf, you know."

He arched an eyebrow and grinned. "Do I?"

"Yes, keen and discerning. They are a lovely silvery gray. But I suppose that is beside the point. You don't want me alone with Morgan."

"Do it for me, Auggie. I know you are used to your independence, but this is no game. These men will not hesitate to hurt you if they think you are getting too close to their operation. Morgan will not be able to save you. He may love you, but his cohorts do not."

"And what about you, Rafe?"

He was about to take another bite but set his fork down. "Are you asking if I love you?"

Her eyes rounded in surprise, and she laughed. "No, I meant what about the danger to you if they find you getting too close?" She rested her elbow on the table and leaned closer, smiling impishly. "But that is quite an interesting question. Is it possible to know you love someone after little more than a day's acquaintance? Perhaps *The Book of Love* will have the answer. Are you going to read it anytime soon?"

He coughed. "I haven't the time right now. Eventually, I will."

"You really ought to. Perhaps a chapter each night."

He resumed eating.

She folded her hands on her lap and stared down into her teacup. "We could read it together."

He coughed again. "Food's a little spicy," he muttered.

But she had to know his discomfort had all to do with her suggestion and nothing to do with his food.

"I overstepped. I'm sorry, Rafe. I should not have been so forward, but I'm surprisingly comfortable around you and forget we don't really know each other."

"Don't be sorry. I feel the same way about you."

She inhaled lightly. "You do?"

"Yes, Auggie. I'll bring you the book tomorrow. Read it at

your leisure, and you can tell me about the important parts."

"Much like Cavendish preparing his reports for you?"

"Gad, no. Those reports are dry as the Saharan desert. I'm sure that book is as spicy as this stew, and I shall likely regret allowing you to read it."

"Allowing me?"

He groaned. "Now you are insulted. You have no idea what you are getting into."

"I am an adult. I'm sure I can handle whatever secrets about love are revealed in those pages."

"Assuming it addresses love and not love-making, which are two entirely separate things."

"I am not a complete dolt. I understand that love is a feeling and the other is merely an act that may or may not involve feelings."

"But you do not understand the impact of them. You are innocent, and the ideas that book will stir in your brain could get you into a heap of trouble."

"Then I will count on you to protect me," she said with a wry smile.

"I am the last person you should count on to protect you."

This obviously surprised her. "Why should I not turn to you?"

"For starters, you are a beautiful woman."

She leaned her elbow on the table once more and eased closer to him. "Do you truly think so? Are you attracted to me?"

"Every man who catches a glimpse of you is instantly attracted. I am no exception. We may behave in a civilized manner in the course of our day, but we are not civilized. Sometimes, it is the thinnest leash that holds us back. Snap it, and you never know what might happen."

She frowned. "Are you speaking of yourself?"

"Of every man. But I would never hurt you, Auggie. I don't mean to imply that I ever would. Quite the opposite, I would protect you with all my being. All I mean to say is that men are not playful, gentle-hearted creatures. We do not share. We often do not play nice. Especially not with each other. We conquer territories, mark them as ours, and chase away all challengers."

He took the last bite of his stew and drank the last of his ale. "I've distressed you."

She shook her head. "No, but you've given me much to think about. Obviously, I know very little about men. All the more reason why I must read that book, with or without you. All right?"

"Yes, all right. I had better get home."

She rose along with him and walked beside him as he strode out. "Rafe, please don't be angry with me. Is it not safer for me to learn about love in a book than get myself into trouble because of my ignorance? And is it not wiser for me to turn to you with my questions than some stranger I do not trust?"

"Auggie, you've only known me for a day."

"No, Rafe. Now you will think I am as dotty as my aunt, but I have known you all of my life. Perhaps not your look or the sound of your voice, but the *heart* of you. It is such a good, strong heart." She sighed. "Never mind. You now look as though you want to run away screaming. It's been a long day. Forget I said anything."

"I have no intention of running from you." He gave her cheek a light caress. "Good night, Auggie."

Her eyes widened in surprise, and she placed a hand to her cheek, stroking it lightly.

She was not wrong about this odd *knowing* they both seemed to feel about each other.

Longing tore through him.

He wanted Auggie.

He hurried off before he proved how uncivilized he could be about it.

The house was quiet when he arrived home. He locked up securely and then went up to Sam's room to give him a kiss. To his regret, the boy was fast asleep. He must have had an active day, for he was usually awake and eager to chat at this hour. Rafe studied his innocent face for a moment longer. Silvery moonlight blanketed his son as it filtered in through the window. "Good night, sweet boy."

He retired to his quarters, stripped out of his clothes, and washed up. He wrapped his towel about his waist, poured himself a brandy, and then settled in one of the padded chairs by the hearth. *The Book of Love* sat on the small table beside his chair. "All right, I give up. Spill your secrets."

He began to read.

Love does not come from the heart but from the brain. It is the brain that sends signals throughout the body, telling you what to feel.

Well, that did not sound right.

His body's response at his first glimpse of Auggie was utterly brainless. He would describe it as instinctive and carnal, in fact. She had been sitting in his chair, his son on her lap. Despite his angry state, he'd immediately noticed every blessed detail about her body, starting with the appealing swell of her breasts.

In that moment, he'd forgotten that his forehead was bleeding or that his mouth and nostrils were filled with soot from inhaling too much smoke. All that mattered was the woman before him and what it would take to get under her skirts.

Of course, his feelings for Auggie had very quickly progressed beyond this. He still wanted to bed her, but his desire was not for a casual dalliance.

He wanted her in his bed for always.

He wanted a life with her.

One shared as husband and wife.

The thought was ridiculous. How could he know? How could he want to marry this woman after an acquaintance of a day?

Perhaps this book would explain how the leap from carnal hunger to wanting to protect and marry her could possibly occur so fast.

A man's sense receptacles do not operate in quite the same way as the female's receptacles do. Nor does a man's brain. A man's brain functions on two levels. The low and the high. The simple and complex. When a man's brain is at its lowest function, he is only thinking of sex.

Rafe began to laugh.

This perfectly described his response to Auggie. He was a respected magistrate, not the sort to lead an innocent female astray.

But…blessed saints…the things he wanted to do to Auggie.

He'd managed to hold on to that thread of civility despite the savage longing she'd unwittingly stirred in him.

But why her?

It is his simple brain at work, the one formed thousands, perhaps millions, of years ago when creatures first crawled out of the primordial ooze. Very little thought occurs when the man's sexual urges are aroused. Perhaps, no thought at all. But that is evidence of his compelling need to breed heirs with any fertile female he comes across.

Breeding was a polite way of stating the thoughts crossing his mind. While that physical ache still existed, Auggie had also become someone important to his heart.

Love is a higher function of the brain. The important function that makes a man feel the need to protect his family. Wife and offspring. Especially when they are at their most vulnerable. Otherwise, he'd merely spill his seed and move on, leaving them to be eaten by wolves. This is why man has been given a higher brain, to enable him to love. However, before he reaches that upper function of intelligence, the man must first be attracted to the female on the simple brain level.

He'd only meant to read the first chapter and then retire to bed. But he continued, taking in the chapters on the five senses. Sight, touch, taste, hearing, and scent. While many women might be considered beautiful and attract his attention, few would ever hold it. Indeed, it was the rare woman who would appeal to all his senses.

His exploded whenever he was around Auggie.

Everything about her aroused him.

He could not recall anyone having quite the same impact on him. The mere sight of her brought on his low brain response. The same for his other senses. Her touch was soft and exquisite.

Her voice smooth and sultry. Her scent, as lovely as the unfurled petals of a rose on a summer afternoon.

Gad, now he was sounding like one of those idiot London peacocks.

He was not about to get on his knee and call her an unfurled petal.

But he did want to kiss her, to taste that sweet mouth of hers.

He finished his brandy, knowing he should set the book aside and go to bed. Instead, he read on. The chapters on expectations and connections sounded interesting. He'd made a mistake in choosing Mary as his wife and did not want to make a second mistake with Auggie. He had Sam to think of now and would never do anything to hurt his son.

As he read the chapter on expectations, he saw what he'd done wrong with Mary. She had appealed to his senses, but that alone was not enough. There were many ways in which two people who were attracted to each other would prove to be a failed match over the longer term.

He had expected Mary to be not only a lover but a partner, someone with whom he could share his thoughts, his hopes, and worries. But she wanted none of that. She was happy to be a vessel and nothing more.

She dutifully gave him her body.

But he wanted more.

As a youth, he had not cared where he'd spilled his seed. He was randy, and women were these beautiful creatures willing to spread their legs for him. But marriage had turned him into a man, someone who appreciated building a life with one woman, raising children together, and building a bond of love.

To this day, he had no idea whether Mary loved him or ever enjoyed the sex between them. It hurt him to think she let him bed her because that was her idea of being a good wife. Within a few months into their marriage, she had completely given up any sense of herself and become nothing more than Mrs. Raphael Quinton. She was no longer Mary Talbott, the young woman with desires, ideas, or opinions of her own.

Perhaps she'd never had a thought or opinion beyond what her parents had told her to think. He simply hadn't noticed. In the early days of their marriage, he had liked her attentiveness. If he wanted fish for supper, they would have fish. If he wanted beef, they would have beef. If he wanted the drapes drawn, they would be drawn. If he wanted them open, they would be opened.

Not that she attended to any of it herself.

They had a cook and a housekeeper. They also employed a laundress, a nanny, maids and a butler, even a lady's maid just for Mary.

Yes, Mary was lady of the house, but she left all decisions to Mrs. Lacey. He wasn't certain what Mary actually did with her time.

These were small things in and of themselves.

But in all the years of their marriage, he had never once heard Mary take the initiative, offer advice, express a preference. After a while, Mary Talbott simply faded from existence. Perhaps another man would have liked this sort of obedient, biddable wife.

Not that he wanted a termagant, but should there not be some give and take between a married couple?

And what of Auggie?

What were her expectations?

As the daughter of a marquess, she could aim far higher than a local magistrate for a husband. He understood she liked him, perhaps was falling in love with him. But would being his wife ever be enough for her?

He could not imagine it was possible.

Life in Exeter was a far thing from the glittering ballrooms and bustle of a major city like London.

He finished the book and closed it.

Yes, he would give it to Auggie to read.

Let her draw her own conclusions. She was intelligent and thoughtful, fully capable of making her own decisions and choices.

He would make himself available to answer any questions she might have. After all, she had never been kissed.

Never felt passion.

There was a lot she did not know.

He meant to be the one to show her.

What would happen afterward?

He simply did not know.

CHAPTER SIX

S AM WAS EXCITEDLY hopping up and down as Rafe strode into the Swan Inn with the boy at his side at the stroke of noon. He had brought the infamous book along, placing it in a folder and intending to give it to Auggie at the end of their meal.

"Papa, this place is so beautiful," Sam said, craning his head to stare up at the gleaming chandeliers and ornate furniture in the sitting areas by the front door. The decor was of the finest quality. There were ferns and large flower arrangements in vases of porcelain and crystal spread atop tables and in niches so that it must have felt to the small lad as though he were walking in an enchanted realm.

"Yes, it is, Sam. But Auggie is the daughter of a marquess, and this finery is what she is used to having."

His excitement faded a little. "Our home is nice, too. Isn't it, Papa?"

"Yes, it is very nice."

Rafe was about to ask for a maid to inform Auggie they'd arrived when he glanced down the hall and saw her approaching. She looked a vision in pale blue silk, her gown seeming to flow like water around her delectable curves as she glided toward them with a lovely smile on her face.

He was never one to notice the details of what a woman was wearing, only how it flattered her body. Everything Auggie wore seemed to fit her to perfection. Of course, her gowns were designed by the finest modistes in London. After reading that book on love, he was acutely aware not only of how much she appealed to him but also of the difficulty he would have in forging a future with her.

Her gown was not merely of silk but was intricately embroidered with pink roses at the waistband and around the hem of the lustrous fabric. Each pink rose had a tiny pearl at its center. He was no expert, in fact, he was pretty much a dolt when it came to such matters. But even he could see the handiwork had been completed with extraordinary care.

This is what Auggie was used to, elegance and expensive surroundings.

How many houses did her father own?

At least one in London and another in his seat of Chelsford. Perhaps another in Bath. Rafe would not be surprised if the marquess owned another in the countryside and one along the seacoast.

The man might have lost count of all his fine, manorial homes.

And Auggie was the pampered only child brought up like a princess as they flitted from house to house depending on the season.

His heart tightened, for there were enormous differences in their upbringing that could not be overlooked.

He had not been raised as a pauper, but his boyhood had been simple. He and Deklan had shared a room throughout their childhood.

She was raised in regal splendor.

That she had turned out kind and thoughtful counted for something, but was it enough to make for a happy future if they were to marry? Could this princess ever be happy with a mere magistrate?

He did not lack for funds, but he owned one residence on a quiet street in a good part of town and did not keep so much as a modest flat in London or anywhere else. He had some investments in properties, but they were not for his personal use. He was not *ton*, and although he liked Auggie, he had no intention of allowing any woman to turn him into something he was not.

Sam tore out of his grasp and tossed himself into Auggie's arms.

She laughed and hugged him emphatically in return. "Don't you look handsome."

Rafe had made sure Sam was thoroughly bathed, scrubbed, and attired in his Sunday best. But boys had a way of finding dirt and sticking their hands in it no matter how carefully they were supervised.

Auggie and her gown seemed to survive his son's assault none the worse for wear. The two of them stood by his side holding hands. Sam was so happy, he appeared to be floating on air. "Thank you, Auggie. You look beautiful, too. Doesn't she, Papa?"

Auggie's eyes glittered with mirth. "Good afternoon, Mr. Quinton."

"A pleasure to see you, Lady Augusta." He returned her smile with one of his own and held up his folder. "I've brought you something. Remind me to leave it with you once we are through with our meal."

"Thank you. I wasn't certain you would permit me the honor of reading your book."

"I said I would, although I'm not certain it is my brightest idea."

They said no more as the majordomo came forward to lead them to their table. But Sam held them up a moment. "Papa, look."

Rafe followed the direction of his son's pudgy finger. "What am I supposed to be looking at, Sam?"

"The sign. There's a dance on Sat…Satur…Saturday night. Can we go, Papa?"

He smiled at the boy. "It doesn't start until eight o'clock in the evening. That's a little late for you."

"But not for you. You should go so you can dance with Aug-gie. You like to dance, don't you, Auggie? You told me so."

"Yes, Sam. I do."

"Papa, see? Auggie likes to dance."

"I'll think about it," Rafe muttered, gritting his teeth. "You know I often have to work late."

"But, Papa—"

"We'll talk about it later." His heart came alive just looking at Auggie. He dared not think of the agony he would endure when actually holding her in his arms for the length of a waltz.

Once he had her in his arms, dancing was not the thing he wanted to do with her.

And that was another thing—he hated these fancy affairs where everyone strutted about like peacocks in their finery, which would always wilt because these parties were a crush and the room overheated as soon as the dancing started.

Hot, sweating bodies leaping about was not his idea of fun. In fact, there were times he became physically ill.

"Will this do, Mr. Quinton?" the majordomo asked.

"Yes, perfect." He'd requested a table by the window so that Sam might amuse himself by watching the activity in the garden if he ever got bored. Not that there was much going on outside other than a gardener pruning some late autumn flowers and a few of the inn's guests strolling along the paths.

For the moment, the boy's attention was fixed on Auggie, and he was clearly besotted. Who could blame the lad?

He was no less fascinated but less obvious about it than his gawking son. "How is your aunt today? And Clara?"

She shook her head and laughed lightly. "Have you noticed a few gray hairs on my head? I would like to say the two of them are better than they were yesterday, but they are not. My aunt is distressed, especially over her lack of gowns. The modiste will return today with one for Clara and several for my aunt, along with accessories for each. It ought to be enough to hold them until their entire wardrobe can be sewn."

"Do you wish to remain with her today?"

"No, she'll be fine once she is with the modiste. I've also engaged two of the inn's maids to remain with her and Clara for the few hours I am gone. Madame Josephine's seamstresses are working around the clock. They'll have a good number of gowns finished within the next few days. My aunt is already talking about hosting her book club here tomorrow."

He nodded. "It is a good thing, is it not?"

"Yes, if that is what they are really doing. She refused to tell me the book they were to discuss, and she wants me gone from our suite while she and her friends are meeting. Does this not sound odd to you?"

"You can visit me," Sam added helpfully.

"Why, thank you, Sam. That is a lovely offer. However, I am afraid to leave my aunt alone for too long. She may need my help with her friends, even though she does not seem to want me around. You see, she is not well and is being stubborn about it. I don't want to be too far away from her, at least for these next few days. But I would love to see you again soon. I'll work it out with your father once we have finished our meal."

"All right." He sounded dejected.

Rafe tried not to show his concern, but the boy was seriously infatuated with Auggie and took everything she said to heart. Had he made a mistake in encouraging their time together? Well, they were here now and were not going to leave.

"What would you like to eat, Sam?" Auggie asked, hoping to cheer him up.

She remained unaware of the doubts swirling in Rafe's head, and he meant to keep it that way.

She was obviously delighted to be in their company.

It meant the world to him that she was so gentle with his boy. But her kindness also made things harder.

What if he and Auggie parted ways?

It was inevitable.

Sam's heart would be broken.

"The nice thing about dining out is that you have choices," Auggie said, continuing to chat with his son while he merely observed. "We may select whatever we like. I think I am going to have the shepherd's pie."

His son looked up at him with trusting eyes. "Papa, do I like shepherd's pie?"

"Yes, you do."

Sam smiled at Auggie. "I'm going to have the same thing."

"Me, too. Sounds good." Rafe placed their orders along with lemonades for the pair and ale for himself.

Auggie cast him a heartwarming smile. "So much for choices. We've all decided upon the same thing."

They ate and chatted merrily, Sam continuing to do most of the talking and Auggie listening with the patience of a saint. This allowed Rafe to quietly think about his investigations, as well as ponder what to do about Auggie.

"I can spell my name, and I know how to count to one hundred," Sam said, showing off to Auggie who had the good manners to look suitably impressed. "I can write all the letters, too."

"That is excellent, Sam. And I know you can read. There is a bookshop not far from here. Perhaps if we have time..." She glanced questioningly at Rafe.

"If we have time. Don't forget, we have other stops to make."

She nodded. "That is true. And I don't want to be away from my aunt for too long. We'll work it out, Sam. If not today, then another time."

"Max is probably missing you and eagerly awaiting your return," Rafe reminded him when disappointment washed over his innocent face.

"Is that a friend of yours, Sam?"

Since Sam was still sulking, Rafe turned to Auggie and responded for his son. "Maxwell is our neighbor's son and the same age as Sam. Right now, they are avidly into marbles."

"No, Papa. That was last week. This week we are playing

spillikins and battledore."

"Ah, forgive my error."

"But his stupid sister, Harry, keeps ruining our games."

Auggie looked to Rafe. "Harry?"

"Short for Harriet. She's only three years old and already runs roughshod over the boys." He arched an eyebrow and grinned. "Be gentle with her, son. She's too young to understand she's stepping on your games."

Sam shook his head. "She doesn't step on them. She beats us every time she plays."

Rafe emitted a deep chuckle. "Ah, I see."

He could see the mirth in Auggie's eyes as they shared a glance.

When they finished, Auggie ran back to her room to tuck away *The Book of Love* and see to her aunt. She returned soon after, sporting a pelisse and carrying gloves and reticule in hand. She'd donned an elegant hat tipped jauntily on her glorious mane of hair. "I'm ready."

They were to take her carriage, something they'd decided upon earlier since the Chelsford crest was emblazoned on it and would give the gallery owners pause if they had a mind to harm Auggie.

Not that he would ever allow them to set a finger on her.

But avoiding a confrontation was preferable to fighting their way out of one.

While her carriage was being readied, she grabbed Sam's hand. "Come with me."

They ran down the street to a nearby bookshop. Rafe followed after them, not in any particular hurry to divert Auggie's attention from his son. He remained by the doorway, his arms folded across his chest as he watched the pair choose several books and a box of tin soldiers.

His son was glowing with happiness.

So was Auggie. "I hope you and Max will have fun with these. Does he read, too?"

"Not yet," Sam said. "But I'm going to help him."

She nodded her approval. "That is very kind of you."

"Papa says it is the right thing to do."

She glanced at Rafe before returning her attention to his son. "Your father is a very wise man."

"I know. Grandmama told me so and so did Mr. Cavendish. But Grandmama Talbott said he is a no—"

"Sam! Let's go." He unfolded his arms and took the packages. "Come along. Auggie and I still have a lot to do today."

"All right, Papa."

Auggie eyed him curiously.

Blast.

She was going to ask questions about Mary and her battle-axe of a mother now.

They returned to the inn, climbed into her waiting carriage, and dropped the euphoric boy off at home.

As the carriage took off for the art gallery, Auggie remained silently watching him and waiting for him to speak. "Your tension at the mention of Mrs. Talbott was palpable."

He sighed. "I am not going to talk to you about Mary or her mother. The woman does not like me. Satisfied?"

"Not in the least."

The air remained thick between them.

"Loss is never something one speaks about easily. It was the same for me, at first, when I lost my mother, brother, and two sisters."

"Auggie," he said with unmasked surprise. "I'm sorry. I had no idea. I thought you were an only child."

She nodded. "I was the youngest and only three years old when they all passed away from cholera. My father and I were saved because we'd remained at home while my mother took my older siblings to visit her sister. They never made it back home. My father has never recovered from their loss. I was raised as an only child, finding it easier on my father to introduce myself as that. It avoids painful explanations. It's been just the two of us for so long now."

He leaned forward and took her hand. "You and Sam referred to me as a wise man earlier, but I can assure you I am an idiot."

"You were remarkably quiet during our meal and also at the bookshop. In truth, I thought you were not happy to be with me. But Sam was having such a delightful time, I just wanted him to enjoy the day, especially if it was to be our last together."

Rafe groaned. "I ended up reading that book last night. I had to see what was in it before I…" He cast her a wry smile. "Before I unwittingly corrupted your morals."

She laughed. "That book has passed through the hands of your cousins' wives and their female friends and relations. After at least a dozen happy matches, I think it is better described as magical rather than unsafe."

"I don't know. It stirred up some pretty bitter memories for me, made me face all the things I'd done wrong in choosing Mary."

She regarded him in confusion. "I…but was it not a love match?"

"At best I would term it a youthful match filled with ignorance and hope. We did not have an unhappy marriage, although I think in time it would have become that. We were two good people who were simply wrong for each other. Sam came out of that union. I will never regret my choice because of that."

Her lips were pursed in contemplation. "How were you wrong for each other?"

"Read the book and then we'll discuss it. That is, assuming you have any interest in talking to me about love."

She laughed and shook her head. "You know I do. I am not very good at hiding my feelings, especially from you. Your wolf eyes are quite discerning."

He cast her a gentle smile. "Not so discerning. I've been wrong in my judgment about you."

"What do you mean?"

"I convinced myself that you were an elegant princess, who

went through life given everything she wanted and having no idea what hardship was about."

She looked hurt. "This is what you thought of me?"

She tried to slip her hand out of his, but he would not let her. "Only partly. I also thought you were intelligent and kind, not to mention beautiful enough to knock the breath out of a man. You are all those things and more. It was the 'more' I was all wrong about. I just assumed you could never understand about loss or pain, but you've experienced both and borne it with grace."

"I had to because my father would have fallen apart other-wise. Perhaps I would have, as well. The sadness remains hidden in that deeper part of me, but it is not something I care to show to others. Nor do people want to hear it. None of my suitors ever bothered to ask. Perhaps they had done their research and already knew my family history."

She shrugged and continued. "Few people ever look beyond my facade."

"I am guilty of doing the same, merely seeing you as the daughter of a marquess. Wealthy, unmarried, beautiful. The world in the palm of your hand. I'm sorry, Auggie. But I am seeing you clearly now."

"And what do you think?"

"Read that book and then we'll discuss it."

"You won't tell me now?"

"No. Read that book first."

She laughed. "Message received. I am to read that book. Do you think it will help? I am about to enter my fourth season. It is a joke. I only do it because it hurts my father to think I am hiding away. He does not want me to spend my life alone and become, dear heaven, like Aunt Priscilla."

He was still holding her hand and now ran his thumb lightly across the palm of it. She wore her gloves, so it was not quite the same as a touch of skin to skin. But he did not intend the gesture to be taken in a sexual way.

He desired her, of course.

But this was about touching her soul.

He cast her a soft smile. "I doubt you are in much danger of that."

"Because of all those proposals of marriage? I can assure you, I will never accept any of those fortune-hunting gentlemen, no matter how often they ask."

What if I were to ask?

But he never got the question out, for they'd reached their destination. Well, he could blame it on that. In truth, he would not have asked the question today. It was too soon. "We're here."

He helped her down and led her into the art gallery.

Mr. Crowell, an obsequious-looking man, hurried toward them. "Mr. Quinton, what brings you here?"

The man had a smile frozen on his face. He tried to appear calm, but the twitch of his right eye and the clench of his hands gave him away.

This often happened with gentlemen thieves. They were not averse to stealing, just to getting caught. They did not like to get their hands dirty. It was so much cleaner to use hired scoundrels for the thefts. How easily they convinced themselves not actually doing the nasty work made everything all right.

Men like these were cowards and easily intimidated when confronted.

"No official business, Mr. Crowell. I am merely escorting Lady Augusta." He made the introductions. "Her father, the Marquess of Chelsford, will request an inventory of Lady Priscilla's remaining possessions."

The man's eye twitched. "Will request?"

"Oh, yes. My father is a very precise man. I itemize everything for him, even down to the ribbons I purchase. I've already written to him and told him of the fire that destroyed his aunt's home. He will be most distressed to learn of it, but I've also assured him the important belongings were miraculously spared. This is why I must make my lists at once."

She batted her eyes and graced the man with one of her enchanting smiles. "My aunt told me about her paintings. I was so relieved to learn they are in your good hands."

Crowell cast her an uncertain smile, his mind no doubt racing to determine whether or not she was having him on and his scheme had been discovered. "Rest assured, Lady Augusta. We will keep them safely stowed for as long as necessary. Indeed, we were about to commence restoration work."

"Oh, and that is another thing. My father will want to know their present condition. I must see them for myself."

"It will not be possible to see them today. We keep them in the warehouse, and they are all safely wrapped."

"Mr. Crowell, perhaps Mr. Quinton did not make clear who I am. I am not in the habit of being put off. We shall wait right here while you bring them in and unwrap them. Or am I to march through the gallery and into your warehouse?"

"No, m'lady! It is not safe…I mean, it is a warehouse stacked with fragile items and not safe to walk about in there."

She tipped her nose up in the air. "Very well, I rarely do this, but I shall compromise. Bring me the two Hansons and the Collingwood."

"Ah, I see you are familiar with Lady Priscilla's holdings."

She cast him an innocent smile. "My father is a meticulous man. Let me assure you, he has a detailed record of every one of his aunt's paintings. He will know if so much as a nick appears on the frames."

Rafe did not think Auggie had it in her to intimidate, but she was managing quite well. He studied Crowell, enjoying that the man was scared witless.

"Lady Augusta, we pride ourselves on our reputation. The paintings are in the best care with us."

"I have no doubt of it, Mr. Crowell. I have no wish to take them from you or interfere with the work you are about to undertake. But as I said, my father has his meticulous ways, and I fear your receipt burned along with my aunt's other possessions. So, let's get through this as painlessly as possible. I have no wish to be late for my next appointment. Would you be so kind as to have your clerk write up a duplicate inventory receipt for me? My father will ask to see it."

He skittered over to his desk and withdrew one of his ledgers. "As you can see, I have it all itemized right here." He held out his chair for her so that she could sit while she inspected it. "Your cousin, Morgan Nesbitt, signed on behalf of your aunt. All properly done and quite in order."

"My dear Mr. Crowell, I did not mean to suggest otherwise. I was relieved to learn he chose your reputable gallery for the work. In truth, I am a bit concerned about the jewelers he chose to care for my aunt's finery. I understand you recommended them, but…"

"Merriwell's is a fine establishment. We have dealt with them for years."

"Then that does ease my mind greatly. Thank you, Mr. Crowell."

Rafe fought to suppress his laughter. Auggie was indeed clever, wheedling the name of the jeweler with little effort and not so much as a suspicion raised.

They now knew where to stop next.

He ought to hire the clever little sparrow as one of his investigators. He was truly impressed by her finesse.

She continued to chat with Mr. Crowell as though he hadn't just given away one of his shady sources. "Did Morgan indicate when he might pick up these paintings?"

"Oh, it would not happen for several months yet. Restoration is delicate work."

"Yes, I'm well aware."

"Ah, of course. The Chelsford collection is renowned."

"Our paintings are always restored at Chelsford. We do not permit them out of our sight. But my aunt's art is not of the same importance. The Hansons and the Collingwood are the only three of any value."

"Yes. This is why you must understand my hesitation in

bringing them to you. The less we move them around, the better."

"I do understand, but I still must see them. Lead us to your warehouse if you cannot bring them to me."

"No, it won't be necessary. I'll have them sent for now. Just give me a few minutes."

"I'll browse your gallery while you prepare them for my inspection. And do have your clerk draw up a duplicate inventory receipt for me in the meanwhile." She turned to Rafe. "Mr. Quinton, walk me around the gallery. There may be something of interest to purchase. My father is always on the lookout for new and interesting artists or pieces to add from his favorites."

"It will be my pleasure, Lady Augusta."

They took their time browsing.

He did not know the first thing about the works on display and was intrigued to know what Auggie was thinking. For the moment, she was playing the role of pampered and demanding daughter of a marquess.

What an arse he was to doubt her strength of heart in any possible way.

Their conversation in the carriage had been a revelation, mostly revealing him to be an oaf in so quickly dismissing her abilities. He had almost talked himself into letting this angel go. What a mistake that would have proved to be.

Even his son had sense enough to realize Auggie's worth.

"Did you notice he did not walk back to the warehouse?" she asked in a whisper, her eyes alight with excitement.

"I noticed, Auggie. Hush. We'll compare notes afterward. You were brilliant."

"Thank you. Oh, I think this must be Mr. Wendall scurrying our way. And look at the clerk he's brought along with him. Red hair. Owlish spectacles. He's the one who must have been overseeing the removal of the paintings from my aunt's house."

"Let Wendall do the talking. Do not get overly confident."

"Lady Augusta, a pleasure to meet you." He bowed over

Auggie's outstretched hand. "I tried to explain to Mr. Crowell that those paintings are buried too far back in the warehouse to bring out today. Perhaps had we known you were coming…but we shall be delighted to schedule an appointment for tomorrow. Or the day after?"

Auggie glanced at Rafe, no doubt hoping for a cue as to how she should respond.

He thought it better to respond for her. "Friday will do. I shall escort Lady Augusta back here first thing Friday morning. Mark us down for ten o'clock."

"But we are just opening our shop at that hour."

"Yes," Rafe said with a nod. "And we shall be here waiting for you."

"But as we are here today," Auggie added, "have your clerk attend to the task of writing out the duplicate receipt I requested. What is your name, young man?"

"He isn't a clerk, Lady Augusta. He is my son, Hugo," Mr. Wendall said.

"Ah, a pleasure to meet you. My father heartily approves of sons following in their father's footsteps. It gives one confidence to know one is dealing with generations. Write that receipt while I continue to browse your shop."

Auggie took a moment to purchase a hideous piece she'd referred to as a vase, but Rafe could not for the life of him see where one would tuck in the flowers or the water necessary to keep them fresh. "Have it wrapped and ready for me to pick up on Friday."

Mr. Wendall had a smug smile on his face as he handed her the hastily scrawled receipt for that vase and the duplicate receipt for her aunt's paintings and other possessions consigned to them. "Until Friday," he said and bowed over Auggie's hand once more.

Rafe helped her back into the carriage, took the seat across from hers, and instructed the driver to head to Merriwell's.

Auggie emitted a squeal and tossed him the brightest smile.

He laughed. "You enjoyed that bit of intrigue, didn't you?"

"Immensely. How did I do, Rafe? Was I really brilliant or are you just saying this to be kind to me?"

He leaned close and cupped her cheek in his hand, lightly running his thumb across it. "Well done, my little sparrow," he said and slowly lowered his mouth to hers.

Her eyes widened. "Are you going to kiss me?"

"Any objections?"

"Not a one." She closed her beautiful eyes and held her breath.

CHAPTER SEVEN

Rafe touched his lips to Auggie's mouth, determined to keep the kiss soft because this was her first, and he needed to make certain it was memorable for all the right reasons.

The heat between them was undeniable.

Scorching, in truth.

He pressed his mouth to hers, sinking a little deeper into the kiss.

Blessed saints, she tasted sweet.

He struggled to keep his low brain in control, banishing raw ache and passion from taking over. Only gentleness would do for this first time. However, a man's low brain was a slippery thing and a little of that rough need pushed through despite the taut leash he kept on his feelings.

He ran his tongue lightly over her full, plump lips and groaned when she opened them to him in honeyed surrender.

He drew her onto his lap without breaking the kiss, intensifying the pressure as he circled his arms around her womanly curves and held her against him. She felt so perfect, small and lithe, but soft in all the right places.

He burned for her.

It was as though the years of emptiness had been quietly building inside of him and were about to release with dangerously explosive force.

In another moment, he'd be unlacing her bodice to taste the

lush fruit hidden beneath. He wanted to suckle her and lick her and leave nothing of either of them but fiery bits and ashes.

Not this first time.

He kept the kiss sweet as the carriage bumped and rattled. The feel of Auggie's luscious body pressed to his was utter agony, especially knowing he was not going to do anything about it.

Not now, but he would next time.

He could not get enough of her.

As the carriage began to slow, he eased his lips off hers with pained reluctance. "Mercy," he mumbled, trying to cool his body as they almost arrived at the jeweler's shop.

He would not blame her if she slapped him.

What they'd just done was madness.

She opened her eyes and smiled at him. "Is this how you reward your investigators for a job well done?"

Her teasing broke the tension, and he emitted a hearty laugh. "I'd be locked up if I did. Auggie, I was not—"

"Hush, Rafe. It was exquisite. I knew you had to be the one. I'm not sorry it happened."

"Nor am I."

She circled her arms around his neck, feeling far too comfortable seated on his lap. As for him, he was in utter turmoil.

Served him right.

Mixing business with pleasure was never a good idea.

He wasn't merely mixing the two, he was diving into a pool of trouble. The last thing he ever wanted to do was hurt Auggie, but that was precisely what he would do if things did not work out between them.

"I was sure my first kiss would occur in a moonlit garden," she said, confiding her innermost thoughts to him as she nestled against him. "I imagined myself stepping onto a terrace to escape a stuffy ballroom only to find the man of my dreams standing in a darkened corner, aching to take me in his arms under a full, silvery moon."

He cast her an affectionate smile. "I see you've given it much consideration."

"I have, but I think a kiss in a carriage is just as divine. Especially with you. You could have kissed me anywhere and I would have enjoyed it. Perhaps it is because you are very good at everything you do, but you made me feel as though you were kissing *me*, Auggie, and not Lady Augusta, the Marquess of Chelsford's daughter."

"It was for you. All for you. Nor am I in the habit of kissing ladies in a carriage, no matter their rank or status. I dare not confess how long it has been since I've even shared a kiss of a romantic sort. All I can say is that it felt right with you."

Her eyes were soft and sparkling as she asked, "Are you hoping for something more?"

"Yes." He placed his hands at her hips to ease her off his lap and back into the opposite seat before he succumbed to the urge to kiss her again. "Much more, but let's leave it at a kiss for now and see if it makes sense to take it further."

"You mean...to bed me?"

"To marry you."

He grinned as her mouth rounded in an 'O' of surprise. "Yes, to bedding you, as well, but only within the bounds of marriage. I mean it, Auggie. You are not a dalliance for me, although you are temptation itself, and it is taking all my strength to resist you. I never meant to draw you onto my lap. I should not have kissed you. Obviously, I am utterly brainless when it comes to you."

She laughed.

"It's true. I am unable to resist you. All my good intentions to take matters between us slowly and carefully have been completely shot to hell. I couldn't hold to my resolve for more than a day. Quite pathetic."

"No, it is completely wonderful. I had no idea."

"Well, now you know. I am a dolt who cannot keep his hands off you. But I am not going to take it a step further. We hardly know each other. More important, you've never experienced romantic feelings before. It's quite possible I am meant to be nothing more to you than your first kiss."

She put a hand to her heart. "Rafe, I think you are so much more."

"I hope that is true. Sam is not the only Quinton who is besotted with you. But time will tell whether a kiss in a carriage is all there will be between us."

"There you go being sensible again. As for me, it is hard to be sensible when my heart is soaring like a bird. But I understand your concern because there is Sam to think about. He took to me so readily, as you've noticed. I could never hurt that sweet boy."

He wanted to pull her into his arms again but resisted. "Let's concentrate on the investigation for now. Appease my curiosity, why did you purchase that ghastly thing you called a vase?"

She laughed. "Because it was ghastly. I wanted to plant a kernel of doubt about my knowledge of art. Let them think I am not as clever as I claim to be. Also, I thought it would be helpful to have an excuse to return to their gallery."

"We already have their receipt and an appointment on Friday morning to see the Hanson paintings and the Collingwood as excuses."

"Yes, but what then? This allows us to return at any time without raising suspicion."

"They are already suspicious. Just don't get too clever, all right? You were brilliant back there, but never forget these are dangerous people."

"I won't," she assured him. "I felt courageous because you were by my side, and I knew you would protect me. Rafe, I enjoy the independence my father and my status has allowed me, but a part of me also adored that I had you standing beside me. It was nice having my very own warrior to guard my back."

They were now in front of the jeweler's shop.

Lord, he wanted to kiss her again.

He wanted to bury himself inside her while he kissed her into tomorrow.

"We're here," he said, trying to douse the torch she seemed

to have no trouble igniting within him. "Tip that lovely nose of yours in the air and march in as though you command the place. However, do not push the man too far. And don't ask for your aunt's jewels back."

"Why not? I will keep them safe at the inn. Should I not ask him to hand over the most precious pieces?"

"I'd rather you didn't. It would allow me to expand the investigation, find out who he uses to make the quality forgeries and to whom the originals are sold. It also allows you to find out why Morgan is so desperate to have these fakes made."

"Gambling debts, no doubt. But for the sake of our family, I do need to know how deeply he has gotten himself caught up in their schemes. All right, I'll just ask for receipts. However, Priscilla enjoys her adornments, and I know she will not feel suitably dressed without a pair of earbobs or a ring. She usually adds a brooch as well. And a necklace. It really was cruel of Morgan to take all of it away."

"Can she not borrow something of yours for now?"

She regarded him as though he were crazed. "My hands are small. My rings will not fit on her fingers. Nor will my necklaces suit her style. She likes larger pieces."

He held up his hands in surrender. "Whatever you say."

Rafe escorted her in and scanned the shop, while Auggie kept the beady-eyed Merriwell occupied. He took note of the clerks behind the counter, the wares on display, especially the shinier pieces. However, he did not know much about jewelry and had no idea how to tell a fake from the real thing.

Auggie asked Merriwell for a duplicate receipt and received the same inadequate excuses as the art gallery owners had given her. But she persisted. When the man went into the back with one of his clerks to make up an inventory for her, Rafe distracted the remaining clerk. This gave Auggie the chance to peek at the shop's register which lay upon the counter.

To keep the clerk's attention on him and not Auggie, Rafe wound up purchasing a cameo brooch.

He'd told the clerk it was for his mother.

In truth, he had Auggie in mind. It seemed the sort of thing she would enjoy, but he was no rakish lord used to purchasing finery for his paramours. Besides, how could he purchase anything for Auggie without tongues wagging?

When they finished, they hopped back in the carriage to return to the inn. Auggie immediately began to tell him what she saw in the register. "Oh, Rafe. We should have thought to bring paper and a graphite with us. I'll rattle off names and hope between us we can remember them until we reach the inn."

He reached into his breast pocket and took out a square of notepaper and his graphite. "Always carry these with me."

He wrote down the names as she repeated them. "Well done, Auggie."

"Do you not find it odd that Lord Whiting was on that list? And I want to take a closer look at the paintings in his home. I thought one of them was not original, but I could not tell for certain. I would have to look at it more closely."

Rafe arched an eyebrow in surprise. "They all looked real to me."

"Exactly as they are meant to look to the untrained eye." She pursed her lips. "Do you think he is involved in Wendall and Crowell's forgery scheme?"

"He could be among the lords who needed funds to maintain appearances. Perhaps he knew to recommend the pair to your aunt because he'd been through this same subterfuge. We'll visit him again in a few days. But Auggie, do not make too much of it. Likely that is the extent of his involvement."

"And if it isn't?"

"Then I do not want us to appear too eager to question him again."

"What do you mean? Why not?"

"If a man of his stature is involved, then he is likely to be running the entire operation."

Auggie gasped. "You think he is the top man? That he ordered Aunt Priscilla's house burned to the ground? I left her in his clutches overnight!"

"I doubt he ordered anything. Their houses are side by side, and his would have burned along with hers had the wind been blowing in the wrong direction." Rafe took her hand and gave it a light squeeze. "His involvement is mere conjecture at this point. Your aunt was not in any danger, not while we all knew she was staying with him. And not while the fire brigade and my investigators were prowling right next door throughout the night."

"That gives me little comfort."

"If he was at all involved, I doubt he meant to harm the ladies. In truth, he is far down on my list of suspects. When you return to the inn, ask your aunt and Clara if they had an appointment they canceled at the last moment that day."

"All right."

"You are still overset."

She nodded. "The man is her neighbor."

"And it is likely that is *all* he is. Whoever is in charge of this forgery operation would never be so foolish as to set that fire or have his name appear in the jeweler's roster. Calm down, Auggie. Perhaps it is best if I continue the investigation on my own."

She looked at him in dismay. "Without me?"

"That is usually the meaning of *on my own*. These next few days are going to be tedious investigative work. I can quietly talk to Merriwell's customers and see if they purposely sold their gems."

"And had replacements made," Auggie interjected.

He nodded. "Or if they have been duped by Merriwell. One of the difficulties in this sort of investigation is in getting at the truth. A wife in need of funds might sell her possessions but never admit she has done it for fear of angering her husband. Similarly, a husband might have had the heirloom pieces sold and replaced with fakes to support his gambling debts or a mistress or merely to ease the crushing burden of entailment. If spouses are lying to each other, they will certainly lie to me."

"Oh, I see."

"Everyone lies." He'd learned this early on.

"I don't."

He smiled. "I figured that out fairly quickly. I wouldn't have kissed you if I didn't trust you."

After taking down the last of the names, he showed Auggie his purchase. "I couldn't think of any other way to distract the clerk, so I bought this piece."

"It is beautiful, Rafe. Truly." She shook her head and sighed. "Merriwell might be a thief, but he knows good quality when he sees it. Your mother will love it. I heard you tell the clerk you were purchasing it for her."

"It was just the first thing that came to my mind. In truth, I was purchasing it for someone else." He eased back against the squabs and studied her face, realizing she was trying to hide her disappointment.

Hellfire.

Did she think he was purchasing it for someone other than her? After what he'd just told her?

He'd kissed her and taken her onto his lap.

Was this not enough to give her a hint?

"Auggie, I meant you. How can you think it would be anyone else? But I cannot give this brooch to you yet. We are already moving too fast." He ran a hand across the nape of his neck. "Seems I cannot be alone in a carriage with you for even a minute without wanting to kiss the daylights out of you."

She blushed but seemed pleased. "We've been alone in this carriage several times. You've only kissed me once."

"But I've wanted to kiss you each time. Just did not act on it."

"I would not stop you."

He leaned forward. "You must."

"Very well, I shall resolve to resist you." She cast him a mirthful grin. "That is one resolution not likely to last beyond ten minutes."

He emitted a pained, laughing groan. "Don't tell me that. Seems we are doomed to corrupt each other, the only question being who will corrupt the other first?"

When they arrived at the inn, he led her inside and escorted her to her suite of rooms. The door was open, and there was a bustle of activity inside. "The modiste and her seamstresses," Auggie said with some relief. "I'm glad they're still here. I worry about leaving my aunt and Clara alone for too long. But they look quite pleased to be fussed over."

"You've done a good day's work, Auggie. I'll see you on Friday." He grazed his hand against hers, daring nothing more at the moment. "Summon me sooner if there's a need."

"Does wanting to kiss you count as a need?"

He groaned. "What happened to your resolution?"

"Rafe, you set my body on fire and—"

"Lord, we're doomed." He swept her into a nearby alcove before they were noticed by her aunt or the seamstresses. "I can't get enough of you." He pinned her lightly against the wall and brought his mouth crushing down on hers.

No gentle kiss, this.

He wanted to envelop her soul.

He was in love with her, and there was nothing on heaven or earth that would ever convince him to let her go. Yet, it was madness to admit such feelings and madness to trust this was real or believe in the strength of these feelings to last a lifetime.

He held her hands against the wall because he dared not let her touch him. He was already in a slow burn, and her innocent touch would set him afire. Her breasts softly molded to his chest, and he felt the rampant beat of her heart against the solid wall of his. "This is bad, Auggie. We mustn't encourage each other to misbehave."

"I love the way you look at me. You have the most beautiful eyes, Rafe. They are like embers and reflect the fire within you. You set me on fire, too. I have never felt this way before. Truly, never once in all my years. I was starting to believe the gossip about me, that I was a cold, unfeeling ice princess. But you make me burn, and I am not ashamed to tell you because, with you, everything feels right."

"So much for caution." He kissed her deeply and possessively, ran his hands along her body and stroked his thumb lightly over one breast.

He wanted to unlace her and taste her.

Make her his.

Lord, he was insane.

He leaned his forehead against hers for a moment before releasing her. "I had better go."

She nodded. "So had I. Thank you for that bit of magic."

"You are the magic. I'm just the big ox who cannot keep his hands off you." He peered down the hall to make certain no one was nearby, then led her out of their alcove. "Until Friday, Auggie."

Her eyes sparkled like sapphires. "Must we wait that long?"

"Yes. Blessed saints, we should not see each other for another month, at least. It will take me that long to cool down."

Nor was that doe-eyed look of hers helping to calm him down.

Those kisses should never have been.

But they were splendid kisses.

She'd liked them.

"It won't do any good, Rafe," she whispered, her eyes now brimming with mirth. "We'll ignite the moment we see each other again."

He cast her a wry smile. "I know. Stay close to the inn tomorrow. I'll come by on Friday to pick you up for that Wendall and Crowell appointment. See you then."

"Give Sam a kiss for me."

"I will." He gave her cheek a lingering caress.

She took a deep breath and strode into her suite.

He stayed back a moment longer and ran a hand roughly through his hair as he watched her greet the seamstresses and then disappear into her aunt's bedchamber.

What was he to do about her?

He pondered the problem of Auggie as he strode off.

The low-brain ape part of him wanted to claim her as his. His heart wanted her as well. But magistrates did not marry *ton* princesses.

How could he and Auggie possibly be right for each other?

It was not long before he marched into his office, hoping he looked ready to conduct business and not like a simpering dolt in love. "Cavendish, get in here! Anything new to report?"

CHAPTER EIGHT

UGGIE ENTERED THE fray and assisted the modiste in selecting more fabrics for her aunt's wardrobe. The marvelous woman had completed one gown for Clara and two for Priscilla, which would hold them until Friday when more gowns were to be delivered.

Her aunt did not appear happy. "I am hosting my book club tomorrow and must have a suitable gown by then."

"Aunt Priscilla, what is wrong with the ones delivered today?"

"One is too formal, and the other is not formal enough."

Clara stood beside her nodding.

Auggie turned in pleading to the modiste.

The woman smiled at her. "It will be done. The gray lace and silk will suit her perfectly. I will have it delivered in the morning."

Auggie cast her a heartfelt smile in return. "Thank you, Madame Josephine."

She ordered tea and cakes brought in, since it appeared the seamstresses would be here for a while longer and had likely not eaten since early this morning. As her aunt and Clara seemed to calm down, she attempted to open up a conversation about the day of the fire by sidling up to Clara while her aunt was busy being pinned for another gown. She began with a few casual remarks designed to get her talking. "Clara, I would like my aunt to keep as closely to her normal routine as possible. Tell me what your plans are for each day. I know she enjoys her book club meeting on Thursdays, but what of the other days?"

"Mondays she meets her friends for tea here at the inn. Tuesdays are the lectures at the botanical society."

"Oh, so that is where you were supposed to be the day of the fire."

"Yes, m'lady. But the lecturer fell ill, so the society's secretary sent word that morning there would be no program that day."

"I see." She listened as Clara prattled about their schedule for the other days of the week, which were not taken up by anything out of the ordinary. Her aunt was home to visitors on Wednesday afternoons and paid her calls on Fridays.

"However, Lady Priscilla did not make her usual Friday calls the week before last, since your cousin, Mr. Nesbitt, surprised us and brought along some of his friends. Good thing Cook had baked fresh cakes that day or we would have had little to offer them."

Auggie was instantly on alert. "Ah, yes. Morgan enjoys a good party."

"Hardly a party, m'lady. He only brought two friends with him."

Was it coincidental that her aunt's belongings were moved out a few days later and her house set on fire the week after that?

Were Morgan and his friends involved? Did they mean to do it? Or had their scheme gotten out of hand?

"Oh, which two friends? I've had the pleasure of meeting several."

"Two polite gentlemen. One of them was that nice young man who supervised the removal of Lady Priscilla's furnishings."

"And the other?"

"Oh, he was quiet. I did not catch his name. A handsome, young man. Perhaps an old schoolmate of Mr. Nesbitt's, for they looked about the same age. Very elegant. I'm sure he was a lord…a viscount or a duke. I could tell by the way he looked down on everyone. My, he was elegant."

"Perhaps I know him then," Auggie said with a cheerful

smile, detesting the man already. Pampered. Entitled. Condescending. "Describe him to me."

"Let's see." She put a finger to her chin as she considered her response. "He was about as tall as Mr. Nesbitt. Blonde hair. Lovely green eyes. Not much of a talker. He did ask a question about gardens."

"Gardens?"

"He was quite interested in Lady Priscilla's botanical society and which lectures she would be attending. Such a lovely young man. Most are only interested in the local gaming establishments. Your aunt thought it was most refreshing. Do you recognize him, m'lady?"

"No, I'm afraid I don't. Oh, well. Not important. But it is nice to know Morgan has friends in Exeter." She was excited about this latest bit of information and could not wait to tell Rafe about it.

They spoke no more, as her aunt was now calling for Clara.

The woman scurried away to attend to her.

Auggie, still feeling proud of the information she'd gleaned from her interrogation, took the book Rafe had given her and decided to find herself a shady spot in the garden to read.

But first, she asked the innkeeper to send word to Rafe on her behalf. "At once, Lady Augusta."

"Thank you, Mr. Perkins. Have your messenger convey it is not urgent. Only that I would appreciate his stopping by later, but only if he has the time." She continued to the garden and settled on a bench in an out of the way corner under a shady apple tree, now eager to read this book she hoped would answer her questions about love.

She had not gotten beyond the first paragraph before she began to blush. "What the…?"

She blushed through the entire first chapter, especially the parts describing the man's lower brain and the frenzied response men seemed to have when seeing a woman with physical attributes they found pleasing.

The shape of a woman's breasts seemed to be absurdly important.

She thought about the kisses she and Rafe had shared, the press of his body against hers, the touch of his chest to her breasts. The raw ache she'd never thought possible could exist. He'd looked at her with those burning, wolf eyes.

Goodness, had he been feeling that low brain frenzy over her?

It made her giddy to think so, and yet he also made her feel…important, as though she mattered to him, and he would always protect her. Yes, two brains working at the same time. Women did not appear to be pulled by these same urges. Perhaps this is how love worked for a man, passion stirred and then culled the flock until only one woman was left to love.

That Rafe desired her stirred the butterflies in her stomach. He was the only one ever to rouse such feelings in her, but what of him? Was she really the only one for him? He did not come across as a rake at all, but how was she to know for certain?

After all, he knew how to touch a woman.

That knowledge was not gained merely by chance.

Well, he'd been married.

But he'd probably gained his prowess long before that.

Every woman in Exeter must have been in love with him when he was younger. The man could melt any woman's heart. As a desirable widower, he would still have his choice of young women eager to soothe him after the loss of his wife.

She put the thought out of her mind at once.

Rafe was a family man who cared deeply for his son.

And he'd purchased a cameo brooch that he said was for her. This meant more to her than any exquisite ruby or emerald or diamond bauble.

She continued reading, and as she turned the pages, she began to understand a little more about men. Rafe had seen something in her that made her special to him, raising her above all other women of his acquaintance. It wasn't her dowry or Upper Crust connections, for he simply was not impressed by anything London had to offer.

She smiled upon finishing the first chapter.

Rafe had exhibited all the characteristics described in those pages. She had never thought of men as having two brains, but how better to describe his needs and urges? His low brain wanted her, and his higher brain wanted to protect her.

Could Rafe be the one for her?

Even if it turned out he was not, she would never forget him and the beauty of her first kiss.

Indeed, every girl ought to be kissed in a carriage.

She could not contain her smile as she read through the next chapters on the senses. These were easier reading and not nearly as naughty. No more talk of males gawking at female breasts and frenzied urges, but a more serious discussion of learning how to properly use the five senses to see people for who they truly are, not what we want them to be.

Was she seeing Rafe clearly?

He was pleasing to all her senses. The look of him alone was explosive. He was a big man and had a hard, warrior's body. His muscles, as he'd wrapped her in his arms earlier, had felt like hot granite.

Perhaps she was the one who was impossibly hot.

He also had the handsomest face, a manly one with well-sculpted cheekbones and a fine, strong jaw. His hair was full and dark, and his eyes were a beautiful, piercing gray and flecked with green.

Wolf eyes capable of seeing into her soul.

One of the inn's servers passed by and offered her a glass of lemonade.

"I'd love one." She gratefully accepted it and gulped down the tart liquid, badly in need of quenching her thirst.

She had never been so aware of a man before Rafe.

Had she been sleepwalking during her last three seasons?

Or was he just that special?

She read through the chapter on the sense of touch. Rafe's

hands were big and slightly roughened from the fights he'd engaged in when bringing in resisting criminals. But the roughness of his skin seemed to arouse the delicacy of her own.

She set aside her book when the modiste approached.

"Ah, there you are." Madame Josephine cast her a cheerful smile. "Hiding out, are you?"

Auggie laughed. "Yes, can you blame me?"

"They are a handful," she said with a knowing nod. "We've done all we can for today. We'll return tomorrow with the promised gowns. If Lady Priscilla is feeling up to it, we'll fit her for several more tomorrow as well."

"Thank you, that will be perfect. A morning fitting because she has her book club meeting in the afternoon." Auggie tucked the book under her arm and returned to her suite, since she was not yet ready to trust the two elderly women to manage on their own. Perhaps she was being overly cautious.

But something was going on beyond the loss of their belongings.

Why were they keeping secrets from her?

Could they not see she was trying to help? Unlike Morgan who had disappeared after taking the valuables.

And what of the book club? Was it in any way connected to Morgan's antics?

If so, how?

And who was that third fellow? Would he ever turn up again now that Priscilla had nothing left to steal?

She tucked the book in her bureau drawer and returned to their shared sitting room in the hope of drawing her aunt into conversation. Instead, it was her aunt who immediately began to question her. "Why did you go to Wendall and Crowell's today? You know Morgan is handling the art restoration for me."

"Yes, and I have no intention of interfering," she said, ignoring the tug to her heart over the lie. "But you know Father and his meticulous nature. He keeps records of everything, and the first thing he will ask to see are the inventory receipts. Since the ones they gave you burned in the fire, I saw no harm in requesting duplicates as soon as possible."

Her aunt did not seem pleased. "Morgan could have taken care of it when he returned."

"Yes, he could. But he is nowhere to be found. Where is he, Aunt Priscilla?"

"Honestly, what a question!" She put a hand to her throat and fidgeted with the lace trim of her gown. "I'm sure I don't know."

"Can you not think where he might be? Never mind about the art and jewels. He would want to know about the fire and dutifully come to your aid."

"You know about my jewels?"

Auggie frowned. "Yes, Mr. Crowell told me about them. He is friendly with Mr. Merriwell. I believe he recommended the man to Morgan. I took the liberty of requesting receipts from Mr. Merriwell, too."

She paled. "Oh, dear. Morgan will be quite put out."

"Why should he be? Is it not expected for me to look after what's left of your belongings? He would do no less were he here. Auntie, someone burned down your house, and we have no idea who or why. They've destroyed almost everything you possess. Thank goodness Morgan saw fit to remove those valuables for you."

Drat, her voice hitched when she lied, but she continued. "What a stroke of good fortune. But we must be more vigilant than ever because the true culprit is still at large, and we do not know who he is or what he might do next."

"Oh, I'm sure there is nothing more to worry about. Who would want to harm me?" She was still fidgeting with the lace at her collar.

"That is the question we must answer. Do not dismiss the severity of what happened. The man who started the fire was found dead, no doubt killed by whoever paid him to set the blaze. Now, are you ready to tell me what is really going on?"

Clara gasped. "Dead?"

Priscilla shot her a quelling look.

Yes, Clara was the weak link in their chain. But how was she to pry more information out of the woman when she rarely left Priscilla's side? "Yes, Clara."

She stared pointedly at her aunt. "The firebug is dead, and more people may die if you don't start telling me and Mr. Quinton all you know. I know Morgan paid a call on you with Mr. Hugo Wendall and another man. Let's start with identifying that third man. Who is he?"

"Really, Auggie! You are too much! It is none of your business."

"How can you say that? You almost died in the blaze." She clenched her hands, attempting to stem her frustration. "And what of your book club meeting tomorrow?"

"What of it?"

"If it is so harmless, why am I not permitted to sit in?"

Priscilla tipped her chin up in defiance. "I have decided to put off the ladies' book club meeting until next week. Clara, tell Mr. Perkins to send word to Lady Whiting. She'll inform the others."

Auggie did her best not to scream in irritation. Is this what Rafe put up with in every investigation? He went up another notch in her already high estimation. "Why the sudden need to delay, Aunt Priscilla? Do you not wish to see your friends?"

"Not with you snooping about."

"I was not going to snoop, although I have no idea why I should be asked to leave. I am not an unruly child. Besides, I love books. Speaking of which, did yours not burn in the fire? I can pick up another copy for you. Just let me know what you were reading and I'll—"

"That won't be necessary."

She sighed. "All right. But there is a bookshop mere steps from here, and I will be happy to purchase any book you want."

"Auggie, you are being tedious again. I think I shall retire for the evening. Clara, inform Mr. Perkins and then hurry back to help me undress."

After seeing that the pair were safely tucked in for the evening, Auggie sought out Mr. Perkins herself regarding her message to Rafe. "No word, m'lady. Shall I send another boy to—"

"No, he's obviously busy, and I do not wish to disturb him. It'll wait until tomorrow." She retired to her own bedchamber, undressed, and then read Rafe's book into the wee hours. She fell asleep to the light patter of rain against her window and awoke to a stronger, howling rain that made her glad she did not have to go anywhere today.

However, it was Thursday, and she had considered sitting in on Rafe's tribunal. She meant to slip away while the seamstresses were attending to her aunt. They'd come to deliver the lovely gray tea gown, and then stayed to work since there was to be no book club meeting today.

But the rain was coming down quite violently, and her aunt and Clara were behaving like frightened hens. "It is only rain, Aunt Priscilla. We are safe here."

"Safe? The heavens have opened up!" Her aunt had a hand over her heart, while Clara was running in circles around the room declaring they were all going to die every time thunder clapped or lightning flashed across the sky.

She and the attending seamstresses had their hands full calming them.

Auggie also felt badly about not seeing Sam.

However, it was for the best. Sam had lost his mother and already viewed her as a maternal replacement. He would be devastated if things did not work out between her and Rafe. Where was he? Why had he not responded to her message?

Perhaps she had assumed too much after those kisses.

What if he was purposely putting distance between them?

She could not blame him, especially because of Sam. She dared not foster an attachment with the boy before she understood what his father's feelings were toward her.

Somehow, in the quieter moments, she managed to finish *The Book of Love.*

The storm finally moved on in the late afternoon, and the sun now burned through the overhanging clouds. Food had been brought into their suite throughout the day on her orders. The modiste and her ladies had been bending over backward to accommodate her aunt and were working feverishly to fulfill her demands.

When they finally left, her aunt and Clara turned in for a nap.

Auggie slipped off to the dining room to enjoy a moment to herself. She was seated alone in a corner and had just been brought a cup and teapot when she caught sight of Rafe.

He noticed her at the same moment and strode toward her.

She could not contain her smile.

He maintained a staid expression, but she saw the glitter in his eyes as he drew out the chair opposite hers and settled his large frame in it. "How are your two hellions doing?" he asked.

She laughed. "Raising hell."

"You looked as though you were enjoying your moment of solitude."

"I was, indeed. The storm had them in fits, but we made it through the day with the help of those saintly seamstresses. My aunt should have five or six lovely gowns ready by tonight. They'll be delivered in the morning. She canceled the book club meeting she had planned for this afternoon."

"Ah, so they have put off their clandestine schemes."

She nodded. "Until next week."

"It troubles you," he remarked, settling back and motioning for their server to bring him a cup of tea.

"Only because I do not understand why she is being so secretive about a simple ladies' club meeting. What is she hiding? And why is she hiding it from me, her loving grandniece, when she knows I am only here to help?"

"Leave it alone for now, Auggie. There aren't many bookshops in town. We can stop at a few tomorrow and quietly nose around."

She nodded. "I had planned to do just that. Would you mind

very much if we included it in tomorrow's plans? It sounds awful, I know. I hate to go behind her back, but she is lying through her teeth, and I need to be sure she and Clara are not stupidly walking into more danger."

"I agree."

"Do you think it is overstepping if I ask the bookseller who else is in the club?"

He shrugged. "Can't hurt to ask, but he might alert the other club members."

She nibbled her lip. "Oh, I wouldn't want him to do that. Perhaps I should wait until next week and just keep an eye on who shows up. Once they are in the suite, I can sneak into the garden and listen in through an open window."

"That might work. But you'll likely be spotted."

She sighed. "My aunt is already on to me. That is why she canceled today's meeting. Rafe, how do you manage not to get all churned up inside. I find this situation most unsettling. Why is Priscilla blatantly lying to me? Clara let slip that Morgan had brought two so-called friends to meet my aunt last week. One was obviously Mr. Wendall's son, with the bright red hair. But there was another man with them, about the same age as Morgan. Blonde hair. Green eyes. Asking about my aunt's schedule for the week. He was particularly interested in her botany lectures, which she attended every Tuesday afternoon without fail...except this Tuesday's lecture was canceled at the last moment."

"Did you get a name?"

"No, Clara did not catch it, and Aunt Priscilla straight out refused to tell me. He had to be the one who arranged for the fire to be set. But what was the point of setting fire to my aunt's home? And what of Morgan? Where did he disappear to? Now I am worried he is in trouble, perhaps abducted or already dead."

"I doubt it. Weasels like Morgan know how to slip out of tight spots. I am working on finding him, Auggie."

"You are?"

"Yes."

"Thank you. Is that what you were busy doing after we parted yesterday? Is that why you could not see me?"

He cast her a questioning look. "You thought I was coming by to see you again?"

She nodded. "I asked Mr. Perkins to send a boy to your office with the request."

"Hellfire. He must have come by while Cavendish and I were out. He probably told the day guard, who forgot to mention it to the night guard."

"It's all right, Rafe. It wasn't all that urgent."

"But you sent word to me, and I wasn't there for you."

He seemed so obviously pained at the notion.

"You would have been if it were something serious." She never intended to accuse him of shirking his duty. If anything, he was the only one helping her. "Please do not ever doubt how much I appreciate all you and your investigators are doing. Do you think it is possible those art gallery owners are holding Morgan captive?"

"Doubtful. He was seen riding out of town on his own a couple of days before you arrived. I expect he was preparing his alibi in order to shake suspicion from himself when the fire occurred."

"Assuming he knew of it. I cannot believe Morgan knew it was planned."

Rafe cleared his throat. "We'll get to the truth once he turns up. He is likely enjoying himself in Bath at the moment. That is the most logical place he would go to be seen and remembered by credible witnesses, since it is popular among the *ton*."

"Once again, assuming he knew."

"I was not able to spare one of my men to ride up there, but I sent a messenger off with a note to the local magistrate. I'll let you know what he says about your cousin."

She sank back in her chair and sighed. "You've thought of everything."

"I hope so. I'm trained for this, Auggie. You are doing remarkably well for someone who is not."

"Thank you, and I've also finished reading *The Book of Love.*"

He grinned. "That didn't take you long. What pearls of wisdom did you glean from it?"

She took a sip of her tea before responding. "That for love to flourish there must be honesty between the couple."

"That is true, Auggie. There cannot be true love without honesty or trust."

"But one must also be honest with oneself. Sometimes we want a thing so badly, we turn a blind eye to what displeases us and pretend all is fine. Love should be something easy, but it can also be treacherous if we refuse to see the hazards before us."

He nodded. "Are you worried about the feelings we seem to have for each other?"

"Aren't you?" Despite her experience on the marriage mart, she still felt as though she was in over her head when it came to matters of love. "After reading this book I understand that merely pleasing each other's senses isn't enough to sustain happiness. I may like everything about you, the look, touch, scent, and so on, but it is no guarantee those are enough."

He turned pensive but said nothing, so she continued. "The frightening thing about it is that neither of us needs to have serious flaws. Even if we are not drunkards or gamblers or unfaithful in our marriage vows, we may still find ourselves unhappy."

She took a deep breath and cupped her hands around the teacup to warm them, even though the day was hotter than usual for this time of year. But her insides had grown cold because there were so many ways she and Rafe might not suit, and it broke her heart. "It is the little things that can destroy us, is it not? For instance, the dance to be held here at the inn on Saturday."

He arched an eyebrow. "What about it?"

She waited for their serving maid to set his cup and teapot in front of him and then leave before she resumed. "I enjoy dancing."

"And I do not? This is what has you worried? It is a trivial thing."

"Perhaps." She nodded. "You were most vocal about it. And you did not seem pleased when Sam mentioned it."

"I will admit that dancing is not something I would ever go out of my way to do. I am not much for parties or elegant soirees."

"You do not strike me as the sort who would be."

"Auggie, what are you taking from this book? A husband and wife do not have to be in complete agreement all the time. In fact, they do not have to like the same things at all."

"How can you say this? Does a married couple not need to have things in common?"

"It helps, but I think I would tear my hair out with boredom if my wife and I were parrots of each other. Our differences would add interest. Lord, I want to reach out and take you in my arms right now."

"I would love to be in your arms, but I know this is neither the place nor the time. In truth, there might never be a right place or time. Yesterday's kisses might be all I will ever have of you."

Auggie followed his gaze as he glanced around the dining room, which was starting to fill with guests. But the tables around them had yet to be occupied. "Damn it," he said, leaning in as close as he dared, "I did not come here to confess what is in my soul. But I don't want you to think that love is a hopeless endeavor. So, here goes…"

He glanced around once more and then proceeded. "Mary and I had little in common but none of it mattered to me. What mattered most, and something I could not compromise on, was her vanishing into nothing. I've told you how she had no thoughts or opinions of her own. She would never tell me if a thing pleased her or displeased her, and I do not mean only in our…marital relations."

Auggie tried not to blush.

They were having a serious conversation, and she was an adult, was she not? She did not want to appear a peahen who turned bright red at the first hint of bedroom matters. "I do not see how she would have had complaints about *that*."

He cast her a wry smile that caused her to melt a little inside. "My point is, I have no idea whether she did or not. She would never open herself up to me. Maybe that's what hurt most, the belief that she did not trust me with her heart."

"I'm sorry, Rafe." Her hands remained around her teacup as she now stared into it. "I would trust you with my heart. It is the little things that worry me the most. As the daughter of a marquess, I am used to hosting teas, charity events, and dinner parties. I would not know what to do with myself if I had nothing to keep me busy. But you are not the sort of man who would like to come home to a ladies' planning committee meeting or to have to dress in formal attire because we are having a dinner party or were obliged to attend a charitable affair."

"Auggie, you must not view this book as a warning of failure."

"How can I not? Is this not the very reason you gave it to me to read? You are also worried that we are not a good match. Dear heaven, should we even be having such a conversation after a few days of knowing each other?"

"I know. It ought to feel ridiculous, but it doesn't."

She took a deep breath and plunged in, wanting him to know how she felt. She could not hide it anyway. This tumbling into love had overwhelmed her, and she did not know what to do about it. "I am falling in love with you, Rafe. But how can it last when we are so different?"

"The differences don't matter. As I mentioned, they are what add interest to marriage over the years."

"But is it not daunting how many ways love can go wrong?"

"You are not Mary. Your conversation is not limited to shopping for new gowns or fretting over dinner casseroles. You have opinions. You will maintain your own identity and not become wholly subsumed by me. That is important to me. I hated feeling as though I had completely taken Mary over so that she no longer knew who she was. But you will always let me know your thoughts and feelings."

He cast her an endearingly rakish smile. "I like that you want to make a mark on society, Auggie. You will do something to improve it. Yes, it will irritate me to come home to a crowded house every night."

"It wouldn't be every night. Goodness, I would go mad myself. And I fully understand a man's home is his sanctuary. I would always take your feelings into consideration."

He eased and drank a little of his tea. "Then where is the problem?"

"But we may not always agree."

He set down his cup. "Would you be willing to compromise?"

She nodded. "Of course. Um, would you?"

He grinned. "Yes, I like to think I am the soul of reason. Just ask Cavendish. He worships me and thinks I am a saint."

She laughed.

He finished his tea and rose. "I never raised a hand to Mary or ever had a cross word with her. I would never raise a hand to you, either. As for cross words, we'll probably have a few because you have opinions and are passionate about them. I like that about you, Auggie. Let's continue the conversation another time. I had better get back to my office."

She rose along with him. "I thought you were through with your hearings."

He nodded. "I am, but now I have to get through the rest of my workload. It isn't too bad. I ought to be done at a reasonable hour tonight, barring any surprises."

"Are there not always surprises in the course of your magistrate duties?" she asked, walking him to the inn's entryway.

"Hopefully not tonight."

But Rafe had not even made it through the inn's front door

before Cavendish burst in. "Thank goodness I've found you!"

"Hellfire, what now?"

"Another body has turned up." He turned to stare at Auggie, so she knew the poor, dead sod had to be someone connected to her Aunt Priscilla's matter.

She put a hand over her heart, for even though she had involved herself in their investigation, she had no stomach for the seedier part of it and felt so terribly sad that someone—perhaps an innocent man—had met a brutal and untimely end. "Mr. Cavendish, have you identified the person?"

"Yes, Lady Augusta...it is Hugo Wendall, the art gallery owner's son."

She gasped. "He was the one who supervised the removal of my aunt's items from her home. Is it somehow connected? How did it happen? When did it happen? Where was his body found?"

"Mr. Crowell came to report it. He looked ashen, so I gave him a seat and a drink, then ran over to let Mr. Quinton know at once."

Rafe let out a roar. "You left him alone in my office to search through my files?"

Poor Cavendish's eyes rounded in alarm.

"Damn it, Cavendish!" Rafe took off at a run.

The poor man ran after him.

Auggie knew she ought to remain at the inn and await a further report. Rafe was supposed to pick her up tomorrow for their ten o'clock appointment at the art gallery.

What if he was too caught up in the investigation to escort her there?

Dear heaven, the gallery could be the scene of the crime.

It was quite possible Rafe would not allow her near there and instead order her to remain at the inn until further notice.

She caught the proprietor's attention. "My aunt and her companion are resting in our rooms. Please have one of your maids attend them while I'm gone. I should only be an hour or so."

She took off at a run for Rafe's office.

How angry would he be when she barged in?

CHAPTER NINE

R AFE'S BLOOD WAS boiling as he tore up the stairs to his office and found that weasel Crowell digging through his files. "I'll have you wishing you were the dead man," he growled, trying to dampen his rage before he actually did harm to the gallery owner.

He also wanted to kick Cavendish's arse from here to London and back for falling prey to the man's obvious trick. But Cavendish was a scholar, not an ounce of guile or scheming in him. He was extremely clever when it came to academics, but as naive as a child when it came to the baser nature of men.

Crowell hastily withdrew his hands, which were buried in his filing cabinet, and held them up in a gesture of surrender. "I meant no harm, Mr. Quinton!"

He wanted to grab Crowell by the throat and shove him into one of the chairs beside his desk, but he managed to control his temper and merely motioned for him to sit. "What were you looking for?"

The man scrambled into the chair and looked up in obvious terror as Rafe glared at him. "Nothing! It was mere curiosity on my part."

"Do not take me for a fool. I'll ask you again, what were you looking for?"

He must have seemed as frightening as the devil himself, for he was barely able to contain his rage. Crowell quickly crumbled and began to talk. "I had given someone a reference and was curious as to how he was doing on the job. I do not give those out lightly."

"Ah, and what did you find?"

"Nothing. I had just opened the drawer to your files when you stormed in and scared the wits out of me."

He would not have found that prison guard's file since Rafe had stuck it in his desk, but he was not about to tell Crowell that. "Who was the man you recommended to me?"

"Well, it doesn't really matter."

He emitted a low growl that had Crowell turning ashen again. "Who?"

"James Kerrigan."

He quickly searched the gallery owner's pockets to make certain he hadn't taken anything from his office and hidden it on his person. "He's been suspended. But I'm sure you knew. Now, why are you really here? Is Wendall's son dead or was that just a ruse to get my assistant out of the office?"

"It's true," he said with a sob. "The boy's dead, and my partner is beside himself with grief. So am I. Look at me, I'm shaking like a leaf."

The man did look as though he was about to faint, and he was noticeably trembling.

Sweating, too.

Rafe leaned against his desk, purposely maintaining his intimidating scowl in the hope of getting the truth out of this weasel.

He heard Cavendish's footsteps on the stairs and a lighter set of footsteps right behind him.

Hellfire.

Auggie had followed.

He strode to the door and waited for them to enter the antechamber. "Cavendish, get back to your desk."

"Yes, Mr. Quinton," he said, looking as though he wanted to dive under it.

He'd deal with Cavendish later.

He turned to Auggie. "You! Sit here and do not say a word."

He pointed to one of the chairs in the antechamber, then walked back into his office and slammed the door shut.

He resumed his spot leaning against his desk, once more intimidating Crowell, who had taken a handkerchief out of the breast pocket of his jacket and was now mopping his brow. "Start talking."

He could see Auggie's shadow against the door and knew she had ignored his command and was listening in. Well, he did not mind. He'd planned to tell her everything anyway.

Crowell took a deep, gulping breath. "Hugo was late returning from a client's home this afternoon. The carters had returned with the wagons hours earlier. So, we went in search of him."

"We?"

"Wendall and I."

Rafe crossed his arms over his chest. "Did neither of you think he might have stopped for a pint with friends?"

"No, he's a good lad. Not the sort to shirk his duties. We got worried, seeing as we'd just had the fire at Lady Priscilla's house, and thought maybe someone was still lurking in Aimsley Square and Hugo recognized him."

"We caught the man who set blaze to Lady Priscilla's home. He's dead now." But Crowell would know this because he and his cohorts had likely killed the scoundrel.

"Well, we were worried this was the work of a gang and Hugo had run afoul of them."

"Where did you find him? And I do not want some made-up story. I know you moved his body before coming here to report it to me."

Crowell's eyes rounded in surprise. "How did you know we—"

He abruptly cut off.

"How did I know you moved the body? Because you are here to report the crime you wish me to see, not the one that really happened. You've tampered with evidence. That in itself is a crime."

Perhaps he had come across as too much of an ogre, for the man buried his face in his hands and began to cry. "It wasn't supposed to be like this."

"Explain what that means, Mr. Crowell," he said, this time more gently. He drew a chair and sank into it to face him. He already knew what the man was going to tell him about the forgery ploy, since he and Auggie had figured out most of it. But he needed to hear about this scheme in the man's own words.

Crowell began to wipe his tears. "It started as an accommodation to our customers several years ago."

"What is *it*?"

"The replica paintings. You see, young Hugo is quite…was quite the artist. Customers had been coming to us over the years asking…"

Rafe arched an eyebrow. "For forgeries?"

"I prefer to call them replicas," Crowell said with a sniffle. "After all, we did not do this without the knowledge and consent of our clients. Surely, you must understand how strapped some of them are with their estates entailed and the necessity of maintaining their standing in society."

"Go on."

"They brought us their paintings, and we…that is, young Hugo made a superb copy for them to hang in their homes, then we quietly sold the originals to private collectors for a generous commission. No one was harmed. Everyone got what they wanted."

Rafe folded his arms across his chest and leaned back in his chair, his gaze still fixed on the art dealer. "And yet, Lady Priscilla's home is destroyed and now Hugo Wendall is dead. Something must have gone wrong."

"I don't know."

"Yes, you do. Mr. Crowell, you must tell me what is going on. What of Morgan Nesbitt? And the third man in his company and that of Wendall's son when they paid a call on Lady Priscilla? Who is he? Is this the man you fear? I cannot help you if you won't tell me the truth."

He shot to his feet. "No…it was a mistake coming here. I have to return to my shop."

Rafe rose along with him, cursing silently as his irritation mounted. "Don't be a fool, you—"

But the art dealer raced to the door, threw it open, and barreled out. Auggie emitted a cry, for she had not managed to get out of the way in time. The door smashed in her face, causing her to fall against the row of wooden chairs in the antechamber.

"*Oof!*" She landed with her gown hiked up to her knees, revealing her shapely calves.

"Auggie! Are you all right?" He knelt beside her, hoping Crowell had not hurt her too badly. She was wincing and now struggling to sit up.

"I'm all right. Go after him."

"Not necessary. I know where to find him." He put his arms around her because she still appeared to be in pain. "You are my priority. Did you bump your head? How is your wrist? Do you think you sprained it when breaking your fall? You have a nosebleed."

He withdrew his handkerchief and gently held it to her nose.

"That rotter," she grumbled, taking the handkerchief from him and tilting her head back as she held it against her nostrils. "I was listening at the door and could not leap out of the way in time. But I'm fine. Truly, Rafe. What do you think he meant to tell you?"

"Not much we did not already know." He turned to Cavendish. "You are to see Lady Augusta safely back to the inn. I'm going to Crowell's gallery. But first, fetch Marbury and Cooper for me. I want them with me when I go."

"What about me?" Auggie asked once Cavendish had hurried off. "You might need my expertise on art."

He brushed his thumb along her cheek in a light caress. "Haven't you had enough excitement for one day? Cavendish will walk you back to the inn once you are steady on your feet."

She frowned at him. "I ought to go with you."

"No, and this is not open for discussion. If Hugo Wendall is truly dead, then something far more serious is going on than merely harmless swaps of paintings for money. Someone felt betrayed and was angry enough to kill that young man."

"An irate husband whose wife secretly traded out the family art collection or their heirloom jewels? We ought to go by Mr. Merriwell's establishment to make certain he hasn't met an untimely end."

Rafe caressed her cheek again for no reason other than he could not keep his hands off her. "We? Rest that impressive mind of yours. You've just been tossed across the room by the force of that blow and likely cannot stand on your own yet. Even if you could, taking you anywhere with me is too dangerous. Something very bad is going on, and I don't want you caught in the middle of a falling out among these partners."

She frowned. "You think Mr. Crowell hurt Hugo Wendall?"

"No, he may be greedy, but he isn't a violent man. Someone else is involved. Ready buyers do not simply turn up in droves in Exeter. Same for the jewelry. There must be a London connection, someone who brings the wealthy buyers to the table. It could be that young man Clara mentioned to you."

"But why would he kill the golden goose? A talent like Hugo's is what makes this scheme possible. If he is killed, then who can paint the fakes? Or perhaps he wasn't meant to be hurt but got in the way accidentally? Rafe, please let me go with you. I think you need me."

He cast her a wry smile. "Oh, I need you. But it isn't for this investigation. I appreciate your thoughts, Auggie. I surely do. But we are beyond the questioning stage now. There may be a war about to unleash between the partners in this operation. I don't know what we'll encounter at the gallery."

She cast him a determined look. "I'll be careful."

"Your nose is still bleeding, and you might have hit your head." He traced his finger lightly across her brow.

"I didn't hit my head. My shoulders absorbed the brunt of the fall. Let me go with you."

He emitted a pained sigh. "Stop arguing with me. You know it is not possible. We're bringing an arsenal of weapons with us because I'm concerned it will be that dangerous. I couldn't bear it if you were hurt. Your eyes look glazed. How are you feeling?"

"I merely have a nosebleed, which will stop in a moment. See, it has already stopped." She removed the handkerchief to show him. "And my nose is not broken. My wrist is fine. See." She moved it around to show him.

"That eases my mind but still doesn't change a thing. You are untrained, and I cannot properly defend myself or my men if I have to worry about you. You would distract me."

"I wouldn't—"

He kissed her lightly on the lips. "You know I'm falling in love with you."

She kissed him back, pressing her sweet lips to his. "I am two steps ahead of you, Mr. Quinton. I am already madly in love with you."

"Blessed saints, this is all moving too fast."

She cast him an impudent grin. "Is it not usually the woman who says that line?"

He rose and moved away from her as his investigators tramped up the steps. "Cavendish will take you back to the inn now. Can you shoot a pistol?"

Her eyes rounded as she gazed at him. "Do you think I need one?"

"Only if you know how to handle it. Do you?"

She nodded. "My father taught me."

"Good." He reached into the top drawer of his desk and withdrew the one he always kept loaded in there. "If that young man Clara described comes around—"

"You want me to shoot him?"

"I want you to *avoid* him at all costs. However, if he manages to break in and trap you alone, then do whatever you need to do to save your life.”

“Rafe…” She tried to rise, immediately paled, and sank back in her chair with a grunt. “Oh, dear. My head is spinning.”

“Lady Augusta!” Cavendish cried. “I’ll run across the street and fetch you a strawberry ice. It will help calm you. Mr. Quinton, should I send one of the boys for the prison doctor?”

“Yes.”

“No,” Auggie said immediately. “Will you not require his services to examine Hugo’s body at the crime scene? Truly, I will be fine in a moment. But I promise to ask Mr. Perkins to send for one when I am back at the inn if this giddiness persists.”

Rafe took her hands in his. “Take another moment to restore yourself. Take as long as you need.”

He then turned to Cavendish. “If she is still woozy after she finishes her ice, then help her back to the inn and make certain the innkeeper summons a doctor for her. Do not let her talk you out of it.”

Cavendish nodded. “I will stand firm.”

In truth, Rafe expected his clerk would wilt the moment Auggie batted her eyes at him. “You are to stay with her until he arrives. I’m also going to assign Wilkins to guard her and her aunt.”

Cavendish nodded. “I’ll make Wilkins aware right now and then bring Lady Augusta her ice.”

Auggie watched him hurry out before turning back to Rafe. “A guard? You believe we are in that serious a danger?”

“I believe all hell is about to break loose among the partners. Setting your aunt’s house on fire was likely a message. Not to your aunt, but to Wendall and Crowell.”

“But to kill Hugo…”

“I doubt it was meant to happen. As you suggested, Hugo likely got in the way by accident, and since he is the talent behind this business, now it is about to fall apart. Who knows what will happen next? I doubt that third man who visited your aunt with your cousin Morgan and Hugo Wendall will bother with either of you. He has to be more concerned with silencing his partners and covering his tracks so no one can connect him to the business."

"But Aunt Priscilla saw him. So did Morgan."

"If Morgan has any brains, he will remain in hiding until we capture this killer. As for your aunt, hopefully, he will not bother with someone he believes to be a dotty old woman. Just be careful these next few days."

He wanted to tell her so much more, but how could he spill his heart in front of his men? He left with them the moment Cavendish returned.

They stopped at the guardhouse to collect weapons for themselves, and he gave instructions to his remaining investigators, assigning one to the home of Wendall, another to Crowell's home, and a third to Merriwell's jewelry shop. "Hold these gallery owners at their houses and Merriwell at his shop until I get around to questioning them."

He also left word for the prison doctor, who was not in his office at present, to meet him at the art gallery.

"Mr. Quinton," Cooper said as they grabbed rifles along with extra pistols. "What do you think we are going to encounter?"

"I'm not sure, but I fear it will be utter mayhem."

CHAPTER TEN

RAFE APPROACHED THE gallery with caution, he and his men having scouted the surrounding buildings first to make certain nothing was awry. But all appeared quiet, and there even seemed to be little activity within the Wendall and Crowell warehouse, which stood immediately behind the elegant gallery.

He wasn't certain whether to be relieved or worried about the silence.

He glanced at his companions, all of them feeling the eerie calm settling upon them like a heavy fog.

The warehouse workers were standing around the loading area, some of them pacing in an agitated fashion and all of them obviously uncertain what to do. No one appeared to be in charge or giving instructions, so Rafe approached the cluster of men with caution and identified himself.

"We know who ye are, Mr. Quinton," one of them said, stepping forward. "We saw ye here the other day with the pretty lady."

Rafe nodded and handed his rifle to Cooper who stood immediately behind him. "Is anyone in charge here?"

The man shrugged. "Mr. Frayne's our foreman, but he fled shortly after Mr. Wendall carried…that poor lad. He was a good lad, Hugo was. Hugo Wendall's dead."

"I know. That is what brings us here. What else can you tell me?" He could have insisted on getting the man's name but felt he would get more information out of him if he permitted the anonymity for moment. "My priority is to find out who killed Hugo Wendall, how and where it happened."

He glanced toward the warehouse filled with crates and wrapped paintings that were piled within. "At the moment I am less concerned about the art forgeries."

A few of the men uttered soft curses, obviously alarmed he knew what had been going on. The air was already charged, and Rafe did not wish it to become even more so.

He held up his hands to calm these workers. "I am not interested in harming any of you. You have my word. Had you been involved in more than merely carting and hauling, you would have run as your foreman did. None of you will be arrested, provided that you cooperate and tell me what we need to know. First, who is presently in the art gallery?"

"Just the clerks. Everyone else has fled. They left poor Hugo and...the clerks may be able to tell you more. They are still inside."

Rafe turned to his investigators. "Marbury, stay with these men and question them. I want to know who else besides the foreman, Crowell, and Wendall has been giving them orders. I want names, descriptions, and where these men might be found. I also want to know where the original paintings are shipped once the forgeries have been made."

He then turned to Cooper. "I'll send one of the clerks out here with an inventory of the warehouse contents. I want every item in here accounted for. Nothing is to leave this warehouse."

He cast his attention on the workers once more. "I've assured you that you will not be arrested so long as you cooperate with us. This also means no pilfering from this warehouse. Anyone caught walking out with so much as a ball of twine will be tossed in prison."

He took back his rifle and strode into the art gallery. Two frightened clerks were standing around looking utterly lost and just as uncertain about what to do as the warehouse workers had been.

"Where are Crowell and Wendall?" Rafe asked the younger clerk, who identified himself as John Grantham.

"They're not here." He stared in fear at the weapon Rafe held at his side. "Mr. Wendall left before…how could he leave his own son?" He shook his head and tears began to flow down his cheeks. "I suppose you are here to see Hugo's body. We didn't know what to do. It felt wrong to just leave him as he was, dumped like that on the floor. But we were afraid to touch him."

He sent the young man off to the warehouse with his inventory ledger and then turned to the second clerk, an older gentleman by the name of Matthew Bishop, who also appeared distraught but was holding himself together better than his companion. "Show me to Mr. Wendall's office."

"Yes, Mr. Quinton. This way." He led him down a hall and into a large, well-appointed office. Hugo lay lifeless upon the carpet. By the blood on his shirt, it was obvious he'd been shot through the heart. The lack of bloodstains on the carpet revealed he must have been shot elsewhere and moved here. But Rafe knew this, for Crowell had admitted as much, and the warehousemen and clerks had confirmed it.

"Hellfire," Rafe muttered, hoping the prison doctor would arrive soon. This investigation would take priority over any other pending matters, most of which were trivial compared to this murder. "Mr. Bishop, tell me all you know."

"Not much, I'm afraid. Mr. Grantham and I were here when the senior Mr. Wendall and Mr. Crowell carried his body in through the back door."

"Where had they been?"

"I don't know."

"Did they mention an appointment with anyone?"

"No. But Mr. Wendall and Mr. Crowell had been arguing this morning. We heard very little, but Mr. Crowell did tell Mr. Wendall to leave things as they were and stop stirring up a hornet's nest. Hugo agreed with Mr. Crowell, but his father would not listen to either of them and stormed out. I assumed he left merely to walk off his anger and expected him to return to the gallery within a few minutes."

"But he did not return?"

"No, so Hugo got worried and went to look for him. Mr. Crowell reluctantly went with him. About half an hour later, Mr. Wendall's carriage drew up behind the gallery and the two of them carried poor Hugo's body inside. Mr. Wendall was beside himself with grief. He kept repeating that it was all his fault. But how can it be? He doted on Hugo and would never have hurt him. Mr. Crowell was also in a state, insisted they go the authorities and muttered that this was too big for them to handle on their own."

"What did he mean by that?"

"I…I'm sure I don't know." He began to wring his hands.

Rafe had been kneeling beside Hugo's body and now rose to his full height. "An old woman's house burned down, and now young Wendall is lying dead at your feet. I've had enough with coy answers, Mr. Bishop. The longer you hide the truth from me, the more likely it is that you and Mr. Grantham will end up as corpses, too."

He turned ashen. "No, we're just clerks. We…dear heaven. I have a wife. Children."

"All the more reason to tell me everything you know. Once this scheme is exposed and you name the players, they will be too busy saving their own hides to bother coming after you. With Hugo dead, it has all fallen apart anyway. Is that not so?"

"I suppose." His shoulders slumped and he nodded.

"You merely suppose? Was someone else working with Hugo on the forgeries?"

"The replicas…"

Rafe refrained from rolling his eyes. "Yes, fine. The replicas. I know the Wendalls, Crowell, and the warehouse foreman are involved. But who else? Give me names. I especially want information on their London connections."

"Hugo was the only artist. He was brilliantly talented. He's been painting for years but could not seem to make a name for himself on his own. About five years ago, his father suggested helping out one of their acquaintances. Hugo's copy was incredible. We could not tell the replica from the original."

"I'll need to see his workroom. Is it here?"

The man nodded and quickly led him to a room hidden behind a set of library shelves. Rafe conducted a quick inspection and jotted down details of what he'd found. Canvas, wood, oils, paints, one painting on an easel, and an identical one carefully set beside it. By Auggie's description of the three important paintings owned by her aunt, he suspected Hugo had been working on the replica for one of hers. "This room is to remain sealed. No one touches a thing."

"Of course, Mr. Quinton."

They returned to Wendall's office where Hugo's body remained. "Tell me about this acquaintance of theirs. Hugo made a brilliant replica of this man's painting, so what happened next?"

"The gentleman had connections in London who took care of selling the original for him."

"Who was the acquaintance, and who was his London connection?"

The man cleared his throat. "I was never privy to the London connection, but the replica was made for...Lord Whiting."

Hellfire, the man had been under their very noses the entire time. Yet, his involvement could have been no more than an introduction five years ago. Or was he more deeply involved? If so, burning down his elderly neighbor's house could have also been a warning to him. "And you do not know Lord Whiting's London connection?"

"I have no idea. Only Mr. Wendall and Mr. Crowell ever had that information. You see, we only ship to a London warehouse. I'll give you their direction. But we were never told where the originals went after that."

Lord Whiting knew, and he would go there next.

But first, he tried to take note of as much as he could off Hugo's body. He searched the young man's pockets for anything that might indicate where they'd been.

Nothing of use.

The prison doctor arrived just as he was finishing. "Rafe, my word. What happened here?"

"Nothing happened in this spot, Milt. Hugo Wendall was shot elsewhere and brought here. His fingernails are clean. There is no sign of a struggle. No soot or grime on his clothing. Dig out the ball and save it for me. Hopefully, we'll be able to tell the weapon used. I'm going to question Lord Whiting now."

"Lord Whiting?" The doctor had just knelt beside the body and now looked up at Rafe in surprise. "What has he to do with any of this?"

"Perhaps nothing. Perhaps everything."

He cast Rafe a wry smile. "Seems to me you believe it is the latter. Be careful, my friend. You are dealing with a lord, and they can be more dangerous than any gang of thieves. I'll take care of this poor soul. I'll have him at the prison mortuary. His family can claim his body there."

Rafe told his men where he was going and sent one of his investigators off to arrange for several of the most trusted prison guards to take on a night watch and keep eyes on the gallery, warehouse, and hidden workroom.

"Highest security until we have all the partners in hand," Rafe said. "Cooper, I'm leaving you in charge here. When you've finished questioning the workers and confirming the inventory, lock this place up tight. The night guards should be along shortly. Once they are on the task, take the inventory ledgers back to my office and lock them in the safe. We'll meet, as usual, in my office in the morning."

"Be careful, Mr. Quinton."

He nodded and took off for Lord Whiting's residence.

He had to pound on the door and threaten to blast it to splinters before the butler would open it. "I'm sorry, Mr. Quinton. I did not mean to keep you waiting, but you caught me off my post. Lord and Lady Whiting are not here."

He frowned. "Where have they gone?"

"I believe they are paying a call on Lady Priscilla and her niece."

Rafe's heart shot into his throat, but he quickly calmed himself as he strode off. He'd placed one of his best investigators to guard Auggie and her aunt. He expected Cavendish would remain close by, as well, since Auggie had taken a door slammed in her face, and it had left her shaken.

Also, he'd given Auggie a weapon.

But would she ever use it? Especially on a couple she believed were friends? And what if this is all they were? After all, a recommendation given five years ago to Wendall and Crowell was no indication of their involvement in an expanded forgery scheme.

Even their recent recommendation of the art gallery to Priscilla and Morgan did not specifically connect them to a bigger scheme.

He tore into the inn and immediately strode to Auggie's suite of rooms. Her door was closed, and Wilkins was nowhere to be seen.

He knocked.

No response.

He tried the door.

Locked.

A maid walked by. "Oh, Mr. Quinton, they are taking tea in the dining room."

"Thank you." He strode there and saw them all seated at one of the corner tables. Auggie, her aunt, the Whitings, Clara, and Cavendish. He had never been happier to see his clerk shirking his official duties. But Auggie was headstrong and likely the sort to insist she was in the pink of health when she was not.

Seated at a corner table not far from them was Wilkins, having a cup of coffee as he kept an eye on them and anyone else who entered the dining room.

He nodded to Rafe.

He acknowledged Wilkins and dragged a chair over to join the small party. Auggie happened to be seated beside Lord Whiting, so he lifted her chair with her still in it and plunked it aside to make room for him between her and Whiting.

"I want a name," he said, not bothering with pleasantries. "Hugo Wendall is dead, and Lady Priscilla's house is burned to the ground. This ends now."

Auggie's aunt gasped. "Now see here, Mr. Quin—"

"Enough, Aunt Priscilla," Auggie interjected. "An innocent man is dead. Two men are dead if you count the ruffian who started the fire. Morgan is missing and could be a third to add to the list. Lord Whiting, you must tell us all you know."

"Me?"

Rafe had reached the end of his patience. "Yes, you. Or would you rather I question you while holding you in a prison cell?"

Auggie's aunt gasped. "Mr. Quinton!"

"And you'll be in the one next to him, Lady Priscilla. I'm done with all of you lying to me. Lord Whiting?"

"Yes, you are right. Of course." He withdrew his handkerchief and began to mop his brow.

Seemed all these elegant gentlemen with something to hide sweated easily.

Well, Rafe knew he was intimidating and had a frightening look about him when he was angry. He purposely encouraged their discomfort in the hope it would get them talking.

"Dear heaven," Lord Whiting muttered. "I should have said something the day of the fire. But we had not seen anything…what we told you was true. I suspected it might have had something to do with the paintings, but how could I be sure? What name are you asking for? If I know it, I will tell you."

"Your London connection. Hugo was the painter. His father and Crowell were the front men people came to in order to have forgeries made of their paintings. What I am missing is the name of the London agent who matched the original paintings with willing, deep-pocket buyers. From what I have been told, you are the one who had that connection and introduced this man to Wendall and Crowell."

He seemed genuinely surprised. "I cannot imagine…it was a referral made years ago."

"But you knew your London connection was still in this trade when you recommended this scheme to Lady Priscilla."

"No, well. Yes. He could have been. I wasn't certain. But they are reputable art dealers and… well, I suppose they are not all that reputable if they are involved in torching houses and taking lives. But until now, how was I to know? How was anyone hurt before this? We sold a painting years ago, and it allowed us to make necessary repairs to my estate as well as maintain adequate staff to attend us. We contribute to our local charities. Support our Exeter museums and the cultural arts."

"A name," Rafe intoned, trying not to grab the man by the lapels and shake him till his teeth rattled.

"Montford and Sons. They are one of the leading art dealers in London. Viscount Montford and I were friends at Oxford. Of course, that was years ago, but even back then he loved art and traveled extensively throughout Europe and beyond. Constantinople. Jerusalem. Damascus. His clientele consists of the elite of Europe. The Montford auctions attract wealthy buyers from around the world. Of course, the real money is made behind the scenes because these wealthy buyers prefer private transactions and not the more public auctions."

"What do you know of the young man who visited Lady Priscilla along with Morgan Nesbitt and Hugo Wendall shortly before her paintings were taken from her home?"

"The viscount's eldest son, Richard."

"Where will I find him now?"

Lord Whiting mopped his brow again. "In London, I presume."

Rafe cast him an intimidating gaze. "Presume again. He is my main suspect in Hugo Wendall's shooting, which happened mere hours ago. Where does he stay when he is in Exeter?"

"I don't know. Perhaps here. It is the finest lodgings in town, is it not? And he is not the sort to stay anywhere cheap. Any contact I had with him or his father was in London. I had no idea he was in Exeter until I happened to see him as he left Lady Priscilla's home."

"You must believe us," Lady Whiting said, clutching her husband's arm. "The young Montford did not even have the courtesy to pay a call on us when he arrived in Exeter. What is happening, Mr. Quinton? We are so very frightened. How can he be the one who shot poor Hugo? It is inconceivable that a viscount's son should do this."

"I doubt it was planned. Still, it happened." Rafe knew the young lord was not staying here because he'd seen the inn's register and did not recall that name appearing in it. Nor would there have been any reason for him to sign in under an assumed name.

Hugo's death may have been accidental, but he had yet to gather all the facts. The consequences to Wendall, Crowell, and the Montfords were now disastrous, and it was quite possible Richard Montford was tearing back to London long enough to grab whatever funds he could from his father and leap onto the first ship out of England. If any of their wealthy customers had paid in advance for the original masterworks that could not now be delivered, the Montfords would have some very angry, powerful people breathing down their necks. They'd have to be worried about being done in themselves.

The wealthy and powerful did not like to be crossed nor did they play by civilized rules.

Lady Whiting shook her head and moaned. "A falling out among thieves?"

"Yes, Lady Whiting. When you introduced Hugo to the Montfords, they must have realized there was substantial profit to be made with his talent. What started as an occasional painting copied and the original secretly sold, over time became a profitable side business, possibly bigger than their daily auctions and gallery sales. And then someone got greedy and wanted a bigger cut of the profits."

"Do you think it was the Montfords?" Auggie asked.

He turned to her, relieved to find her eyes clear and the color back in her delicate cheeks. "I have no idea. But there was obviously dissatisfaction among the ring of thieves. Lord Whiting, do you have any other names for me?"

"No. The Montfords were my only connection." He rested his elbows on the table and buried his face in his hands. "What have I done?"

Lady Priscilla harrumphed. "You have done nothing wrong, Lord Whiting. None of us could have known what would come of this arrangement. Now I am worried for poor Morgan. I will have nothing to give him. I cannot even openly sell the paintings without the Marquess of Chelsford's permission. You must speak to him, Auggie. He is so angry with Morgan, I doubt he will give in to my pleas."

"I cannot promise anything, Aunt Priscilla. Where is Morgan now? I will go with him to talk to Father, but Morgan has to own up to his responsibilities eventually. He cannot continue in his profligate ways and then count on his family to rescue him at every turn."

Auggie's aunt was being stubborn again. "If that is your attitude, then I am not telling you a thing."

"For pity's sake, Aunt Priscilla! Where is Morgan?"

The old woman tipped her chin in the air. "I cannot say."

Auggie frowned at her. "Cannot? Or will not?"

"Morgan has nothing to do with any of this intrigue. You are being tedious again, Auggie." She turned to her companion. "Clara, I am tired and wish to return to my room."

Rafe discreetly caught hold of Auggie's hand beneath the table and gave it a light squeeze. She was not going to get any information on her cousin's whereabouts here and now. He'd leave it to her to question Clara later, assuming the woman knew anything at all.

As for him, he wanted to question the senior Wendall next, then Crowell immediately afterward. Once done with those two, he would ride to London and report the crime to the London magistrate. He would not waste his time looking for the younger Montford in Exeter because the man was likely in a panic and already halfway to London.

If Auggie's father was in town, he would also pay a call on him to report what had transpired and get a sense of the man.

But official business first.

His mother was a Brayden, and he had plenty of Brayden relations in London, so finding lodgings for himself was not a problem. He had his choice of where to stay. However, much as he would have liked to see his family, he only intended to remain long enough to file his report with the London magistrate and grab the younger Montford before he fled.

The matter could be wrapped up within a day or two which would allow him to be back home within the week.

He rose, now satisfied he'd gotten all the information possible out of the Whitings.

More importantly, he'd been a magistrate long enough to know when people were lying to him and when they were telling the truth. He could tell the innocent from the guilty, and Lord Whiting and his wife were innocent. At worst, they'd sold a painting that should have been passed down the Whiting bloodline.

Any punishment for their deception was a matter to be addressed by Lord Whiting's heir. Not likely to happen while said heir, Lord Whiting's eldest son, was dependent on his father's good graces to keep him living in the lavish style to which he had become accustomed.

Rafe's greatest relief was in knowing they did not pose a threat to Auggie or her aunt. Once he was certain Lord Montford's son had fled for London, his heart would ease. He did not want that bastard with a dozen miles of Exeter.

He did not want him anywhere near Auggie.

He bade them good day and strode out.

Auggie chased after him. "Rafe! I know you are busy, and I do not want to interfere. Will I see you tonight? Or tomorrow?"

He led her to a quiet corner of the inn's foyer. "No, I need to question Hugo's father and then Crowell. After that, I am heading to London in the hope of stopping Montford's son before he flees England."

She put a hand to her heart. "Please be careful. Not only for my sake but for Sam."

"I will. That boy means the world to me."

"I know. Do you mind if I see him while you are gone? He'll miss you. My taking him and your mother for an outing one afternoon might ease his worry. But I won't do it if you object." She cast him an imploring look. "Please don't object because you are afraid he's already gotten too attached to me. I would never hurt him, no matter what happens between us."

"I know you will be gentle with my son. I trust you, Auggie." He ran a hand roughly through his hair. "But about us...think carefully what marrying me will mean for you."

She inhaled lightly and then released her breath with a smile. "Are you proposing to me?"

"I'm considering it," he said, returning her smile with a wry one of his own. "My son and Cavendish will never forgive me if I let you go."

"How do *you* feel about letting me go?"

"I'd probably regret it for the rest of my life. But what about you? Both of us need to be happy if there is to be a marriage. Auggie, you blew into my life on an October breeze, and now I cannot imagine living it without you. Do you think you can make a life here with me? I am Exeter's magistrate, and I love what I do. But my work can be dangerous at times and often requires my keeping late hours. My point is that my roots are here in Exeter, and I am not going to move to London."

"Duly noted, Mr. Quinton. This is a point upon which you will not compromise. So, it is up to me to decide whether I can accept to give up my former life and make a new one here with you and Sam. Perhaps I ought to read *The Book of Love* again, particularly the chapters on flaws, expectations, and compromises."

"I suppose I am not being fair to you. I just want to be honest about what is important to me." He took her hand. "Anyway, we'll talk further when I return."

"Assuming I am still here." She slipped her hand out of his and started back toward the dining room.

"Auggie, wait."

She turned to him, and he noticed tears clouding her eyes. "Do what you must. I am not going to cry."

He gave her cheek a light caress. "Yes, you are. You're just too proud to do it in front of me. But what I said earlier about falling in love with you…"

She arched an eyebrow. "Ah, you wish to take it back?"

"No, I've spouted off a list of things I want, but I've left out the most important item. You. The fact is, I'm not merely falling in love with you. I *am* in love with you. I'd marry you this minute if I could. But I suppose I haven't properly asked you, just told you what I wanted in my highhanded way."

"Tend to your business, Rafe." She reached up and quickly bussed his cheek. "I'm glad you are in love with me. Let me think about all you've said. We'll talk when you return."

She ran back into the dining room.

He missed her already.

Yet, it was mad for either of them to know their feelings so soon.

To trust those feelings.

He shook out of the thought and put his mind to Hugo's murder. Much of what had happened was already clear. But who had been the greedy party demanding a bigger cut?

Wendall and Crowell?

Or Montford?

CHAPTER ELEVEN

AUGGIE HOPED RAFE would not be too angry with what she did next, for why should she not go with him to the Wendall residence and assist in his questioning? Would she not be helpful? She saw him in the distance striding up the street and took off at an unladylike run to catch up to him.

He must have heard her light footsteps coming up behind him, for he turned and frowned at her.

She cast him a breathless smile. "Rafe, wait for me."

He looked so big and handsome as he stood in the crisp sunshine, looking not at all pleased. "I told Mr. Cavendish I was going with you and asked Mr. Wilkins to keep a close watch on my aunt. I did not have time to grab my hat or reticule. You won't make me go back, will you? Because I think I am the perfect one to question Mrs. Wendall and their staff, while you deal with Hugo's father."

She took a deep breath and continued. "And there may be paintings in his home that I can identify as genuine or fakes. Won't that be helpful to you? I was also thinking that while you are gone, I could be of help to Mr. Cavendish and your investigators. They'll need an art expert to assist in confirming that the paintings in the art gallery warehouse are what they are listed as being in their inventory. What do you think? Would I—"

"Yes, Auggie." He cracked a smile as he took her hand, placed it on his arm, and continued up the street. "You win. In truth, I was missing you already. But know I am allowing you to come with me because I believe it is safe. If I thought for a moment Montford's son was still in Exeter, I'd have hauled you back to the inn."

She nodded. "Nor would I have come after you had I thought there was any danger. Give me some credit, Rafe. Are there any questions, in particular, you want me to ask Mrs. Wendall once we're there?"

He cast her another affectionate smile and gave her a few suggestions. "But mostly go with your instincts and follow up with more questions depending on the answers. All right?"

"Yes, I won't fail you."

He gave her hand a light caress. "You seem fully recovered from the bashing Crowell gave you when he barged out of my office. Just don't overdo it."

He slowed his pace to accommodate her shorter strides and cautioned her again as they reached the Wendall residence which turned out to be not all that far from his own residence, Auggie noted. "Is Mr. Crowell's house close by as well?"

"Yes. I hope we'll find him there when we finally get to him. He may have gone into hiding. He was terrified, as you may have noticed."

The Wendall household was in disarray, and the door was already flung wide open when they approached. Auggie exchanged a glance with Rafe when she heard the sound of crying. A moment later, a tearful butler rushed forward. "Mr. Quinton, thank goodness you are here. I will let Mr. Wendall know. He has been expecting you."

He led them to the visitors' parlor and then scurried off to summon his employer. It was not long before he scurried back. "Please follow me, Mr. Quinton. He awaits you in his study."

Auggie remained seated. "Do tell Mrs. Wendall that Lady Augusta, the Marquess of Chelsford's daughter, is eager to see her."

His eyes widened in obvious surprise, for the Wendalls could not have been used to entertaining higher society at home. They may have served a wealthy clientele, but only in their business dealings. "At once, m'lady."

She was leaping out of her skin to know what Hugo's father was going to tell Rafe, but she also had her work cut out for her.

Mrs. Wendall rushed in a short while later. "Do forgive me for keeping you waiting. I've ordered refreshments to be brought in for us."

"Oh, my dear Mrs. Wendall. I did not mean to put you to the trouble. But I insisted on coming along with Mr. Quinton to pay my condolences and tell you how impressed I was with your wonderful son. Do come sit next to me and we'll chat."

Auggie had been pondering how to ask the necessary questions without having it sound like an interrogation, but she needn't have worried. As soon as the refreshments had arrived and they were once more alone, it was obvious the woman needed to unload her grief. "Mrs. Wendall," she said, taking over the chore of pouring each of them a cup of tea because the woman's hands were shaking too badly to manage it, "I know everything about the replica paintings and their Montford and Sons connection. Men get mixed up in all sorts of things in their business. But I had to come to you as his mother, a very good one who raised a fine son, and let you know how sorry I am for your loss."

"Thank you, my lady." Then the words began to flow as though a floodgate had been opened. Auggie felt guilty about her subterfuge, but she hadn't really been lying about wishing to lend her comfort. "I told my husband not to confront his London people, but he would not listen to reason. He is not a crook, and this arrangement was turning into something beyond merely switching out paintings. Those wicked men were demanding Wendall and Crowell help them with other things."

"Stolen artwork?"

The woman's eyes rounded in surprise. "How did you know? Has Mr. Quinton been investigating this matter all along?"

"He doesn't tell me his business, but I would not be surprised. Very little gets past him. Do go on, you may be able to provide information about those odious men that he does not know yet. The more you cooperate, the more favorably he will look upon your husband. Is it not important to save him now?"

She nodded. "Well, Hugo wanted out as well. He'd only ever intended to do a favor or two for a few of our regular customers. After all, Hugo was the one with all the talent, and he did not wish to spend his life imitating masterpieces created by others."

"That is understandable. So, they met here with the London man? I understand he is Viscount Montford's son."

"Yes, this is who my husband stormed off to confront. But they met elsewhere, not here."

"Was anyone else at the meeting?"

She shook her head and cried some more, but Auggie could not tell if she was nodding in agreement or merely shaking her head. "That villain would not deign to step foot in our humble home. They met at his place…well, it is not his, just loaned by a friend of his while that friend was traveling."

"Do you know where this friend lives? Is it far from here?"

"I don't know." The woman leaned closer. "But I can tell you, he quickly turned that residence into a den of iniquity. Women of ill repute coming and going at all hours. Drinking. Shameless goings-on. That's what my husband told me." She tipped her chin up and sniffed. "And he thinks we are beneath him!"

"So, your son and husband met him there? Where is this meeting place?" she asked again because she knew Mrs. Wendall was holding back. "I do not mean to insist, but it is important for the magistrate to know. Perhaps he can catch this fiend and—"

"It won't bring my Hugo back." She burst into tears again.

"No, of course, it won't. But it might give him justice."

"Justice? There is no justice in this world." She shook her head furiously. "His father is a viscount. That family is above the law."

"Well, my father is a marquess, and that is above a viscount."

Both cups of tea were getting cold, and the cake brought out was left uncut, but Auggie ignored these niceties set out, instead wondering what she might do for the Wendalls. "Forgive me for pressing you on the matter, but it burns me up to think such a low fellow can act with impunity. Perhaps my father can do something to help. Even if it is only to warn his friends about the sort of men these Montfords are. Their duplicity deserves to be exposed."

"Yes. Yes, I see." She told Auggie where the fiend had been staying. "My husband meant to go alone to confront him. Hugo realized what he was doing and rushed to tell Mr. Crowell. They both went over there to stop him. Dear Hugo, he was such a gentle boy. He didn't want a bigger cut of the profits. He just wanted a way out of this situation. A peaceful way out. He was willing to ease out gradually. But my husband insisted their London partnership had to stop at once."

"I see. He wasn't asking for a bigger share but demanding an abrupt end to their operations."

She nodded. "He wanted so much to free Hugo to work on his own paintings, to make a name for himself."

"Did your son and Mr. Crowell come upon your husband and Lord Montford already arguing?"

"That beast was drunk and brandishing a pistol, shouting at my husband to get out or else he would shoot him. Hugo stepped between them to keep them apart, but both men kept shouting...and suddenly, Montford stumbled, and his pistol went off."

Mrs. Wendall tried to pick up her teacup to drink, but her hands were still shaking too badly, so she set it down with a clatter. "Accidental death will be the verdict on the inquest, won't it? Montford's boy will get off without so much as a slap on the wrist. He is an evil, callous fellow. He did not stay around to help but immediately fled for London. His father will protect him now, and there is nothing you or your father can do to help us. But I do appreciate the offer."

"He may not be touched by the law but losing Hugo will

make some powerful people very angry. Especially if they have paid in advance for something that cannot now be delivered. He will not get off lightly."

"I do not care, my lady. Nothing that happens can bring our Hugo back."

Rafe came to collect her not long afterward, and they walked over to Mr. Crowell's residence. She quickly related all that Mrs. Wendall had told her.

He nodded. "Her husband told me much the same. He and Crowell panicked, carried Hugo into Crowell's carriage, and brought his body back to the gallery."

"I suppose he died instantly. Did they not think to take him to a hospital? Or a surgeon?"

Rafe's expression was grim. "They were completely brainless and left Hugo's body in the art gallery office. Just left him there while they ran around like chickens with their heads cut off."

"I suppose they will be ruined once the scandal breaks. They'll have no business. Who would ever trust them again? And while the wealthy and powerful might go after the Montfords first, they are also likely to come after Wendall and Crowell, don't you think?"

He shrugged. "Possibly. But I hope it can be avoided. That's why taking inventory of their stock is so important. Once the inquest is over, we'll supervise the shipment of the most valuable works back to their rightful owners and work down from there until everyone has the items they left in the care of the gallery. The owners can do whatever they like with their paintings afterward. It isn't my lookout. But I will be keeping Wendall and Crowell in custody. Not in prison but confined to their homes. They were branching into other things that were clearly illegal."

"Those are what will ultimately send them to prison?"

"Their sentence will be left to the judge at the next Assizes. Murder and theft at this level are beyond the scope of my authority. I would not be permitted to rule on the matter."

"But your opinion would hold sway with the judge, would it

not?"

"Perhaps." He held the gate open for her as they reached the Crowell residence and marched up the walk. "Auggie, do not go soft on them. They planted a spy within my prison which suggests to me that more was going on…or about to start going on than the mere painting of replicas to accommodate their customers. They were dealing in forgeries. Probably in stolen artifacts, as well. I doubt these deceptive practices were limited to consenting parties."

"And what of Mr. Merriwell?"

"The jeweler? Probably involved in selling stolen jewelry. I've had a man watching his shop since yesterday. He isn't going anywhere. Once we are through with Crowell, I'll drop you back at the inn and head to Merriwell's, as well as inspect the actual scene of the crime."

"Then off to London?"

"Yes."

She took light hold of his arm. "We could examine the scene of the crime together."

"No, Auggie. It is too dangerous. Montford might still be lurking about."

"But you are convinced he fled Exeter right after the shooting."

He nodded. "But I could be wrong. I'll take a couple of my men along with me to complete a thorough search." He arched an eyebrow. "Don't even think to argue with me. What if he didn't run? We know he is drunk, scared, and carrying a loaded pistol."

"I won't argue with you. I know it is asking a lot of you, but don't leave Exeter without stopping by to see me again. I want to kiss you properly…and then I want to think about what I will be giving up if I were to remain in Exeter."

"Fair enough." They spoke no more as the Crowell butler opened the door to let them in. He appeared as devastated as the Wendall butler had been, perhaps more so because he hadn't the presence of mind to lead them into the visitors' parlor. So, they stood in the entry foyer listening to the echoing sobs and wails from abovestairs.

"Show Lady Augusta to the parlor," Rafe told the butler when he returned with Mr. Crowell.

Auggie knew better than to protest, for Rafe must have had a reason to speak to the man alone. She waited in the parlor, the staff too distracted to offer her refreshments, and Mrs. Crowell too distraught to come out of her bedchamber.

It did not take Rafe long to finish questioning Mr. Crowell.

"What did he say to you?" she asked as he led her back to the inn. The wind had picked up and cooled a little so that she felt a light chill run through her. She burrowed a little closer to Rafe as they walked, not minding that he had quickened his pace so she had to take two strides to one of his own.

"Nothing we did not already know. He just confirmed the story Wendall told me."

She wanted to ask more questions but found it hard to talk and keep up with him. "Rafe, slow down."

"Sorry. I just want this investigation over and done. It is like a snake with many heads. Lop off one and more appear. They were caught up in far more than occasional forgeries, and I don't believe they've told us all of it yet. Crowell had a shifty look in his eyes. I don't like shifty looks."

"What else do you think they were up to? Beyond fake paintings and possible stolen artifacts."

He rubbed a hand across the nape of his neck. "I don't know yet."

"Well, since they are art dealers it is likely any illicit activity involves art. Perhaps art theft? I mean, people's homes are broken into on occasion. Museum thefts? Jewelry thefts? They are partnered with Mr. Merriwell as well as the Montfords, and the jewelry could be a lucrative side business since it is much easier to walk out with a diamond in one's pocket than a priceless tapestry or painting."

Rafe grinned at her. "If we were in a carriage, I would kiss you again. You are a clever sparrow."

She laughed. "My father would be appalled to know what we have been doing in his carriage."

When they returned to the inn, he took her aside just before reaching her quarters. "Auggie, I am not going to stop here again. I'll be off once I am through at Merriwell's, the crime scene, and a quick return to the Wendall and Crowell gallery to bring my investigators up to present. Cooper is my best man, he'll be in charge while I'm gone. My only stop after that will be home to pack and give Sam a hug."

"I understand."

He glanced around and drew her into the alcove near her suite of rooms. "Close your eyes."

She closed them and tipped her head up.

He gave a soft chuckle. "I think this is the first time you've ever done a thing I've asked without tossing questions back at me."

"I—"

His arms closed around her like steel bands, and he crushed his mouth to hers, kissing her so thoroughly, that every limb, organ, and pulse in her body tingled.

There was not an inch of her left unscathed.

Not an inch left unkindled.

Their bodies were wrapped around each other so that she could feel the hard length of him, his muscled arms, broad shoulders, and powerfully built torso.

"Next time I have you like this," he said with a deliciously deep rasp to his voice that shot more tingles through her, "we will both have our clothes off, and I will not be stopping at kisses."

After a moment, he groaned and drew away.

She smiled up at him. "That was extraordinary."

He kissed her on the nose. "You are extraordinary. Be careful while I am away. Don't go anywhere without one of my men to accompany you."

He was now looking at her in a burning, possessive way.

For someone who prided herself on her independence, she was awfully eager to give much of it up for this man.

She had to give their relationship serious thought.

It was one thing to be giddy and excited now because everything was so new to her and she'd never felt this way about a man before. But what would happen if they married?

He was no milksop to be easily led about by the nose.

Would he allow her to participate in other investigations? Or was this a one-time indulgence and all would change the moment they exchanged wedding vows? And what about her life in London?

Well, that horrid marriage mart was an easy thing to give up.

But what of her father? Could he manage without her? Would Rafe allow her to see him as often as she liked? And that was another thing, why should a wife need to seek permission from a husband for her every move?

Rafe was right when he'd said earlier that things were moving too quickly.

How confining would marriage be to a man like Rafe?

CHAPTER TWELVE

RAFE COULD NOT bear the disappointment in his son's eyes as the lad sat on his bed and watched him pack. "When are you coming back, Papa?"

He withdrew several shirts and cravats and set them down beside his son. "In about a week, Sam. The time will pass quickly, you'll see."

"No, it won't," he grumbled, his sad expression making Rafe's heart turn to crystal and shatter.

"Tell me what your plans are while I'm gone. Will you be playing with Max? What games are on your schedule for this week?" He tossed his shaving gear into his pouch and ignored his housekeeper's clucking over all the things he was forgetting.

"Mr. Quinton, you'll get to London and find yourself half undressed! Let me finish this for you."

"Fine, Mrs. Lacey," he said with a chuckle and allowed her to take over the chore, while he settled in a chair by his bedchamber hearth and took Sam onto his lap. "Tell me, son."

"We're going to play with the soldiers Auggie bought me."

"That sounds like fun. And what about the books she got for you?"

He nodded. "I'm going to read those to Max and Harry. She listens better than Max does and already knows her letters. She thinks she's so smart." ·

Rafe could not contain his grin. "She probably is. Girls are more clever than we are about many things."

Sam nodded. "Like Auggie. Is she smarter than you, Papa?"

"Possibly," he muttered, casting his son an affectionate grin.

"Grandmama says I can take dance lessons. Max wants to take them, too. Then Harry began crying because she wants to take them, and I said she's too little and couldn't. She wants to do everything I do."

"Because she admires you. It is a compliment that she likes you and thinks you are special. Wouldn't it be helpful to have her with you, since she's a girl and you can dance with her?"

"I don't want to dance with her. I want to dance with Auggie."

"Yes, but how are you going to practice? Isn't the point of your lessons to learn how, so Aggie will be impressed?"

"I guess. All right, I'll do it. But Harry had better not cry. Why won't you dance, Papa? You really should because Auggie enjoys it, and I think it makes her sad that you won't. I don't want her to feel sad." Sam cast him such a look of admonition, that one would think the lad was the parent and he was the unruly child.

Rafe chuckled. "Tell you what I'm going to do. You take those lessons with Max and Harry, and when I get back, I'll take you all to the next dance at the Swan Inn. How does that sound?"

"Thank you, Papa!" He threw his arms around Rafe's neck and hugged him fiercely. "You don't have to worry about Auggie. She'll be happy to dance with me and Max. She won't even notice you."

Lord, he loved this boy.

"Glad you have my back, son."

"Always, Papa."

His housekeeper was wiping a tear from her eye. "Oh, Mr. Quinton. You be careful in London. Come back to us quick."

"I will, Mrs. Lacey. No place I'd rather be than home." He grabbed his now stuffed pouch, knowing Mrs. Lacey had thought of everything he'd need on his journey, and headed downstairs with Sam.

His mother was waiting by the door. "Don't you fret about a thing, Rafe. We'll take good care of the boy."

"I know." He kissed her cheek. "So, my son is to have dance lessons?"

She smiled. "Every afternoon. It's all been arranged. I'll look in on Lady Augusta and her aunt as well. Our ladies' auxiliary will make certain they have all they need."

He gave a nod of approval and strode to the mews to collect his mount. After securing his pouch to the saddle, he rode off to London without looking back. Parting from Sam felt like a physical tear to his heart, but he was comforted in the knowledge his son would be distracted by those tin soldiers Auggie had purchased for him and those dance lessons.

He wished he could be there to watch his son, that gritty look of determination on his pudgy face as he, Max, and probably Harry attempted to conquer the intricate steps.

The weather held up for him on the road to London, the occasional rain passing quickly and leaving few puddles. The city was already bustling with activity by the time he reached the outskirts, even though it was barely after sunrise. He went straight to his cousin Joshua's townhouse, since his cousin was the army liaison to Parliament and had close connections to the London authorities. Joshua would help him move swiftly to detain Viscount Montford and his son, as well as obtain permission to search his home and gallery.

He would seek his cousin Finn's help once they had the Montford ledgers, for no one could fool Finn when it came to spotting fraud. Well, that was for later. First, he had to get the Montfords detained.

To his relief, Joshua and his wife were awake and ready for the day. "Well, I'll be damned," Joshua said, striding forward to give him a hearty embrace. "What are you doing here, Rafe?"

"Official business." He next greeted Joshua's wife, Holly, a beautiful woman who bore a resemblance to the Farthingale women he'd met several months earlier in Taunton, the very ones his cousins Shayne and Lorcan had married. He understood why his Brayden cousins had fallen hard and fast for the young ladies in that family.

Auggie, although not part of the Farthingale family, had the same look and demeanor. Intelligent eyes, soft and delicate features, but also a quiet strength about her.

"We were just sitting down to breakfast. Join us," Joshua said, wrapping an arm around his wife's waist as he led them into the dining room. Apparently, his cousin did not even consider keeping Holly out of their conversation. He liked that, for this trust and eagerness to seek her opinion was exactly what Rafe hoped to have with Auggie.

Of course, he could not say yet if she would marry him.

They had an extra place at the breakfast table prepared for him, then all of them settled in their seats and began to chat over eggs and coffee.

Holly sat beside her husband and listened intently as Rafe told them the reason for his presence in London. "I've seen that son of Montford's around town," she said, pursing her lips. "He's an arrogant knave, the sort who only thinks of himself and what he can grab from others."

Joshua nodded. "Sounds like he overreached this time. But if what you say is true, that he stumbled and the pistol went off, then he's never going to be punished."

"True, he won't be held on that charge." Rafe drank his coffee and set the cup back down. "It's the forgeries and stolen artifacts I'm after. The actual thefts, not the copies commissioned by the owners themselves. That is what I believe the Montfords had branched into doing. Expert replicas take too long to paint. I think they were getting greedy and not willing to wait, so they simply started stealing art instead. Art, jewelry, antiquities. I'll need to talk to the London magistrate and get his cooperation."

"You'll need my help. I'll come with you," Joshua said.

"I think you ought to take the Duke of Edgeware with you, too." Holly turned to Rafe. "He's married to my cousin, Dillie."

Rafe grinned. "We'll call on him if it proves necessary. Is everyone in London married to a Farthingale? Why am I not surprised? Everywhere I turn, you ladies seem to be stealing hearts. Mostly Brayden hearts."

Holly laughed softly. "Not yours, I expect. Your cousins handed that book off to Lady Augusta Nesbitt to deliver to you. Well?"

Rafe cleared his throat. "Hellfire, I am not going to answer that."

"You already have. I saw the look in your eyes at the mention of her name. I'm glad. She seemed lovely, although I only met her briefly at Donal's wedding."

He groaned. "What about you, Joshua? Were you involved in that bright idea to hand her the book to deliver to me?"

He raised his hands in surrender. "I had nothing to do with it." He turned to Holly and cast her a rakish grin. "Holly did not want that book either when her sisters attempted to shove it at her, so she stole next door to hide it. She got an eyeful of me and instantly fell in love. Don't fight it, Rafe. It's no use. There's no escaping the power of that book. Right, Holly?" He cast her another rakish grin. "She still thinks I am magnificent."

She coughed and set down her cup. "Shouldn't the two of you be off to find the London magistrate? In the meantime, I shall prepare a guest room for you, Rafe. You'll stay here with us, of course. How long do you plan to remain in town?"

"Not long. I'm hoping no more than a couple of days. I need to return to my son as soon as possible."

"Of course," she said with a nod. "He must be missing you terribly. Would you mind if I had the family over tomorrow evening, just a light supper, so they all have the chance to see you?"

He pursed his lips. "I don't know where this investigation will lead us. There's a lot to be done and it might take my working late into the evening. Perhaps overnight. Put off the family gathering for another time. All right?"

She nodded. "I understand. I won't say anything to the others."

Joshua laughed heartily. "I'm sure word is already spreading. My mother will descend on us like an enraged harpy if she finds out you were here and didn't see her."

Rafe gave a mock shudder. "Aunt Miranda? I'll make certain to call on her before I leave London. Glad to hear she hasn't mellowed with age."

He and Joshua rode off for the magistrate's office located on Bow Street shortly afterward. They strode up the marble staircase and were quickly admitted to see the presiding justice, Lord Farnham, a man perhaps ten years older than Rafe but still full of vigor. "Mr. Quinton," he said, coming around his desk to shake Rafe's hand, "a pleasure to meet you. Your reputation precedes you."

"All good I hope, my lord."

"The best. You've done a remarkable job in Exeter. Have a seat, gentlemen. I assume this is not a social call."

"No, and it is rather a pressing matter." He quickly related all that had happened in Exeter. "I need warrants issued to conduct a search of Viscount Montford's home, gallery, and any warehouses that handle his merchandise. I'll also need the assistance of your constables."

"So, you think the viscount and his son are involved not only in forgery but theft? I don't know, Mr. Quinton. This may be a matter beyond the scope of my authority. In any event, I'll need proof. The Montfords are well respected in London society. We cannot simply barge in on his lordship and demand to question him and his son."

"My word is sufficient proof of their involvement. The younger Montford will run off unless we stop him. Perhaps he has already. I hope not. He shot Hugo Wendall. Yes, it was probably accidental. But I want young Montford separated from his father while questioned. One of them will crack and reveal more about their operation. We need to conduct a search of their gallery and warehouse, seize the company ledgers.”

“I don’t know,” he repeated, now frowning as he listened to Rafe’s requests. “I will have to consult with our legal counsel. It is a close thing, and I am not certain I can issue such orders. We may have to seek out a justice of the criminal court.”

Joshua shook his head. “He’ll require a hearing, and we’ll lose all element of surprise.”

“I know, but it’s my neck on the line if I overstep. I am sympathetic to you, believe me. However, our constabulary is still fairly new and not everyone is convinced of its viability. One wrong step…or overstep…and there will be an outcry.”

Rafe raked a hand through his hair in frustration. He hadn’t come all this way merely to be dismissed. He was about to say more when there was a knock at the magistrate’s door. “Enter,” Lord Farnham called out, obviously eager for the distraction.

The Duke of Edgeware strolled in. “I hear there’s been some excitement.” Though his manner was polite and he appeared every inch the wealthy gentleman, there was a glint in his eyes that spoke of intelligence, power, and an iron determination.

“Your Grace.” The magistrate shot to his feet, as did Rafe and Joshua.

“Holly must have rushed straight over to Dillie’s the moment we were gone,” Joshua muttered.

“I’m glad she did,” Rafe whispered back. Praise heaven for good connections. It was imperative to have them when dealing with the elite of London society. No one was more elite than the Duke of Edgeware.

Rafe quickly filled him in on all that had transpired.

He nodded. “We had a flurry of thefts reported in Bath over the summer. Another major theft was reported two days ago by Lady Manchester here in London. Several museum thefts. These may all be connected to the crimes you are investigating in Exeter. Lord Farnham, dispatch your constables to the viscount’s home immediately. I want him and his son detained and his home searched.”

"But Your Grace—"

"I see you are distressed."

"Not distressed so much as uncertain. Under whose authority may I do this? I don't think I have the power as magistrate to act on such matters."

"Let me make it easy for you. You are to take them into custody and issue those search warrants in the name of the Crown."

"Royal authority?" His eyes widened. "Yes, Your Grace. It will be done at once. I'll have my constables summoned."

"Give me every man available. Rafe. Joshua. I'll leave the matter of questioning the Montfords to you. The constables will go with you and search his home under your supervision."

"What about the gallery and warehouses?" Joshua asked.

"Agents of the Crown will attend to those under my supervision." He arched an eyebrow and grinned. "You've done good work, Rafe. We were busily trying to connect the pieces, then Holly strolls into my home, kisses my wife and children, and proceeds to tell me the entire scheme. She laid out all the relevant players. We've been trying to figure out who they were for months, and she blithely hands them over to me on a silver platter."

Rafe groaned. "She suggested we go to you first, but I dismissed the notion. I did not think their operation was as broad as you've made out."

Joshua folded his arms and grinned. "There's something about these Farthingale women. They may look sweet and demure, but they save lives, smash international spy organizations, and then go about their business as though they've done nothing extraordinary."

Rafe nodded. "I think Lady Augusta is shaped from the same mold."

Joshua slapped him on the shoulder. "Sounds like it from the way you speak about her. Don't be an idiot and let her go."

The duke said nothing, but Rafe saw something deep and raw

in his expression. He'd heard the gossip, of course. The duke who'd vowed never to marry being forced to marry in scandal. But who ever believed such gossip? It was obvious this man could never be made to do anything against his will.

He wanted to marry Dillie Farthingale.

Probably burned with a need to have her and not merely for one night. A woman like that wrapped around a man's soul.

Rafe understood enough about such feelings having gone through his own lack of it in his marriage, one he would never consider failed because it had given him Sam. But any flame of attraction had soon snuffed itself out. He would never blame Mary, nor would he blame himself. It was not her fault that he needed something more than a pretty face to greet him coming home. After polite greetings, they'd had nothing to say to each other. Not a blessed thing. Their conversation had dried up like a pond besieged by drought.

As for the Duke of Edgeware, who could doubt he was a man in love? Not only in love but bound to his wife with all his heart and soul.

This is what he hoped for with Auggie, but could it ever happen?

Was he hoping for too much?

He returned his attention to the matter at hand and listened while the duke continued. "A few of those stolen pieces were heirlooms belonging to foreign royalty. These were actual thefts, not some family member switching out the real thing for a fake and pocketing the proceeds. The brazenness of it leads me to believe the Montfords have been at this game for some time and thought they'd outwitted us."

"Which they had," Lord Farnham intoned.

"True, but no more. They recently expanded into museum thefts as well. Several priceless artifacts were taken only last week."

Joshua gave a low whistle.

The duke nodded. "Separate the father and son, question

them about their contacts. I want to know who they hired to conduct the actual thefts. I want the names of those thieves. I want the names of the deep-pocket buyers willing to pay for the stolen goods. I want to know which jewelers were involved. Did they employ artists other than Hugo Wendall to paint forgeries? Did they have spies planted inside the museums? Inside Lady Manchester's house? You get the idea."

"We'll get it done," Rafe assured, determined to get this scheme unwound and all the participants revealed as quickly as possible so he could return home. He was eager to take the measure of the viscount and his son, determine who was the weaker one, and question that one first.

"Meanwhile, I'll be poring over the gallery and warehouses with my agents. I hope we are in time to prevent shipment of those priceless artifacts and gems out of England."

"Assuming we are not dealing with an English buyer," Rafe said. "Such a one would be hard to trace without ship manifests to point us in the right direction."

"We ought to call in my brother, Finn," Joshua suggested.

The duke shook his head and laughed. "He's probably awaiting our summons since Holly happened to mention she was off to visit Belle next." He turned to Rafe. "As I expect you know, Belle is Finn's wife."

Joshua emitted another chuckle. "No wonder those Fellows in the Royal Society are afraid to admit women into their fold. They'd wipe the floor with those old stodges."

Joshua and the duke proceeded to toss a few more jests between them about their accomplished wives, but Rafe felt none of their merriment. Mary would never have done what Holly just did. She would not have listened in on their breakfast conversation or thought to help bring the right people into this investigation.

On the other hand, that is exactly what Auggie would have done.

But he'd given her that stupid ultimatum. Exeter or nothing.

And he'd set down the gauntlet after claiming he could compromise.

Had she made her decision?

Would she refuse his offer of marriage?

He followed Joshua out once the constables had been gathered. Lord Farnham hurried after them. "This is the biggest thing that's happened in London in years. I'm not missing out on the action. Tell me what to do and how I can help."

Well, it would free him and Joshua to interrogate the Montfords while Lord Farnham supervised his constables. These Bow Street men were tough and intelligent. Lord Farnham, despite his initial concerns, now looked eager to participate in bringing down the Montford operations.

The streets of Mayfair were quiet at this hour, which was still too early for the well-heeled to be up and about, even though the working class had long since been astir. There was a bite to the air and a trace of stench off the Thames that reminded him of rotted fish.

The others were obviously used to it by now and made no passing remarks. Rafe preferred the scent of Exeter, the waft of pine from the surrounding woodlands as it swept across the rolling hills into the ancient market town. When the wind shifted, it also carried in a hint of salty air from the nearby coast.

No, London was not for him.

Exeter was in his blood.

Could he work this out with Auggie?

Lord Farnham ordered his constables to surround the elegant Montford townhouse. "No one leaves the premises, not even a mouse." He withdrew his firearm and knocked at the door.

No one responded.

"Open up under the authority of the Crown!" Tossing aside politeness, he pounded on the door, then turned to Rafe with a grin. "I've always wanted to say that. Feels good to be doing something other than sitting at my desk."

Rafe stepped down to cautiously peer in one of the front

windows. "The visitors' parlor," he muttered. "No one's in there."

Joshua did the same at another window. "Lord Montford's study. No one there either. Are we too late? Have they run off?"

Finally, the door opened, and a terrified butler popped his head out. "Gather the staff," Lord Farnham ordered, striding in and immediately taking command. "But first summon Lord and Lady Montford and their children."

The elderly servant shook his head furiously. "His lordship is not here. Nor is her ladyship and their children…well, just their eldest daughter, Lady Grace. But surely you cannot mean—"

"Advise her we are here." Rafe stepped forward, knowing he had a rougher look about him than Joshua or Lord Farnham and would intimidate the man. "We also know Richard Montford is here. This is a Crown matter. Anything less than your full cooperation and you'll all be thrown into—"

The man emitted a cry and clutched his heart.

Hellfire.

Was he that frightening? He didn't want the man's heart to fail.

But in the next moment, the butler caught his breath. "Lady Montford and the youngest children are at their estate in Hampshire. Only Lord Montford and his eldest son were in London. Well, Lady Grace, too. But she merely remained to complete fittings for her new gowns. She is to make her debut shortly. I am telling you the truth. The gentlemen are not here now."

"How long since they fled?" Rafe asked.

"No more than an hour ago," he said, his breaths now shallow and fast.

"Where did they say they were going?" Lord Farnham asked.

"They didn't say, m'lord."

Lord Farnham shook his head. "You'll have to do better than that." He then turned to Rafe. "Mr. Quinton, I'll leave two of my men outside to watch the house and bring the others in to search it."

Rafe nodded before returning his attention to the trembling butler. "What is your name?"

"Hodgkins, sir."

"Take me to the rest of the staff while Lady Grace readies herself. Someone must have overheard something. Do not think to save Lord Montford and his son by stalling us. It will only go worse for all of you."

While Hodgkins might have felt some loyalty to his employer, it turned out much of the staff did not. Rafe was soon scribbling names, directions, and other useful information as they hastened to give up every useful bit that came to mind, often speaking over each other in their haste to tell him what he needed to know. They also confirmed the two Montfords had fled to the docks.

Lady Grace confirmed their story as Rafe and Joshua questioned her.

In truth, Rafe's heart went out to her, for the girl was obviously unaware of what had been going on and was clever enough to understand the repercussions. "Richard is my half-brother. We have the same father, but my mother is his second wife. I never suspected a thing until yesterday. Richard did this. My father is not a dishonest man."

Joshua cleared his throat. "The thefts have been going on for several years."

It was a sad thing to see a girl's heart crumble before one's very eyes, but that is what he and Joshua witnessed as she realized the extent of the damage she and her younger siblings were facing.

She buried her face in her hands and cried silently, but after a moment, she looked up at them with a fragile composure. "This is my fault. My father kept going on about my securing a wealthy, titled husband, and how important it was for us to make a good showing. I did not think...I never imagined." She emitted a ragged breath. "I came to London to be fitted for new gowns, the very best. Ridiculously expensive. I never wanted any of this."

The girl was pretty and might have landed one of the *ton's* most eligible bachelors had her father's activities not been discovered.

Nothing but ruin faced her now, and she fully grasped it.

Too bad, for she appeared to be a good sort.

"May I return to my mother, or must I stay here?" she asked. "I think the servants will all abandon us now. Perhaps Hodgkins will stay on to properly close up the house. I don't know. You'll be tearing the house apart, I expect."

She looked up at the ceiling when she heard Lord Farnham and his men's footfalls overhead. "I see you are already at it."

"I'm sorry," Joshua said, "but it must be done. Do you have any other family in town?"

"No." She dabbed at her tears. "No one."

Rafe and Joshua exchanged glances, obviously thinking the same thing.

Rafe nodded.

Joshua offered her his handkerchief. "I'll summon my mother. You may have heard of her. Miranda, Lady Grayfell? You'll be safe under her wing for the next few days until we can make arrangements to get you to your mother."

She cast them a grateful smile. "Thank you. I won't be a bother to her."

Joshua could not help but give a light chuckle. "You needn't worry about that. My mother has the hide of a rhinoceros. She will take good care of you."

While Joshua remained with the Bow Street men to complete a search of the house, Rafe and Lord Farnham headed for the docks, accompanied by two of his best constables, experienced Bow Street runners. However, the Montford pair had gone deeply into hiding and it took him and the runners hours of scouring the dockside, the local taverns, and numerous inns before they finally found father and son hiding in one of the seedier taprooms that lined the wharves.

It was nearing midnight by the time the Montfords were hauled back to the magistrate's Bow Street office and placed in separate rooms to await interrogation.

Rafe started with the viscount first, for he looked far more haggard than his son. It was understandable, for the man had a lot more to lose. He had a wife and children to worry about while his puffed-up peacock of an heir had no one but himself to consider.

Rafe was fairly certain this expansion of their criminal activities had more to do with the greedy son taking over than the old viscount having a sudden desire to leave his heir an illicit and illegal legacy.

It took a certain brazenness to commit such crimes and a conceit to believe they would never be caught. This sounded like the son's nature, not the father's, but the father had obviously been dabbling in such activities early on and foolishly went along when the son suggested they fully dive in. They would now suffer the consequences. "The Crown will be lenient toward your wife and younger children if you start cooperating. Give us the names of those involved in your operations. Give us the locations of the stolen goods."

Lord Montford withdrew a handkerchief from his breast pocket and used it to mop his brow.

Ah, yes.

The handkerchief with which to mop the beads of sweat away.

So typical of these elegant gentlemen to capitulate once they were caught. They did not regret their deeds, only that they had been found out. Now all they could think about was how best to avoid punishment. He suspected the viscount was like all the other caught rats, ready to squeal until his lungs were raw, willing to give up anyone and everyone to save his pampered hide.

"All right, Mr. Quinton. Where shall I start?"

Chapter Thirteen

T O RAFE'S FRUSTRATION, he was required to remain in London for over a week while goods were recovered, culprits tracked down and apprehended, and affidavits taken. The Duke of Edgeware and Lord Farnham were more than qualified to handle the matter, but for some reason, the viscount had chosen to speak only to him, so he was brought in whenever there was new information and questioning was required.

He missed his son terribly. Auggie, too, and could not wait to take her in his arms again. Seeing his Brayden cousins so happily married and content with their wives was enlightening for him. Not just Joshua and Finn, either. He had about a dozen cousins around his age, mostly male, and all of them having made strong, successful marriages.

It was surprising, considering how unruly they'd all been in their younger years. His Aunt Miranda had taken to calling them wildebeests because that was what they were as growing boys—wild beasts who could not be contained when they were all together. They ate like beasts as well, for Braydens were big and always hungry.

But the women they married had tamed them and become partners to them in every way. Despite this partnership, their wives maintained their own hopes, dreams, and convictions. They had opinions and were not afraid to express them.

That is what he wanted for himself, what he hoped would

exist between him and Auggie, assuming she would have him.

He had another day before he was free to return home, and he wanted very much to pay a call on her father. But first, his Aunt Miranda. Her proper title was Lady Grayfell, and she proudly considered herself the matriarch of the family.

She was indeed the one who held the Brayden family together, no small thing considering the Brayden men were tough and preferred to give orders rather than take them. But family was important to all of them, so if Aunt Miranda summoned you, then off you went.

"Rafe, dear boy," she said, sweeping into her parlor where he had been placed to await her. "It is so good to see you. I know how busy you've been while in London, so you are forgiven for not calling on me sooner."

He gave her an affectionate hug. "We had a lot to do, as I'm sure you've heard."

"Yes, Montford's daughter told me about your ripping their house apart. That poor girl. What a sweet thing she is. She's back with her mother now, but I've invited her to return here and stay with me once she gets her mother and younger siblings settled. I'll see what I can do for her. There'll be no debut for her, of course. It is out of the question now that her family is disgraced. But perhaps I can quietly introduce her once the scandal dies down."

Rafe nodded. "It will take a while. These thefts were no small matter. We are still digging through Lord Montford's homes, his clubs, his gallery, and his warehouses. I thought to be here no more than a day or two, but we keep uncovering new information every day."

"And now your stay has stretched into more than a week. I know how badly you must miss your son." She waited for her butler to roll in the tea cart and then leave before she resumed conversation while pouring their cups and offering him a slice of ginger cake. "You are right. This theft ring you've uncovered is all the gossip and shall likely remain so for a while. Poor Lady

Montford. What's to become of her and the younger children? Will they be left with nothing?"

"I doubt Edgeware will be so heartless as to advise the Crown to take it all away. He'll make certain they are left with enough to live on, but not in the grand style to which they were accustomed."

"In truth, I think Grace will be relieved not to be paraded in front of the *ton*. She has a quiet nature. Not that anything we say matters. They are all quite ruined. It is tragic. She did show quite a bit of promise."

"I can see by the glint in your eyes you have a plan already formulated."

She bobbed her head, her hair appearing redder than he'd last seen it. But this was his aunt, a warrior queen with blazing red hair, and she was never going to admit she colored it with a henna dye. "Just the kernel of an idea."

Rafe laughed. "Lord help the man you have in mind."

"It is not set yet, just a possibility. Too bad the viscount did not take his heir in hand and straighten him out before they got in too deep. But, I suppose, he was greedy as well."

"Yes, lured into things he should never have done. Most of the recently stolen goods have been recovered. The Duke of Edgeware and Lord Farnham will continue to dig into the matter, hopefully, recover pieces from older thefts as they track down the buyers. I think they will reach out to Deklan for retrieving the stolen goods from foreign shores," he said, referring to his brother. "Working for the Crown in England is risky enough, but on foreign shores? I'm not sure I would have had the courage for that. It takes a man with steel running through his very core."

"Deklan certainly has that."

There was something in the way she said it that had Rafe's eyes widening in horror. "Oh, no! You cannot mean him for Grace Montford. Have you gone mad, Miranda? He is the worst possible choice. Do not even consider it."

"Fine, I won't. Who knows where he is now anyway? What is

next for you, Rafe?"

"Back to Exeter for me, but I may return at Christmastide with Sam and my mother. I think they'll enjoy being with the family."

"Yes, please do. Your mother, being a Brayden herself, knows us well. But young Sam knows very little about us. He'll have a delightful time here. And what of Lady Augusta?"

He groaned. "Does everyone know about her?"

"Yes, we were all there at the wedding when Donal and Lucy asked her to deliver the book to you. We all knew what would happen. She seems a lovely girl."

He ground his teeth.

Of course, Auggie was lovely. He was mad for her. But whose business was it other than his and Auggie's? "Nothing has been decided. Her life is here in London. Mine is in Exeter."

Miranda leaned forward and placed her hand over his. "Brayden men can be stubborn and set in their ways. I'm hoping the Quinton part of you will soften your edges. The people in your life are what matter most, not a place or thing. Just remember this."

They spoke a while longer, catching up on family news. Miranda seemed to know everything about everyone, even his cousin, Caleb, and Caleb's wife, Faith, who were happily settled up north in Scarborough. "Faith is about to have their second child. I hope it is a girl this time. We have far too many Brayden men already."

"We haven't turned out too badly, have we?"

His aunt laughed. "You've all done well for yourselves. Makes me feel rather useless now."

"Never that," he said, rising to leave. He had yet to see Auggie's father and wanted to attend to it today. "It was lovely to see you, Aunt Miranda. But I must be off. I'll be calling on the Marquess of Chelsford next."

"To ask for his daughter's hand in marriage?"

"No, I'm not saying a word until I know Auggie's feelings on the matter."

His aunt pursed her lips. "Do you think she does not reciprocate your affections?"

"She does. I have no doubt of it. But we have a lot to think about before we dare leap into marriage. I understand what you said about people being important, not places or things. But it is more complex than that."

"It's that book, isn't it? It's led you to love, but also warned you how it can go wrong. Now you are afraid it might not work out because she was raised as the daughter of a wealthy marquess, and you cannot offer her a title or that sort of London life. Don't think too hard, Rafe. Love is magical. And, by the way, you won't find the Marquess of Chelsford in London."

He shook his head and frowned. "But Edgeware said he was in residence only a few days ago. When did he leave? Do you know where he is now?"

"Of course, I do. Your Aunt Miranda knows everything." She cast him a wide smile. "He left yesterday for Exeter."

Rafe's heart shot into his throat. "Why? Has something happened to Auggie? Is she hurt?"

Miranda put a hand on his arm to calm him down. "She wrote to him and told him a cousin of hers had returned to Exeter."

"Morgan Nesbitt?"

"I think so."

"Hellfire, I have to go." Rafe tore out of his aunt's elegant townhouse and, after bidding a hasty farewell to Joshua and Holly, rode out of London for home.

Morgan Nesbitt had finally shown his face in Exeter.

Why hadn't Auggie written to him about it?

She had to know where to reach him.

Or had she made her choice, and this was her way of cutting ties with him?

He wasn't going to let it happen.

He had to make things right with her, although how he was

going to do it and what he was going to say eluded him at the moment.

His clothes and hair were covered in dust by the time he arrived home two days later. He'd come into Exeter at the twilight hour, catching the sun's golden glint upon the rooftops and the cool breeze that hinted of approaching winter.

Sam emitted a squeal and leaped into his arms, giving him barely a chance to set down his pouch as he strode into their house. "Papa!"

"It's good to be home." He gave the boy a fierce hug. "Have you been behaving? Not giving your grandmama any problems?"

His mother bustled to the door. "He's been an angel."

"And I can dance, Papa! So can Max. But Harry can't remember the steps. Max called her a baby."

"Let me guess, he made her cry."

Sam nodded.

He chuckled. "Poor Harry. She'll learn them eventually."

"Are you hungry, Rafe? I'll have Mrs. Lacey warm up supper for you while you unpack."

"Yes, I'm starved." He carried his travel pouch and his clinging son upstairs, dropped the pouch on the floor of his bedchamber and his son on the bed. "No jumping on the bed, Sam," he warned when Sam kicked off his shoes and was about to do just that.

The boy sighed and sank to his knees. "All right, Papa."

Rafe shrugged out of his jacket.

Mrs. Lacey came in carrying an ewer filled with fresh water and juggling soap, a stack of cloths, and some freshly laundered clothes. "I'm sure you'll be needing these, Mr. Quinton. I'll warm your supper now. Ring for me if you require anything else."

"This is perfect." He shut the door for privacy while he removed the rest of his dusty clothes.

Sam was still on his knees and bouncing lightly on the bed while he watched Rafe take off the last of his travel garments and toss them on the floor. Rafe stifled a chuckle, for Sam obviously considered bouncing on one's knees not at all the same thing as jumping on the bed. He did not bother to correct his son, for the boy was too happy at this moment, and Rafe's heart was full just being home with him again.

He poured the fresh water from the ewer into a basin, grabbed the soap and a cloth, and began to wash his body. He did the same with his hair, giving it a thorough rinsing to remove all the travel dust built up along the journey.

Sam chattered all the while, filling him in on all that had happened while Rafe was gone. Of course, it was from a boy's perspective, so he heard all about the games he and Max played and watched Sam as he showed him all the steps he'd learned from his dance lessons. "Impressive, son."

"Auggie came by to watch us at the beginning, but she couldn't come again because her cousin came to town and now her papa is here, too."

"So I've heard." Rafe tried to keep the disquiet out of his voice as he slipped on a clean pair of trousers. "I'm going to stop by the inn to see her tonight."

Sam nodded. "Do you think her papa is here to take her away from us?"

"I don't know. I hope not." He donned a decent shirt and then selected a suitable cravat but did not bother to put it on yet. He would do attend to that chore after he ate.

"I hope not, too. Auggie promised she would dance with me at the big party at the inn. She wouldn't break a promise, would she?"

"Auggie's an honorable lady. If she could not attend the party, it would be because of something out of her control. She would never purposely break a promise to you, but she might have no choice. Maybe her father will make her go back to London with him in the next day or two."

"That would be mean of him," he said a little breathlessly, resuming his bouncing on the bed.

Rafe ran his fingers through his mane of damp hair to give it a semblance of order. "Did you ever think that maybe Auggie misses her home? That maybe her father would take her away because he knows she'll be happier in London. That is where Auggie lives."

Sam shook his head. "No, she's happier here."

"Did she tell you that?"

Rafe never got his answer because Sam took an awkward bounce and hit his chin against the bed's footboard. He let out a wail. "Botheration, son. I told you not to do that."

He responded with another wail.

He drew the boy into his arms and settled him on his lap. "Let's see. Did you bite your tongue? Knock your teeth? Are you bleeding?"

But the boy was fine, other than a slight redness where his chin hit the wood.

He continued to hold Sam until his tears subsided. "Come downstairs with me while I eat. I'm starved."

"All right, Papa. Are you angry with me?"

"No, I'm just glad you weren't badly hurt. I missed you a lot while I was away. I didn't have a chance to bring you back a present. How about we pick out something for you tomorrow? A new game for you and Max to play?"

He burrowed his face in Rafe's shoulder and nodded. "All right."

Rafe carried the sniffling boy into the dining room and allowed his mother and Mrs. Lacey to fuss over the lad while he ate the remains of a delicious lamb stew. He spent most of the meal answering questions about London and his mother's Brayden relatives.

"Oh, I do miss them all, especially dear Miranda. She and I were very close growing up."

"I was thinking we might visit them this Christmas. Miranda's extended us the invitation. Sam might enjoy meeting his cousins."

His mother clapped her hands. "That's an excellent suggestion. I'll start planning our trip right away. We'll have to reserve rooms at suitable coaching inns along the way."

"Auggie will know the best ones." He used it as an opening to ask a few questions about Auggie in the hope his mother had more information to give him.

"That cousin of hers, Morgan Nesbitt, sauntered back into town earlier this week," she said with a sniff of disapproval. "Oh, that man rode in as smug as you please and brought along a few of his wastrel friends. Well, I call them wastrels, but I suppose others might consider them eligible bachelors because they're titled. Courtesy titles for the moment because their fathers are still very much alive and controlling their allowances. One is heir to an earl. The other is heir to a marquess. They toss their money about as though their fathers are bottomless wells they can dip their buckets into at any time. Reckless, if you ask me."

Mrs. Lacey nodded. "Worthless knaves. I'm sure your Lady Augusta wants nothing to do with them. The fact they have rank, wealth, and good looks is not going to impress her."

Rafe laughed. "Indeed, what young lady wants that for herself?"

Mrs. Lacey clucked at him. "There's no substance to them. They are nothing but preening peacocks. She would never choose one of them over you."

"I guess I'll find out soon enough." He finished the last of his stew, kissed Sam goodnight, and left him in his mother's care. Sam rushed downstairs as he was about to leave. "Tell her you love her, Papa. She needs to know."

"Did she tell you that?"

"No, but a man knows these things."

Apparently, his little boy was wiser than he was about romancing a young woman. "Go up to bed, Sam. We'll talk about it in the morning."

A blustery wind blew through the streets as Rafe walked along in the familiar darkness toward the inn. He quickened his strides and soon arrived. The establishment was brightly lit and bustling with activity, as usual. Fires blazed in the massive hearths, and candlelight shone from the many tapers in the large, center chandelier. The proprietor hurried toward him. "Mr. Quinton, good to have you back. How was London?"

"Busy," he replied, glancing around in the hope of spotting Auggie.

The proprietor grinned. "She's having a late supper with her party. They're in the dining salon."

Rafe nodded and headed there.

To his relief, he saw Wilkins seated in a corner of the room, his back to the wall and his gaze on all who came in and those who left. The place was crowded, and it took him a moment to spot Auggie at one of the larger tables in a corner. With her were her Aunt Priscilla, the companion Clara, and four men he'd never met before.

He assumed the eldest was her father.

As for the others, he did not know which one was Morgan Nesbitt and which were his friends. They all had a dissolute look about them.

He went to Wilkins first. "Who are those men with Lady Augusta?"

His man laughed. "Good to see you, too. How was London?"

"Quite successful. The Montfords were into a lot more than mere art forgery. Agents of the Crown got involved and, with their help, much of what was recently stolen has been recovered. Are Wendall and Crowell still under house detention?"

"Yes, just as you instructed. We caught them attempting to flee a time or two, but they never made it past their front doors. Their gallery and warehouse remain under constant watch, as well. The contents have been recorded, and Mr. Cavendish spent the past ten days comparing them to the inventory ledgers. Lady Augusta assisted him until her cousin and father arrived. She's stayed put at the inn ever since. Mr. Cavendish has a full report sitting on your desk, and the ledgers are locked away in your safe."

"Good. I'll review them first thing in the morning." He

glanced over at Auggie, who had yet to notice him. She seemed to have all the men at the table enraptured as she spoke. Who would fail to be enchanted by her? "Which one is Morgan Nesbitt?"

"The gentleman with blonde hair, wearing the green cravat. There, he just tossed his head back and laughed at something Lady Augusta said."

"They all seem rather cheerful," he grumbled. "Have the Nesbitts forgotten he was trying to take Lady Priscilla's life savings?"

"I'm sure they haven't forgotten. The elder gentleman is Lady Augusta's father. He isn't pleased with Morgan, but you wouldn't know it to look at them now. I suppose this is what the rich and titled do, keep family matters private and put on a show of one big, happy family for the rest of the world to see."

"Has anyone questioned Morgan Nesbitt?"

Wilkins shook his head. "No, just kept our eyes on him. We thought you would prefer to do the honors."

"Indeed, I would." He slapped his hands to his thighs and then kicked back his chair.

"Oh, hell. Are you going to take him in for questioning now?"

"I'm not sure any of the Nesbitts would ever forgive me if I did. No, it can wait until tomorrow. But I fully intend to order him to my office first thing in the morning."

"Shall I keep watch over him in the meanwhile?"

"Yes, but do not try to stop him if he attempts to flee. From all I've learned, he's not really involved in these art thefts beyond attempting to fleece his aunt."

"I don't know, he's been tossing his blunt about quite freely these past few days."

Rafe sighed. "The idiot. You have full authority to stop him and toss him in a holding cell if he steals anything in Exeter." He rose and approached Auggie's table, immediately noticing the array of elegant food and bottles of finest champagne set on it.

Auggie stopped her conversation and stared at him. "Mr.

Quinton, you're back. Papa, this is Mr. Quinton."

Her father studied him with avid interest. "So I gather. Won't you join us? I understand you've spent the last few weeks in London."

"Thank you, my lord." He took a seat beside Auggie's father and across from her. "Yes, you may have heard of the goings-on. Gossip spreads very quickly."

"Indeed, I have been following your activities with avid interest. You've managed to bring down the Montfords. Quite a shocking development. My daughter is friendly with Montford's eldest girl, Grace."

Rafe nodded and turned to Auggie. "I'm afraid she will need a good dose of your kindness. She'll be shunned by society now that her father and eldest brother are disgraced."

"What is to become of Wendall and Crowell?" Lady Priscilla asked.

"I'll leave the ultimate decision to the agents of the Crown. They'll be held in custody in their homes until the Crown's men arrive. They'll also be interested in your nephew. I assume that is what concerns you most."

The man Wilkins had identified as Morgan leaped to his feet, as did his friends. "I dare say, I will not be held like a common thief. I've done nothing wrong!"

Rafe had just taken a seat beside the marquess and was now up on his feet again. "That remains to be determined. Lady Priscilla's house burned down, and you brought the very man responsible for ordering its torching into her home a few days beforehand. You took her paintings and her jewelry. I would appreciate your presenting yourself at my office at eleven o'clock tomorrow morning, and we'll sort it all out then."

"The hell I will! As a matter of fact, my friends and I were planning on leaving Exeter this evening."

"Try it, and I will lock you and your friends in my prison."

"Who's to stop us?" One of the friends replied. "You?"

This friend of Morgan's had a walking stick with a fancy

handle that he now twisted open and withdrew a sword blade. "Dare to stop us, and I will run you through, *Mr.* Quinton." He stressed the fact that Rafe was no lord, his disdain so obvious, Rafe was tempted to haul off and punch him.

"Put that thing down before one of my men shoots you. Do you think I have not had all of you watched from the moment you rode into Exeter? Drop it now and keep out of this business if you have any sense about you."

"You're bluffing," the second companion said with a sneer.

Lord, he wanted to punch that supercilious oaf as well. "I do not bluff."

Auggie now looked quite distressed. "I'll bring Morgan myself to your office in the morning. Please, Mr. Quinton. Everyone is staring at us. Go before there is any bloodshed."

He turned to her father. "My lord, I trust your daughter to keep to her word, but I doubt your nephew will oblige her. I'll need your word on the matter as well."

Her father eyed Auggie and Morgan before returning his gaze to Rafe. "You have it. My nephew will not bolt."

"Uncle! This is absurd! I will not be treated like a common criminal."

"Which is what you are," Auggie's father shot back, his expression stern and forbidding. "You'll stay and face Mr. Quinton's questions or I shall personally see you carted off to prison. Have I made myself clear? As for your friends, they may leave if they wish."

"We're not leaving Morgan to face this ogre's inquisition," the one whose sword remained drawn said. "I have powerful connections. We'll see who wins the day. You won't be Exeter's magistrate for long if I have my way."

"I am quaking in my boots. You go do that. You'd be doing me a great favor if your complaints worked. Then I would no longer have to deal with worthless arses such as you and your friends. You have to the count of three to set down your sword, or I shall shove it so far up your—"

"Rafe!" Auggie put a hand to her throat and her face paled. "You needn't rile them. My father and I gave you our promise. Now you are just goading them for sport. It is not well done of you."

How was he in the wrong? "Lady Augusta, with all due respect, no one draws a weapon on me without facing consequences. He has to the count of three to tuck it back into his walking stick or I shall stuff it far enough up his exalted personage that it never sees the light of day again."

"Rafe, for pity's sake." She sank back in her chair with a shake of her head. "Lord Rutledge, kindly do as he asks. Mr. Quinton is quite serious. I can assure you, you are no match for him. So spare your head from a good cracking and put away your weapon."

"I shall do so because you have asked me. As you know, my heart can refuse you nothing." Lord Rutledge sheathed his sword.

Auggie shook her head and groaned.

Rafe clenched his hands to stem his irritation.

Perhaps he ought to have waited until tomorrow to approach Morgan, but it was too late for reconsideration now. Lady Priscilla was tossing daggers at him with her look, as were Morgan and his friends. Auggie's father showed nothing in his expression, but he'd spoken sharply to Morgan only a moment ago, so he could not be pleased with his nephew.

He doubted the man was pleased with his oafish performance either.

Auggie looked furious.

And now Sam would kick his arse for behaving like a jealous ape.

He relaxed his hands and nodded toward the marquess. "Thank you, my lord. Until tomorrow then."

He spared not a glance at Auggie, for his heart was in too much turmoil as he strode out of the inn and inhaled a gulp of cool air to calm himself down. She appeared so comfortable among these elite oafs. Is this the life she wanted?

It irritated the hell out of him.

He loved her.

Were their lives too different for marriage to ever succeed?

To see her so comfortable with worthless toads like Morgan and his friends was galling. These so-called elite of society were enjoying a fine repast and behaving as though Morgan bore not a whit of responsibility for all that had happened to his aunt.

Blast it!

He also wanted to throttle Lady Priscilla for so adamantly siding with her grandnephew. Where had the toad been when fire raged through her home? It was Rafe who had saved her, but she showed not an ounce of gratitude toward him.

Of course, he hadn't saved her for the acclaim.

He'd run into the flames because it was the right thing to do, and he would do it again without hesitation.

But the sense of privilege ingrained in them had his blood boiling.

"Rafe," Auggie called softly from behind him as he strode down the street in the cold night air. She placed her hand on his forearm. "I'm so sorry. I know my family and Morgan's friends were unpardonably rude to you."

He shook his head. "Auggie, it's only you I care about. I suppose I came on like an enraged bull."

She grinned. "You certainly did."

"Not going to win points with your father, I suppose. But he can't seriously be considering Rutledge for you, can he? What about you?" He shook his head. "Hellfire, don't answer that. I don't think I can take an honest answer from you right now."

She laughed. "Then let's save our discussion for tomorrow when you are a little less irritable."

She shivered, for she'd come out wearing only her elegant evening gown and had nothing to warm her bare shoulders.

He took off his jacket and wrapped it around her.

She smiled at him. "It has your scent. Insanely attractive, you know."

He eased as he gazed into her beautiful face. "So, you don't hate me?"

"Not at all. Will you tell me and my father what happened in London? Do you think Morgan is involved beyond assisting Aunt Priscilla? Well, he was only assisting her in order to take it all for himself. Odious man. You had better keep at least one of your men on him because he's just the sort of weasel who will give his word to my father and then sneak off in the night with those worthless clots he calls friends."

"So, you find Rutledge insufferable?"

"Heavens, yes." She rolled her eyes. "I would sooner marry a warthog before I would ever consider marrying him. His head is so big, he has difficulty fitting it through doorways."

Rafe cast her an affectionate smile and caressed her cheek. "And what of me? Do I rate above a warthog? Because I surely do want to marry you."

"That is a relief. I was certain you wanted nothing more to do with me or my family. I wanted to grab Lord Rutledge's weapon and crack it over the heads of all three of them, Morgan, Rutledge, and Clivedon—he's the third man in their party. My father is livid as well, but you will never see him respond to their antics in public beyond a stern but quiet warning."

"Unlike me."

She laughed softly. "You are a big ape, but it is hard to keep one's temper in check when they are so infuriating. I missed you so much, Rafe."

"I was in agony missing you, Auggie." He shook his head. "Sam lectured me before coming over here. He thinks I am going to mess things up with you. He'll never forgive me if I do. I do not deserve you, but I surely want you with all my heart. I intended to stop by your father's residence when I was in London, but he'd already come to Exeter. I know you and I still have things to work out."

She stopped him with a short, sweet kiss on the lips. "We don't."

"We don't?" He still had his hand on her cheek and was running his thumb lightly along the line of her jaw.

"I'll be happiest wherever you are. If it is to be Exeter, then that is where I am content to be. You've built a life here for yourself, and I want to be a part of it."

"And I want you in my life something fierce, my beautiful Auggie. Does this mean you will marry me?"

"Are you proposing?"

"Hell, yes." He reached into the breast pocket of his jacket and withdrew the cameo brooch he'd bought with her in mind when they'd investigated Merriwell's. He hoped it wasn't stolen merchandise. Too late to worry about that now, he decided, as he helped her pin it to the lace at the bosom of her gown.

He'd buy her something special if it turned out to be stolen and he had to turn it over as evidence.

"What do you think, Rafe?"

"Looks nice on you." He got down on one knee, ignoring the crowd now gathering around them, for he had not made it far beyond the inn before Auggie had stopped him in front of a row of carriages awaiting their owners.

Her father must have followed her out, for he was now standing among the onlookers.

Lord, he could not botch this.

But he already had, for he ought to have spoken to her father first. Well, too late now. Add one more demerit to his standing. The marquess likely considered him rude and boorish. By not coming to him first, he would also add disrespectful to the list. "I'm probably doing this all wrong, but I hope you'll see into my heart and know I love you. I fell in love with you at first sight."

She cast him the softest smile. "You did?"

"Cupid's arrow straight through the heart. So did Sam. I would be honored to have you as my wife. Will you marry me?"

Her smile was now as bright as a moonbeam, and tears glistened in her eyes. "I—"

"Augusta, do not answer him," her father said, elbowing his

way through the onlookers and was now upon them. "Come with me, Mr. Quinton."

"As you wish, my lord."

Auggie looked at Rafe in utter dejection.

He rose and placed her hand in the crook of his arm, keeping hold of it in an effort to console her. No one was going to take her away from him. She was his. He was going to marry her.

However, she loved her father.

Rafe was not going to do anything to put a rift between them.

"Papa, what are you going to say to him?" she asked as they returned to the inn and marched toward her father's guest quarters.

She looked so forlorn, Rafe wanted to wrap her in his arms. He wanted to scorch her with his kisses just as she scorched him with her smallest smile.

Those kisses would have to wait for later.

Her father's expression wavered between angry and irritated.

Rafe was no green youth and had never been any good at bowing and scraping. He wanted her father's approval, but for her sake and not for his. Auggie was of age to marry, and he did not have to ask for her father's consent nor did he have to say a blessed thing to her father.

But he would never be rude to the man because it would break Auggie's heart. "My lord, if it is terms you wish to discuss, then I shall make it simple for you. Whatever your daughter desires is what I am willing to give her."

"That is good to know." Her father nodded. "But what do you plan to take from her in return? That is what worries me most."

CHAPTER FOURTEEN

"**P**APA, HOW COULD you? Rafe is not some soul-sucking leech who will bleed me dry." Auggie's hands were curled into fists, and she had a stubborn look in her eyes that warned her father was not going to win any argument with her, certainly not when her happiness depended on the outcome. "He isn't trying to *take* anything from me. How can you even suggest such a thing? Love is about giving. And Rafe loves me."

Rafe fought hard not to grin as Auggie strode into her father's guest chamber still swallowed up in his jacket and looking utterly delicious.

She also looked determined.

Her father's chamber turned out to be an opulent suite of rooms occupied by him and his valet. The marquess dismissed the man. "Crenshaw, go have a cup of tea in the dining room."

"Yes, m'lord."

He turned to his daughter as soon as the door closed behind his valet. "Be reasonable, Augusta. Were you not the one who told me Mr. Quinton refused to leave Exeter? That he would not marry you unless you agreed to settle here?"

She tipped her chin in the air. "I did tell you that. But I've also come to realize that I cannot be happy unless I am with him. So, I am going to stay in Exeter. Father, do you honestly believe Rutledge or Clivedon are better prospects for me? They are low, horrid creatures."

"There are other men who—"

"But I am in love with Mr. Quinton." She smiled up at Rafe.

He loved the warmth reflected in her eyes as she turned back to her father and continued. "Leaving London is a compromise I will gladly make. The matter is settled. I am marrying him. I gain not only a husband but a son and a mother. Rafe, I hope you know I would never ask your mother to move out."

"So, this is how it's going to be?" Her father's smile was wistful. He obviously wanted his daughter to be happy, but it also meant she would no longer be with him.

It had to be particularly hard for the marquess since it had been just him and Auggie for most of her life. Auggie had been his to love and care for since her mother and siblings had died all those years ago.

She was his heart, his happiness.

Probably his salvation.

The fire went out of Auggie as she came to the same realization a moment later. "Papa, do not look so downcast. Settle here as well. What is so important to keep you in London? We can both remain close to Aunt Priscilla and make certain Morgan does not get his greedy hands on her again. And you have yet to meet Rafe's son, Sam. You will fall in love with him just as I have."

"No, my child. My life is in London."

"No, no." She shook her head vehemently. "It is just a place. Everyone you love will be here. Are we not what matter most?"

Her father cast her another wistful smile. "*You* are all that matters to me."

"Then stay here, Papa. Return to London when Parliament is in session but make your home life here with us."

"My dear, the answer remains no. You may be willing to sacrifice for Mr. Quinton, but I am not."

The sparkle diminished from her eyes. "I thought you were happy for me. I thought you approved of my marrying him."

"I can see how much you love him. And I do not doubt he is a good and honest man."

"But?"

"Marriage is for a lifetime, and you are not the sort who would ever survive in a typical *ton* marriage where the husband and wife lead their own separate lives. You need love. Affection."

"Something I will have with Rafe. Ours is a love match. Is it not obvious?"

"I understand his nature better than you do, my child. He may love you, but he will also leave you to eat alone, to wait up for him into the wee hours because he is wrapped up in business affairs…and how long before he might entertain other affairs?"

Auggie gasped. "He never would!"

Rafe stepped in as well. "I will never be unfaithful to your daughter, my lord. My fault is in being too wrapped up in my work, I will give you that. However, it's going to change." He glanced at Auggie. "I give you my promise. I owe it to you and Sam."

She nodded.

He turned to her father. "But as for the suggestion my eye may roam, it will never happen. I love Auggie and would sooner cut out my heart than ever hurt her."

"Your words may be sincere, but your actions will speak louder. I am not saying I will refuse your suit of my daughter, and I fully understand she is madly in love with you. Indeed, I know she would marry against my will if it came down to that. She is of age and does not require my consent."

"Yes, but it would crush her heart. Nor is it fair of you to force her to choose between us. She wants both of us and will never be truly happy if you are miserable. You know this to be true, my lord. Do not wield this as a sword against her."

The marquess nodded. "I never would. Her happiness is all I care about. But you cannot have it all exactly as you wish, Auggie. You've given me twenty years of abundant joy. But do not resent me for using caution. The fact remains, as between you and Mr. Quinton, you are making all the sacrifices. You are doing all the giving. What is he giving up in return?"

"He just told you. He wants me and not any dowry that comes along with our marriage."

"It is an empty sacrifice. You are my only child. He knows I will never leave you lacking. Besides, you already have plenty of your own."

"So does he. He turns over his salary to pay for his staff because he believes in protecting the citizens of Exeter. He will fight with all his being to protect me, as well. As for his behavior toward Morgan, you and I both know Morgan is a spoiled weasel who respects nothing and no one."

"That is a family matter."

"And Rafe will be a part of this family. I need to be by his side. I don't care if I appear to be doing more of the sacrifice. In truth, I am gaining everything. He is a big, proud ape of a man..." She paused and smiled at him. "Sorry, Rafe."

He folded his arms across his chest and chuckled.

She turned back to her father. "And yet he was not too proud to get on bended knee to ask for my hand in marriage."

"He should have come to me first."

Rafe now spoke up, eager to have the father-daughter dispute brought to an end. "Perhaps the proposal should not have tumbled out of my mouth, but I've made no secret of my feelings for your daughter. I intended to see you in London but learned you had already come here." He pursed his lips. "Auggie, why did you not write to me about Morgan?"

"I did. In fact, I sent that message off first. But I wasn't certain where you were staying, so I had it delivered to Lucy's father. Well, I supposed it was all right to send it there since the secret is out and everyone now knows she is the Duke of Wooton's daughter. Then I realized I ought to have told my father as well, so I wrote to him next. Goodness! Did my letter never reach you?"

"No. It's probably sitting on Wooton's desk awaiting his return. He's back in Dartmoor helping Lucy and Donal clear up her maternal grandfather's estate."

"Oh, how stupid of me. I ought to have realized."

Rafe took her hand. "No, Auggie. It was logical. I should have let you know I was staying with my cousin, Joshua."

"Which only proves my point," her father said. "You did not think to write to my daughter."

"No, Papa!"

Rafe's heart sank, for the man was right. "Auggie, do not make excuses for me. I was busy, but never too busy to take a moment to send word to you. I should have done it. I assumed you would simply ask my mother if you ever needed to get hold of me. She would have sent word to my Aunt Miranda, and I would have received it within an hour of its arrival. But I only gave thought to my assignment."

"You got on bended knee for me, and I know you would not have done this for any other woman."

"There will never be anyone else for me, Auggie. I'm glad you know this."

"But my father doesn't." She looked up at him with big, sad eyes. "Rafe, make him see sense."

"My lord, you will always be welcome in our home. Think about it, for Auggie loves you and will worry about you every moment you are apart. As for me, I will devote my life to making her happy. Yes, I am not perfect, but I will try with all my heart to be a good husband to her." He turned to her and smiled. "Bring on your charity teas, your book clubs, and anything else you wish to support. I know you love to dance…as my son has made sure to remind me. I shall dance with you every night of my life if this is your wish."

"Rafe, you hate to dance."

It was more than simple dislike, but he was not about to get into how ill it made him feel, those bodies crushed together, the heat and nauseating perfume. "But you love it, and I will do whatever it takes to make you happy. My lord, I would like your blessing to marry your daughter. It isn't for my sake, but for Auggie's."

He responded with silence.

Rafe watched with mounting pain as Auggie removed the cameo brooch he'd just given her and handed it back to him.

He tucked it back in her hand. "No, keep it. We are right for each other. No one will be happy if you choose not to marry me."

"But my father—"

"Wants to be certain I will make you happy."

"But you do make me happy."

"I know it, but I have to prove it to him."

"Oh, that is ridiculous. How are you going to prove it?"

CHAPTER FIFTEEN

"**S**AM, I NEED your help," Rafe said, sitting down to breakfast early the next morning.

His son's eyes widened in delight, and he quickly swallowed the eggs he'd just put in his mouth. "You do?"

He took a sip of his coffee and nodded. "Yes, to practice my dance steps."

Sam gasped. "So you can share a dance with Auggie?"

He nodded again. "Will you help me?"

Sam threw himself into his father's arms. "Of course, I will. It is the perfect gift for Auggie because it is something she loves to do, and you have to make her happy."

Gad, how did his son understand things so much better than any adult? Especially him, for he was used to having his way in all things, everyone accepting his commands. Well, he did not give orders to his mother or Mrs. Lacey, nor had he ever snapped orders at Mary.

But they had indulged him.

And what of Sam?

How many nights had he forced himself to stay awake in the hope of sharing supper or receiving a goodnight kiss from his papa and been disappointed?

"Sam," he said, his heart tightening in dismay, "do you feel I've neglected you?"

His big eyes widened. "No, Papa. I know you are a busy man

and very important."

He hugged the boy. "Never too important for you. I hope you know that."

Sam nodded. "I do. When do you want your dance lessons? We don't have much time. The inn's big party is Saturday."

"How about we start tonight? Or earlier if I can get away from this investigation I'm working on." Of course, he knew how to dance. He just hated to do it, although he'd probably like it just fine if he only had to partner Auggie. But he was out of practice and would need a refresher on most of the fashionable dances.

And he wasn't going to practice under the vigilant eye of some priggish dance instructor.

Hell, no.

Sam would be the perfect tutor.

His mother and Mrs. Lacey were grinning from ear to ear.

Despite the momentary setback in his wooing of Auggie, he knew all would work out in the end. First of all, they loved each other.

Being a father himself, he understood the Marquess of Chelsford's concerns. He only wanted the best for his daughter. For this reason, Rafe was not storming about like an enraged bull.

He gave his son another hug and a quick tickle that had the boy giggling, then left for his office.

The hour was still early, but the sun was already bright in the sky. The wind had yet to warm, but it was less biting than last night's breeze.

When he reached his office, he waved to the familiar guard, climbed the stairs, and after unlocking his door, spent the next hour catching up on the piles of paper on his desk. He also reviewed the ledgers Cavendish had locked away for safekeeping.

He'd just finished looking them over when Cavendish arrived. "Mr. Quinton, you're back."

Rafe grinned. "So it appears. Have a seat. You've done an excellent job with this inventory. Not only the Wendall and Crowell gallery but Merriwell's stash of jewelry. This will be very helpful to the London magistrate and the Crown agents, but I need to hold onto this one. Would you prepare a duplicate inventory to send to them?"

Cavendish nodded. "I thought you might ask, so I've already done it."

Rafe threw his head back and laughed. "Of course. How could I doubt you? Careful, Cavendish. I might just have to increase your salary."

"Then I should not admit how much I enjoyed performing this work. Being out in the field was most invigorating." He cleared his throat. "I don't suppose you've had the chance to see Lady Augusta yet."

"I did, last night." Rafe winced. "She was dining with her family, including her wastrel cousin, Morgan Nesbitt."

"And her father, I presume."

"Yes. He'll be bringing Morgan here at eleven o'clock today…assuming the bounder hasn't fled with his no-good friends. I hear he's been tossing his blunt about quite freely. Any idea where his sudden wealth came from?"

Cavendish shrugged. "He claims to have had a good turn of cards while in Bath, but I find it hard to believe. It is just as likely he sold one of his aunt's valuable items…or he might have stolen an item from someone else and sold it. I'm inclined to believe theft over his winning a fortune at the gaming tables. The man strikes me as a reckless idiot. But who can be sure?"

"My sentiments exactly. I'll ask Bath's magistrate to nose around. One would think Nesbitt would be quiet about his sudden wealth, especially if he'd obtained it illicitly. But neither he nor his friends struck me as particularly clever, just full of themselves and certain they are above the law."

"Well, at least you got to see Lady Augusta."

Rafe winced again. "I'm not sure it was one of my best ideas. I had words with her cousin and his friends. I don't think I made a good impression on her father."

"If it is any consolation, I don't expect anything you say or do will make the marquess happy just now. After all, you are not only the man who plans to arrest his nephew, but you are also the one about to take his beloved daughter from him."

Rafe raked a hand through his hair. "Yes, if he chooses to view it as that."

They spoke no more about Auggie or her family as they reviewed the other matters piled on his desk.

At the stroke of eleven, Auggie and her father appeared.

Rafe dismissed Cavendish and came around to the front of his desk to greet them. "I don't suppose your nephew will be joining us."

A pink flush sprang into Auggie's cheeks. "Morgan ran off in the middle of the night with his friends and left their rooms unpaid. I know you had a man watching my cousin. Obviously, he and his friends gave him the slip…is this the right term for it? They certainly are slippery wretches. My father will take care of their account, but I'm so sorry, Rafe. We promised to deliver him to you."

"I suspected it was an impossible task. Not because of his involvement in the Wendall and Crowell affair, for what I've uncovered so far points to his involvement being nothing beyond assisting Lady Priscilla to sell her goods."

Auggie put a hand to her throat. "That's a relief."

Her father frowned. "If you knew this, then why insist on questioning him?"

"Because he'd convinced Lady Priscilla to give over her life savings once everything of value in her home was sold, thereby leaving her destitute. Well, he knew you would ensure she remained in comfort, but does this not concern you? I had hoped to put a little fear into him. Should he not feel a shred of remorse?"

"Yes, he should." Auggie's father nodded. "I ought to have taken him firmly in hand, but Priscilla is so attached to him."

"And he is using her love to grab all he can from her. That nonsense about his big win at the gaming tables is just that, stuff and nonsense. Those three were up to no good in Bath and fled before I could discover it under questioning."

"Do you have proof?" the marquess asked.

"Not yet, but I've been at this long enough to pick up on what is going on. As for giving my man the slip, I instructed him not to stop Morgan from fleeing unless he was seen doing something illegal in Exeter. We'll know soon enough when he reports back to me. In any event, those fellows are a bad mix. You'll do your nephew a great service by separating him from that pair, especially Rutledge. He's a bad egg."

The marquess groaned and sank into one of the offered chairs. "I owe you an apology, Mr. Quinton. I think, perhaps, I allowed Priscilla and Morgan to sway me because I wanted to believe the worst in you. But it is impossible to overlook Priscilla's dithering nature or the fact that Morgan is no longer a harmless man. He has preyed on his own aunt. Yes, that is something I must attend to as soon as I get my hands on him. If it is any consolation, Auggie never wavered in her support of you."

Rafe cast her a wink.

She grinned back.

"So, I am here at my daughter's urging not only to report my missing nephew but to let you know…you have my blessing to marry. Consider yourselves officially betrothed. I'll have my solicitor draw up a betrothal contract and deliver it to you for your review."

"Oh, Papa. How long will that take?" Auggie did not look at all pleased.

Her father laughed. "If I said an hour, I believe it would be too long for you. Child, you have won. You have my blessing and will be married to Mr. Quinton before year's end since I doubt I can keep the two of you apart any longer than that. He does not strike me as a patient man."

"I'm the one who's impatient," she shot back.

"Indulge me, Auggie. You must have your betrothal contract. I am your father and will never forgive myself if I do not protect you, even if it proves unnecessary. I'll leave for London in the next day or two to attend to it. Do you plan to marry here in Exeter? Or will you consider a London wedding?"

Rafe did not care where the ceremony took place. "Whatever Auggie prefers is fine with me."

"Would you consider London, Rafe?" She glanced up at him, worry in her eyes.

"If that is your wish, of course. In truth, I had planned to take Sam there to see my family this Christmas."

"So, we could hold the wedding at Christmas? But Rafe...it is over a month away."

The dismay in her voice warmed his heart. "I'll marry you tomorrow if that is your wish. Sam will be bouncing with glee when I tell him," he said with a chuckle. "He is desperate to see us married and was so afraid I would botch my proposal...which I did, but I hope it turns out all right anyway. One thing I will never botch is my love for you."

Her eyes took on an exquisite sparkle. "I know."

He took her hands in his. "I'm glad you do, Auggie. Never doubt it. But I also intend to prove it to you."

She laughed lightly. "You do? It isn't necessary. I believe you."

"It is necessary."

"How will you prove it?"

"You'll find out soon enough. Sam and I have something special planned for you."

"Rafe." She threw her arms around him and hugged him fiercely.

He laughed and wrapped his arms around her slight body to return her hug. "I love you, Auggie. I always will. This is my sacred pledge to you."

"As I shall always love you."

Cavendish suddenly appeared at his door. "Mr. Quinton...Marbury, Wilkins, and Cooper have just returned with his lordship's nephew. They are awaiting us in the...er, in the conference room."

"Thank you, Cavendish. I'll be right there." Truly, the man deserved a raise for his tact alone. They had no fancy conference room, for any meetings were held in his office. What they did have were interrogation rooms. The marquess would have been howling if Cavendish had called it that.

However, Rafe was not pleased about Morgan being hauled back. He'd told Wilkins not to stop him if he attempted to flee unless he'd been caught doing something shady.

Hellfire.

What had the idiot done now?

The marquess must have been thinking the same thing. "Mr. Quinton, would you mind giving me a moment alone with my nephew?" He raked a hand through his mane of gray hair. "I take back any reluctance I had about you. Indeed, I think you and Auggie need to marry and get about the business of producing heirs as soon as possible or that spoiled nephew of mine will inherit the title and that will be disastrous for all."

He walked off with Cavendish, leaving Rafe alone with Auggie.

She was smiling at him, her eyes gleaming with mirth. "Rafe, he's given his approval. I did not think beyond our marriage. But to have your children…ours…I hope we are so blessed."

"I'll try my best to make it happen." He shut the door and wasted no time in drawing Auggie's delicious body up against him.

Her eyes widened. "Are we to start here and now?"

"No, love. Just a warm-up." He lowered his lips to hers and kissed her with the incendiary force of the fire raging in his heart. He felt the soft give of her breasts against his chest as she molded to him, lost in her own innocent desire.

He wanted to pleasure her, make her melt at his touch.

Were she anything but innocent, he would have had her atop his desk or up against the shelves for a quick tumble. But not for the first time, and definitely not when anyone could burst in at any moment. Some women felt heightened pleasure by the thrill of discovery, but Auggie would simply want to shrink into the woodwork in embarrassment.

Nor did he consider it pleasant for himself to have to draw off suddenly.

No, her first time had to be private.

He meant to go slow and pleasure her thoroughly.

He trailed kisses down her neck but went no further. Low brain dolt that he was, he wanted to peel away her gown and get at her body...her breasts, of course. But the gown was too intricate to take apart and put back together in time. Still, he so badly wanted to taste her. Well, he could...lower the bodice...tease her with his fingers and tongue...but again, not for a first time.

Auggie had no experience with men.

Lord help him, every blessed thing he did to her, every lick and every caress, would show on her face and everyone would know.

"Rafe, I'm so happy," she said breathlessly. "We are going to have a wonderful life together."

"That is what I want and hope for." He steadied his own breaths and eased her out of his embrace. "You must always tell me if you are unhappy about anything, Auggie. Don't hold your misery inside." He cupped her face in his hands and caressed her warm cheeks. "And don't ever give up who you are."

"Rafe, you have such a serious look about you. Are you jesting? I will soar with your support. Why do you think I fell in love with you? Yes, I love that you are big and protective, but you are also kind and generous. Goodness, we have not discussed so many things. There's still so much to learn about each other. But I know you want me to be a true partner in our marriage. You've mentioned how important it is for me not to get lost in you as Mary did, to remain true to who I am. You will help me become the best person I can be. I know you will encourage my dreams. I knew it the day I met you, the moment I saw how happy Sam was to see you and how you encouraged him to leap into your arms." She laughed softly. "Of course, it did not hurt that I also saw you without your shirt. I have been wantonly lusting after you ever since."

She regarded him in earnest. "I hope you don't mind that I had naughty thoughts about you. Or still have them. But truly, I never felt this way about anyone before you."

She had no idea how hot his dreams had been about her.

He cast her a wicked grin. "Care to know what I've been wanting to do to you?"

"I would much rather you showed me."

She was clever and sweet and beautiful, and he wanted to have her panting his name and howling as he brought her to pleasure. He wanted her in his bed and in his life. He wanted to fall asleep with her in his arms and wake to find her curled like a kitten against him. "I am marrying you before the week is out."

She laughed. "Is that a demand or a suggestion?"

"It is a plea." He kissed her lightly on the lips. "You leave me in agony."

"I think my father can be convinced to give his consent to that. After all, the two of you are clever enough to agree in principle to the terms of our betrothal. The marriage contracts can be signed later. We can save the larger wedding breakfast celebration for Christmas in London with our friends and family."

"That sounds perfect." He opened the door upon hearing footsteps on the stairs and knew Cavendish was returning. "Time for me to question your idiot cousin."

"May I sit in?"

He shrugged. "Why not? Your father is still with him, and I doubt he will agree to leave either."

"Thank you, Rafe."

He shook his head. "Don't thank me. It isn't a pleasant task. And do not say anything, no matter what insults he tosses at me. He will hurl them at me, you know. I don't need you to defend my honor."

"All right. I will keep my mouth shut and let you ask all the questions."

He smiled. "No, you won't. You'll probably leap across the table and punch him."

"He deserves it." She sighed. "I shall remain a lady."

Morgan cast Rafe a disdainful look when he settled across the table from him. Auggie took a seat beside her father. Morgan cast her a wry smile as she settled at the end of the long table. "Ah, my beautiful cousin. I hear you are planning to marry beneath you. My condolences. It will never work out. He is a low fellow, not of our class. He'll never treat you as the princess you deserve to be."

Auggie shook her head. "Honestly, Morgan. Do stop spouting nonsense."

"I would have married you. You could have been my marchioness. After all, I am your father's heir. We would have made a good marriage."

"First of all, we would have had the most horrid marriage imaginable. Second, you are clinging to the hope I will not have sons to kick you off the line of succession. Rest assured, I will work most diligently to accomplish that."

"Auggie, you don't even know what that means. You always were a naive fool. Quinton will have at you with the finesse of a rutting boar."

"He will not. He loves me and will always treat me gently." She tipped her head up in indignation. "We are not here to talk about me."

Morgan cast her a wistful smile. "Ah, my lovely cousin. You don't get it, do you? All of this has been about you."

"What do you mean?"

"Quinton understands. I'm sure fire tore through him the moment he set eyes on you. Do you think any of us are different? Me. Rutledge. Clivedon. But how do we tempt you when we are forced to wait years before stepping into our titles? Do you think it is easy for any of us to toady up to our fathers, or in my case, my uncle, and beg for every spare shilling? And then Quinton comes along and you choose him? Why Auggie? You could have had your choice of London's elite."

Rafe silently gave thanks she'd chosen him.

Morgan was right, she could have married a prince if she'd had the slightest inclination.

"I am happy with my choice of Mr. Quinton." Her chin was still tipped in indignation, and she looked magnificent. "It isn't about wealth or rank or material possessions, but about trust. Respect. Sacrifice."

Morgan regarded her as though she was spouting gibberish.

"Mr. Quinton has all those qualities, which is more than I can say for you and your friends. How can you think I would ever consider marrying you when you are nothing but a conniving weasel and a petty thief? Why did Mr. Quinton's men haul you back to Exeter? What did you steal this time? And how could you sneak out of the inn without settling your account? You are depraved and despicable. No woman will have you if this is all you have to offer."

Rafe sat back and listened to Auggie excoriate her cousin.

So much for her assurance to keep quiet.

In truth, he did not mind.

Morgan was now confessing to taking a diamond stickpin from one of the inn's guests. "But I did not steal it. The pin fell off the man's tie, and he did not bat an eyelash when he realized it was gone. So, why should I return it when he did not miss it? How can this be considered stealing when he lost it and I found it?"

"You knew it belonged to that guest," the marquess intoned. "Where is it now?"

Morgan folded his arms across his chest. "Mr. Quinton's men have it. I suppose you are going to return it to Lord Archer."

Rafe nodded.

"It is a pity. It had a very pretty diamond in it."

"What of your adventures in Bath?" Rafe asked. "What did you steal there?"

"I didn't take anything. I told you, I had a run of good fortune at the gaming tables. You'll see. I am telling you the truth."

Rafe leaned in. "Rest assured, the magistrate there is investigating and will report back to me soon. I will know if you are lying."

"So help me, Morgan," the marquess interjected. "If you are deceiving us about this, as well, I shall leave you to rot in debtors' prison."

Morgan's handkerchief came out, and he began to mop his brow. "I promise you, Uncle. It was a good run of cards."

Rafe doubted it.

Auggie's cousin and his friends either stole from the well-heeled set in Bath or they worked together to cheat at cards. Yes, that was likely it. A coordinated scheme to cheat the other players. The fools were fortunate not to be found out.

Rafe stared at Morgan as he continued to mop his brow.

"All right, blast it." He was now mopping the beads of sweat on his neck. "Rutledge worked out a simple plan. Clivedon and I..."

Rafe listened as the man spilled all about their marked cards and how the three of them lured their target into a game.

"There, I've told you all. May I go now?"

Was he jesting?

The man was a cheat, a thief, and a liar.

But he was also under the Marquess of Chelsford's protection.

Rafe glanced at the marquess.

Was the man going to let his nephew rot in jail?

Or use his influence to spare his pampered hide?

CHAPTER SIXTEEN

"**P**APA! HURRY UP or we'll be late," Sam chided, staring up at him as he straightened his tie. It was Saturday night, and they were preparing for the dance at the Swan Inn. These affairs, best described as a country ball, were formal affairs. The men were required to wear black tie and tails, while the women garbed themselves in their finest silks and satins.

Even Sam and Max were fashionably dressed with their hair slicked back, although each boy sported a cowlick that would not stay flat.

They looked adorable.

Rafe shot a grin at his mother. "Ready?"

Children were not usually permitted to attend these functions, but Rafe was a man of clout in Exeter. If he wanted children to attend, then by heaven, they would attend.

"The coach is here, Papa!"

The marquess had sent his conveyance around to pick them up. The boys scrambled onto the plush leather seats and bounced on them the entire way. Rafe and his mother sat across from the boys and stopped them only when their heads were about to smack against the windows. "Papa, will you remember what I taught you?"

"I will, son. Don't you fret." He bit the inside of his cheek to keep from laughing.

Auggie and her father were waiting for them in the foyer as

they strode in. Morgan, to everyone's relief, had been shipped off to one of the Chelsford estates along the Scottish border to learn what it meant to work.

Rafe hoped the toil would give him purpose. Perhaps seeing all that developed from the fruit of his labors might have a good effect on him. He'd been too coddled growing up, especially by Lady Priscilla, and it was time for him to stop strutting about like a preening peacock and learn to walk like a man.

The marquess took his mother's arm. "Mrs. Quinton, will you do me the honor?"

"I'd be delighted, my lord."

Rafe held out his arm to Auggie. "You look beautiful."

It was an understatement.

She looked like an angel in white lace and silk.

He wanted to say more to her but not in front of the boys.

Auggie took hold of Sam's hand, while Rafe held onto Max. "Harry fell asleep," Sam told her when she asked about the little girl. "This is her bedtime. She cried and cried but couldn't manage to stay awake. Their papa said it was all right for Max to join us by himself."

Max nodded. "Because I'm big."

"Well, I'm glad you boys made it here tonight." Auggie's smile took Rafe's breath away. "I am looking forward to dancing with each of you."

The musicians were already playing the opening quadrille, and guests were twirling around the crowded dance floor. Sam wasted no time in asking Auggie to partner him. Rafe could not stop himself from puffing up with pride, for Sam was surprisingly good for someone so young.

Max took a turn next, also doing a commendable job of leading Auggie through the intricate steps, although Rafe was certain she was doing most of the leading. In the meantime, Sam danced with Rafe's mother.

The third dance, he was informed, was to be a waltz.

"Do you not dance, Mr. Quinton?" the marquess asked.

Auggie, his mother, and the boys had just returned to their table as he answered. "I try my best to avoid it."

Auggie nodded. "He hates it, Papa. But I am quite content to be escorted by these dashing young men. I am also not averse to dancing with you."

Her father shook his head. "We'll have our dance later. But your betrothed should be asking you. You're a sweet girl, Auggie. Do not let him take advantage."

"But Papa—"

"Your father is right," Rafe said and held out his arm to her as the musicians played the beginning strains of the waltz. "Will you do me the honor?"

She glanced at the dance floor, then back at him. "But you detest dancing."

"But I love you."

"Yes, but…what are saying, Rafe?"

"I don't like dressing up. Nor do I care to hop about amid a crowd of sweating bodies. But you enjoy it, do you not?"

She laughed lightly and nodded. "You make it sound so appealing."

"I will dress up, hop and skip to the music every Saturday night if I must. I will never deny you something you enjoy. Nor will I ever gripe about it because if you are happy, then I am happy."

She cast him a dazzling smile. "I see. This is your sacrifice. The proof that you love me."

Rafe arched an eyebrow. "Pleasing you is no sacrifice. Your smile is worth everything. Will you dance with me?"

"I would love to, Mr. Quinton."

He led her onto the floor and tried his best to avoid the crush of dancers while he placed his hand at the small of her back and began to twirl her in time to the music. He could feel the warmth of her body beneath the thin layer of silk that separated his hand from her soft skin.

She was warm, but he was burning as they moved in a swirling wave along with the other dancers.

They may as well have been alone, for he noticed no one but Auggie and loved the feel of her in his arms.

"Rafe, you are a wonderful dancer."

"Surprised?" He smiled. "Sam's going to take all the credit for teaching me, but I've always known how to dance. I've just hated it immensely." More than hated it, for he often had a physical response to the crush of bodies. He felt it coming on now and wanted to stop dancing and walk outdoors to catch a breath of air. "The room is crowded." All he could smell was hot, perspiring bodies.

"Rafe, are you all right?"

"Yes."

"Are you sure? You have nothing to prove to me."

"Auggie, I do."

"Fine, but you do look green. Just let me know if you want to stop."

"I am going to finish this dance."

She sighed. "As you wish. I have something to tell you."

"What?"

"I've discovered Priscilla's secret and now know why she wouldn't let me sit in on her book club. That's why she and Lady Whiting exchanged those glances, and why she and Clara did the same."

He grinned. "And what is that deep, dark secret? Not a book club but a rebel spy ring?"

"Nothing like that. You know how *The Book of Love* is about finding true love? About the feeling and not the act."

"Blessed saints. Don't tell me their book club is all about the act. They read those sort of books?"

She nodded. "I did some snooping at the local bookshops while you were in London."

"Why, those naughty old ladies. Good for them. Let them enjoy."

"You aren't shocked?"

"No, what business is it of mine what books they read?"

"That's very enlightened of you."

He shrugged. "Murder is shocking. Poverty, illness. A group of ladies reading saucy literature is low on my list of concerns. If they enjoy it and it harms no one, why should I disapprove? But I'm glad you solved your mystery."

"And you look like you are about to toss up your accounts. No wonder you hate dancing. Is it the spinning motion that makes you dizzy?"

"Maybe. That and all these damn bodies. The sweat. The perfume to mask the sweat."

"Enough. I am taking you outside."

"The waltz is not over yet."

"You are not an enemy prisoner, and I have no intention of torturing you further."

He laughed as she took the lead and forced their way onto the terrace. As soon as they were outdoors, he removed his jacket and wrapped it around her shoulders, for her gown was of the lightest silk, and it hugged her exquisite body to perfection. There was a refreshing chill in the air which carried the scent of pine and the lavender sweetness of Auggie's skin.

He drew her close and placed his lips against the slender curve of her neck for a long moment before easing away and resuming their waltz. "I promised you, and I am going to keep to that promise."

"Oh, Rafe. I've never danced in the moonlight before."

"Like it?"

She nodded. "Very much."

"I'm glad, love." He captured her mouth with his and gave her a lingering kiss while they slowly spun together in the darkened garden. No torches had been lit, and the only illumination came from the argent rays of the moon and the interior candlelight.

Her mouth felt warm against his, soft and plump and giving. She arched her body to meet his in sweetest surrender, and they danced this way until the waltz ended. He eased his lips off hers. "Sam and Max are spying on us."

"Oh, Rafe." She started laughing. "Do you think they will report us to your mother and my father?"

"I have no doubt. Do you mind? You'll be my wife by this time tomorrow. Less than a day, and it still feels like an eternity. I cannot bear to let go of you."

"You'll never have to after tomorrow. It is amazing how right this feels. I am dizzy and happy and lightheaded, and I've not had a sip of champagne yet. Thank you for dancing with me tonight. I won't make you do it again."

He tucked a hand under her chin and tipped her gaze to his. "Don't say that, love. If you wish to dance, then I shall dance with you. I wasn't saying this merely to impress your father. I love you."

The music started up again.

Auggie glanced toward the inn's crowded ballroom. "That is odd. They're playing another waltz."

"I bribed the musicians while you were dancing the quadrille. Care for another turn? It's too cold for you outside. I'll be all right if we try this again indoors."

"Not a chance. You can take down hardened criminals, but you cannot hold down the contents of your stomach when twirling about a ballroom. Consider this a compromise. We'll dance, but outside." She nodded, quite pleased with how she'd worked it out. "It's such a pretty tune. Such a lovely waltz. No wonder they call it the dance of love."

"It shall be our tune. Our dance. Our love." He kissed her again.

She looked like an angel.

The air carried the sound of Sam and Max's giggles.

CHAPTER SEVENTEEN

London, England
December, 1821

"I CANNOT BELIEVE we have the house to ourselves, Rafe." Auggie's heart beat faster as she undressed for bed in the room that had been hers while growing up in London. Indeed, the Chelsford townhouse was one of the finest in Mayfair, and even Rafe had been impressed while walking through it earlier in the day. Rafe's mother and Sam had come to town with them but were staying at the home of Rafe's aunt, Miranda.

"I haven't had a night to myself in too many years to recall." He removed his jacket and untied his cravat. "It feels strange…wonderful, but strange. I hope Sam isn't missing us too much."

Auggie laughed. "He is not going to give either of us a second thought, not with all those Brayden cousins and their children about. I'm glad he'll have the chance to be with them, although poor Harry and Max. They will count the minutes until his return. Sam said Harry burst into tears when he ran next door to say goodbye. She's very attached to him."

"He's like a brother to her."

Auggie waggled her eyebrows. "For now. That will change as they grow up."

He groaned, casting her a mockingly dubious glance. "Don't you dare pass *The Book of Love* on to Sam. He's too young."

"I agree. Wouldn't dream of it. Although you ought to be thinking of who will get it next. I considered Mr. Cavendish, but he has taken a fancy to the young woman my father hired to care for Aunt Priscilla and Clara. I'm sorry they could not travel with us, but it is best they remain in Exeter under the watchful care of Hester," she said, referring to the genteel young woman just hired on as companion. "It is no surprise Mr. Cavendish offered to look in on them every day. Have you noticed the way he and Hester blush around each other?"

Rafe groaned again. "It is hard to miss. So, we are agreed, Cavendish has no need for the book. And don't you dare think of giving it to Morgan."

"Heavens, no! Although my father wrote that he seems to be thriving on our farm, the one along the Scottish border near Berwick. I'm glad. He's a dolt, but I always thought there was promise in him. Father should be on his way back to London now, probably arriving here tomorrow. Do you think your brother will come for Christmas?"

"Deklan?" Rafe shrugged as he removed his shirt and helped her unlace her gown. He planted a hot kiss on her neck as he did so. "I hope so."

He wrapped her in his arms and continued to plant light kisses down her neck as they spoke. She loved the feel of Rafe, the touch of his lips, the rough texture of his hands. The scent of his skin. The heat of his rippled body. He was big and muscled. Possessive and yet gentle. "Um…that feels nice…so, is that a yes to your brother?"

"A yes that he will be here for Christmas or a yes to giving him the book? Oh, hell. Auggie, you cannot be serious."

"Why not him?"

"My cousins, Donal and Lorcan, have taken on some pretty dangerous assignments for the Crown. But Deklan is in a class of his own. He can take down an entire army. In fact, he's done it. He's England's most lethal weapon. There isn't a single Brayden or Quinton fearless enough to undertake the foreign missions he has been assigned. He has steel coursing through his veins instead of blood."

Auggie glanced at the book sitting atop her dresser, its leather binding taking on a soft, red glow in the candlelight. "But we're supposed to give this book to someone else now that we are happily wed. Shouldn't it be Deklan? Don't you want to see him happy?"

"Of course, I do." He left her side to sit on the bed and tug off his boots. "My little brother?"

"Why not? You obviously love him. He is brave and valiant. Why are you so reluctant?"

He shook his head and laughed. "I'm not. I just…all right. Yes, him. Absolutely, him. *Bloody hell.* Auggie, that is priceless. Although I cannot imagine the sort of woman who might tempt him."

"We'll find out soon enough." She patted the book. "You mentioned he stays with your Aunt Miranda whenever he is in London. Does he have an assigned room?"

"Yes, he uses Tynan's old room. Tynan is the Earl of Westcliff and the eldest of Miranda's boys. Tynan, Finn, Joshua, and Ronan. They're all married now and set up in their own homes."

"Perfect, we can place the book on the bureau of his bedchamber and see what happens."

Rafe was holding his sides and still laughing. "He is going to kill me when he finds out what we've done. But the rest of the family will be in stitches watching his romance unfold. He will hate us all forever. All worth it, of course."

Auggie undid the pins in her hair and joined him on the bed. He wore only his trousers and had settled on his back, his head propped on the pillows and his hands casually clasped behind his head as he studied her body.

She was clad in a prim, woolen nightgown, which, by the rakish smile on his lips, was not going to remain on her much longer.

"You get more beautiful every day." He nudged her down

beside him and rolled atop her, now propping on his elbows so that he did not crush her with his weight.

She closed her eyes and sighed as he eased the gown off her and then removed his trousers so that they were lying skin to skin, heart to heart. Her soft curves pressed to his hard muscles.

He took her in his arms, cradling her as he suckled one breast and then the other, his touch light and even more gentle than usual as he licked his tongue across her sensitive peaks.

All of her seemed to be sensitive lately, her body so quickly aroused by his touch. Even the intimate spot between her legs was throbbing and ready for him before he'd even touched her there. Yet, when he did finally put his fingers to her, she responded immediately. Stars exploded behind her eyes and tingling waves of heat flowed through her with such intensity, tears formed in her eyes.

"Auggie, love," Rafe said with a gasp, swallowing her in his arms. "Have I hurt you?"

"No, it isn't that. I don't know what's wrong with me lately. Every emotion is heightened, even the pleasure you give me when we're together in bed. I cry when I'm happy, and I cry when I'm passionate. I cry when I pour myself a cup of tea."

"Oh, love."

"And look, I've scratched your shoulders. I did not mean to cling to you so tightly."

"I don't mind." He kissed her and held her until she'd calmed, and at her urging continued their coupling, for she did not want to leave him unfulfilled. He would never complain about it, but she wanted this just as much as he did. She sighed in pleasure as their bodies began to move in one fluid motion, joined to each other, attuned to each other, the music they made uniquely theirs.

Being alone with Rafe freed her to express herself as he brought her to passion, her moans of delight echoing off the walls and obviously stirring Rafe as well. She felt the tense coil of his body, the feral magnificence of it as he let go of his control and loved her with abandon.

Their coupling was wild.

Frenzied.

Wonderful beyond imagination because despite Rafe's obvious hunger, despite his raw desire, there always remained the need to be gentle and protect her, the promise never to hurt her.

She clung to his shoulders as he suckled and kissed her, explored her body, and memorized her every curve.

They reached their crests together, still craving each other, hungry for each other as they tumbled together.

"Blessed saints, Auggie," he said as they lay panting from their latest exertion. "That was good."

This.

This was truly their dance of love.

"I thought you did not like hot, sweating bodies," she laughingly teased.

"I love yours." He drew her into the circle of his arms, their breaths rapid and bodies sticking to each other as they floated to the ground together.

She continued to hold onto Rafe, never wanting to let him go. "Oh, dear."

"What is it, love?" he asked when she suddenly gasped.

"I'm going to cry again. Why am I suddenly unable to get through a single day without bursting into tears?"

"It's all right. I love you, Auggie. Blessed saints, I love you so much." He set his hand gently across her stomach, warming her with his touch. "And I will also love the child you carry. Our child. How far along do you think you are?"

"You notice everything, don't you?"

He smiled and kissed her on the forehead. "Your tears made it evident. The size of your breasts was another clue."

"We've only been married seven weeks, so I cannot be very far along. At most, six or seven weeks."

He kissed her. "Are you cold, love? Let me help you put on your nightgown."

"All right. I think I had better," she said, tugging it back on. "And that's another thing, I need to peel off my clothes one moment and, in the next, I'm cold and piling on layers."

He took her back in his arms. "Shall I fetch another blanket?"

"No, Rafe. I am perfectly comfortable right where I am. I am in your arms, and this is exactly where I belong."

"Always, love."

"Rafe, do you realize this is our first Christmas together."

He kissed her on the forehead. "The first of many, I hope."

"Me, too. Happy Christmas."

He kissed her again. "Happy Christmas, love."

They fell asleep to the crackle of wood in the hearth and the gentle fall of snow on the ground.

Also by Meara Platt

FARTHINGALE SERIES
My Fair Lily
The Duke I'm Going To Marry
Rules For Reforming A Rake
A Midsummer's Kiss
The Viscount's Rose
Earl Of Hearts
If You Wished For Me
Never Dare A Duke
Capturing The Heart Of A Cameron
Tempting Taffy

BOOK OF LOVE SERIES
The Look of Love
The Touch of Love
The Taste of Love
The Song of Love
The Scent of Love
The Kiss of Love
The Chance of Love
The Gift of Love
The Heart of Love
The Hope of Love (novella)
The Promise of Love
The Wonder of Love
The Journey of Love
The Dance of Love
The Miracle of Love
The Dream of Love (novella)

DARK GARDENS SERIES
Garden of Shadows
Garden of Light
Garden of Dragons
Garden of Destiny
Garden of Angels

LYON'S DEN SERIES
The Lyon's Surprise
Kiss of the Lyon
Lyon in the Rough

THE BRAYDENS
A Match Made In Duty
Earl of Westcliff
Fortune's Dragon
Earl of Kinross
Earl of Alnwick
Pearls of Fire*
(*also in Pirates of Britannia series)
Aislin
Gennalyn
A Rescued Heart

DeWOLFE PACK ANGELS SERIES
Nobody's Angel
Kiss An Angel
Bhrodi's Angel

About the Author

Meara Platt is an award winning, USA TODAY bestselling author and an Amazon UK All-Star. Her favorite place in all the world is England's Lake District, which may not come as a surprise since many of her stories are set in that idyllic landscape, including her paranormal romance Dark Gardens series. Learn more about the Dark Gardens and Meara's lighthearted and humorous Regency romances in her Farthingale series and Book of Love series, or her warmhearted Regency romances in her Braydens series by visiting her website at www.mearaplatt.com.